AWAKENING

A DARK MAFIA ROMANCE

STASIA BLACK

LEE SAVINO

D1528307

Cover Design by Jay Aheer

"The god of Love has conquered me . . ."
Orpheus, Ovid's Metamorphoses Book X

ONE

CORA LEANED against the giant window in the expansive living room of the most expensive penthouse in the most expensive hotel in New Olympus.

Far, far below, people scurried like ants down the narrow sidewalks. Cars crawled through rush hour traffic.

If Cora waited long enough with her face pressed against the glass, would she see a woman, young and beautiful with stars in her eyes, step off the bus and spin in a slow circle, mouth parted in awe at the magnificent cityscape? Maybe the young woman would look up and imagine someone like Cora, diamonds in her ears and hair sleekly coiffed away from her made-up face.

Would the young woman be wistful, wondering what it'd be like to live in the penthouse and float in the beautiful world above the streets? If she could hear Cora whisper, *Get back on the bus, run away,* would the young woman escape before the darkness swallowed her whole?

Cora backed away from the window, chest heaving. Only months ago, she'd been that young woman. The city had been beautiful, overwhelming and alien, a far cry from the blue skies and waving wheat of the farm she'd grown up on back in Kansas.

She been full of so much hope. She'd ascended the heights and now she lived in her husband's penthouse, with everything she could desire. Diamonds and dresses, fine art decorating the elegant apartment.

Every morning someone delivered fresh flowers to a giant vase on a pedestal by the door. The blooms filled the open space with their delicate floral scent. The lilies of the field, plucked and cut and perfectly arranged to live one day at the height of their beauty. And tomorrow? Tomorrow they'd be gone. Thrown away.

Cora crossed to the front door and ran a finger over the silky petals. Here was a rosebud, tightly furled. She could pull it out and place it in a cup of water. It wouldn't look as grand, but it would still be here tomorrow. She could save one flower. It might be enough...

Crossing the room, she caught a glimpse of herself in a giant gilt mirror. A young face stared back at her, pale and lovely under layers of artful makeup. She'd spent all day at Armand's spa and every inch of her skin was plucked, smoothed, and polished. Her hair had been cut and styled as well.

When she'd lived on her mother's farm, she'd wear old overalls, t-shirts, a farmer's tan and freckles her only adornment, and go months without examining herself closely in a mirror.

These days, every inch of her was scrutinized, first by her stylists, then by society when she went out on Marcus's arm. The wife of a wealthy businessman must look the part.

Especially if that man's business had deep ties to the city's criminal underworld.

Marcus Ubeli, the ruler of New Olympus' underworld. Her husband.

When *he* stood by the window, he only saw his kingdom. His abject subjects scurrying far below. They saw only what he wanted them to see, an elegant businessman, handsome and shrewd, with a new and pretty wife.

They applauded his philanthropy and patronized his legit businesses—and only half listened to the whispers about his dark dealings. Only the rich and ultra-powerful knew the truth about Marcus Ubeli. He had a representative on every shadowy street corner. Cops, judges and juries were in his pocket. Even the mayor owed him favors.

By the time you learned the truth about Marcus Ubeli, it was too late. He owned you, too.

And Cora was his most prized possession.

Yes, she lived a grand life, far above the masses. Weekly spa visits, shopping sprees, meals in the finest restaurants, entry into the glittering nightlife of New Olympus high society. Beautiful clothes, a magnificent penthouse with its amazing view.

She preferred volunteering at the animal shelter downtown and curling up on a couch with a book, but it didn't matter. She was a cut flower in a gorgeous vase, beautiful and elegant and dying a little more each day.

Oh yes, she played her part perfectly in exchange for this new life her husband had given her. Because that's all it was: an even exchange.

Four months ago, she'd thrown herself in front of a bullet for him and saved his life. So now he'd given her all the freedoms she desired, even those that he himself had once denied her... She thought back to those days, miserable but also sort of wonderful through the haze of recollection.

Because back then she'd been naïve enough to believe her husband could one day love her.

He'd disabused her of those notions while she lay on her hospital bed after being shot, just coming out of a coma. He didn't know she'd overheard him, which made it all the worse because it meant he'd been telling the truth.

Cora was always a chess piece for me to play against the Titans. And she served her purpose... As an added bonus, wifey dearest made herself a shield and took a bullet for me. I'd say that's mission accomplished as far as she's concerned, better than I ever could've hoped for. Plus, she's a great lay, so...

She was just a possession. That was all she'd ever be to him. He'd never loved her. He'd seen her as a commodity and a tool to use against his enemies. And as someone convenient to warm his bed at night. It was all she would ever be to him. He simply wasn't capable of feeling anything more. At least not for her, a Titan.

Not after finding out that her mom, Demi, had murdered his sister in cold blood. And come back fifteen years later to finish the job on Marcus himself, no matter the fact that Cora had begged her not to do it, to put the gun down, to *stop*.

Cora had chosen Marcus.

And taken the bullet meant for him.

She still had the four-inch scar on her stomach from where they'd had to operate to take the bullet out.

But after her recovery, what had there been to come back to? This life, stuck in the no man's land between two rival gangs, shunned by one because of who she loved but never fully embraced by the other.

"Cora." Marcus's deep voice rolled across the room.

She jerked her head up in surprise.

Her husband stood next to the floral bouquet. When had he come in? She hadn't even heard the front door open, she'd been so deep in her own head.

Marcus was as handsome as ever, the most gorgeous man she'd ever seen, if she was being honest. His hands were in his pockets and his face was tilted into the shadows enough that she couldn't read his expression. Not that she'd be able to read him even if the room were lit with a hundred blinding light bulbs. She didn't even try anymore.

She knew who he was and what was in his heart. She'd heard him loud and clear. In the days and weeks following the coma, his coldness toward her only reconfirmed everything he'd said that day.

He was solicitous towards her. He provided the best medical care money could buy. He continued giving her countless gifts but he never delivered them himself. His driver, Sharo, drove her to rehab every day for two months as she regained her strength.

But Marcus worked dawn till dusk and she could go entire days, once an entire week, without seeing him. He was awake before dawn and back long after she fell asleep. Often he'd sleep in the guest bedroom, saying he didn't want to wake her with his erratic hours.

He never came to any doctor's appointments yet still seemed to know every last detail of her care regimen. When he did talk to her it was to remind her to take her supplements or to ask if she'd eaten enough. And the day the doctor pronounced her well enough to resume physical activity, he came to their bed at night and made love to her in the dark.

The sex was as intense as ever. Their chemistry in bed was undeniable. Some nights his kisses felt frantic as he wrapped his arms around her and pulled her against him so tightly it was like he was afraid she'd disappear.

Sometimes it was fast, his mouth or hands on her working to bring her to a desperate, wild release and then he'd bury himself inside her and spill within minutes. Only to wake her up hours later in the middle of the night with his need pressing against her backside, and then he'd take her slowly, so achingly slowly that she thought she might die.

But always in the dark. And when morning came, he was gone as if the night had never been.

Tonight he wore his signature suit, and he looked just as fresh and unwrinkled as he had when he first put it on the day before. His effortless, controlled perfection was as much a mystery to her as on their first day of marriage. He tucked his hands into his pockets and, black hair falling across his brow, looked her up and down.

She stared back out the window, unmoving. "You're home early."

"We're going out tonight—remember? I thought you'd be ready."

She had on makeup, high heels, and a coiffed updo fresh from the spa, but the rest of her was still wrapped in a robe.

She hadn't forgotten but still she said, "We're going out?"

"The concert at Elysium. New act. A big one."

She looked Marcus's way again as he shrugged and she watched his face carefully. She found herself doing this more and more lately—poking the bear to see if she could get some reaction out of him, some proof that he was really human and could show genuine human emotion. As usual, though, his poker face gave nothing away.

"I always give a photo op on opening night," he continued.

"I didn't forget," she said, turning fully towards him and letting the light christen her hair. He had to squint to try to see her. "In fact, I went shopping for just the right outfit."

"Did you now?" He rubbed the dark shadow around his jaw, the only evidence of his long work day.

She undid her robe and let it fall in a rustle of silk. As she moved closer, she watched her husband's eyes grow hot as they took in her body. A black lace camisole with built in bra cupped her breasts. A sexy garter belt was slung low around her waist, holding her sheer black stockings up.

Cora felt satisfaction at the intense look on his face. "What do you think?"

This was all they had between them.

Sex. Fucking. That was how Cora thought of it now—as fucking. Or at least how she tried to think of it.

Marcus liked fucking her.

She was a good lay, after all, right?

Her teeth ground together at the memory. It was just another reason she'd chosen her outfit so carefully. Sex was a weapon that plenty of women used to control the men in their lives, right? No one would ever control Marcus but if she could even get the slightest edge up on him, it would be something. She was determined that the next time they had sex, it would be on her terms. In the light where he'd be forced to see her face.

Marcus studied her carefully, letting the silence lengthen between them. He smirked, the barest upward quirk of his lips.

"I think the paparazzi will eat it up."

He prowled forward, put a commanding hand to the back of her neck, and drew her head to his.

She told herself not to open to him, to play hard to get—after all, what would entice the man who had everything more than being denied the one thing he seemed to crave?—but the second his lips touched hers, her body went liquid. Such was his power over her. Damn it all to hell.

How did he always manage to do that? To get the upper hand? She'd been so determined to master *him* for once.

But when Marcus pulled back for a moment, his dark eyes catching hers, a jolt of pleasure shot through her.

"I like finding you like this," he whispered. "Waiting so eagerly. Wanting."

He lifted her up and settled her on the small makeup bureau. Kneeling, he parted her legs and leaned forward to inhale deeply, his teeth catching at the top of her lace panties. "I like smelling how much you want me."

Cora felt her face flame. For as calm, cold, and professional as Marcus was on the outside to everyone else she'd ever seen him interact with, it was still shocking how crass and brutish he could sometimes be in bed. Or on the makeup bureau, as it were.

She rubbed her legs together but he wasn't having it. He shoved her thighs open wide and stepped between them as he rose back up, the front of his fancy suit pants jutting obscenely. He made quick work of unbuckling and unzipping them. And all her plans went out the window. She just wanted him inside her now, whatever way she could have him.

She thought he might shove into her quick and harsh, like he often did in the dark. No matter how many times she told herself, *not again,* she always ended up welcoming him into her arms, clinging to him, and spending all day living for the half hour at night when his hands would reach for her in the darkness.

In those moments, it was so easy to let herself forget the truth of their situation. That to him, she was only a trophy of his latest victory. Because he *had* been victorious in quelling the brief insurgency the Titans had attempted on New Olympus. It had been months and there was no word from the gang her mother now apparently ran.

Marcus had triumphed, as he always did. There was no point resisting him. He had a will unlike anyone she had ever met and that was saying something, considering that she'd been raised by Demi Titan.

And yet still Cora had to cling to her sense of self. She couldn't let herself be obliterated by Marcus completely. It was why she continued her futile campaign to gain the upper hand in this marriage. She might never escape him but it didn't mean she had to be tormented forever by her unrequited love for him.

But wait, no, she *didn't* love him. It had merely been infatuation.

And it was an infatuation she would cure herself of, one way or another... But she'd been trying for months with no success.

In the meantime, she meant to gain more of an even footing with him. It was why she'd thrown herself so violently into society life. She was determined to have a life apart from him. And maybe, if she asserted herself more in their bed play, then she wouldn't feel so completely overwhelmed by him each time and so shattered in the aftermath.

She could only piece herself back together so many times.

Because while she knew in her head that to Marcus it was only fucking, to her stupid heart it often felt like making love.

Which was why she'd put on her armor today and surprised him in a full-frontal assault.

But five minutes later, he had her on her back and one hand splayed ever so gently across her throat.

His dark eyes searched hers for a quick moment and her breath caught. He was so gorgeous, his face sculpted with sharp lines and commanding angles. Even through the tux she could feel the power of his large body, muscles bulging against the expensive tailored fabric.

She lifted a hand, reaching toward his cheek. How long since she'd seen him like this in the light of day?

But he grabbed her wrist before she could make contact and slammed her wrist to the bed above her head, pinning it there. She couldn't help the whimper that escaped her at the commanding move. Everything he did turned her on. Everything he was.

She thought he would pull himself out and take her right there. She was only a few seconds away from begging for it.

Instead, though, he pulled back and flipped her over so that she was on her hands and knees. He didn't make her wait long, though. He dragged her lace underwear down and immediately stroked inside her. She was drenched and his passage was smooth.

Apparently he wasn't looking for smooth.

He pulled out and rammed into her roughly and gods, it felt so good. Like he was claiming her. Like she'd actually managed to rile him up for once.

She shifted her backside needily against him and he swore, clutching her hips in a punishing grip as he continued to pound into her.

She tried to look over her shoulder at him but he wasn't

having it. He put a hand on her neck urging her down to the bed, ass up.

He followed, his body dominating hers as his relentless thrusting continued. "Next time you think to tempt me with such slinky little underthings, goddess," he hissed in her ear, "remember to be careful what you wish for. You only make me want to remind you who you belong to."

She'd been on the edge since he first thrust into her but his words sent her over. He was hitting that perfect spot deep inside. Yes, oh gods, *yes*.

In order to stop herself from howling Marcus's name as she came, she thrust her face into the pillow.

But he knew her too well. He pulled back and stopped thrusting right as the first astounding bloom of her orgasm hit.

She cried out with the loss of it and he wrapped his arms around her, holding her still. "Say my name," he commanded in a low, guttural voice. "Say who you belong to."

She shook her head in an attempted denial but he just gripped her tighter and gave her a slight shake. "Say who you belong to."

His cock teased at the edge of her entrance, tormenting her, her pleasure was so close and yet so far away.

"Marcus," she finally wailed and he slammed back into her, immediately lighting her back up. She screamed his name again as her pleasure ramped higher and higher and then exploded like a night full of firecrackers.

Marcus thrust himself to the root right as she clenched and spasmed around him, his grip on her body never lessening an iota.

Together, they came, as the light of sunset streamed through the window.

As the pop and sparkle of her orgasm finally dissipated, she panted, short of breath, her entire body alive but languid with satisfied pleasure. And Marcus still held her from behind, though he rolled them so that they lay on their side. Him spooning her, his cock still hard inside her and every few moments he'd thrust again, like he wasn't ready to let go no matter the fact that he'd already spent.

His fingers trailed the back of her neck. "I missed this."

Her heart was heavy, full to bursting with the things she wished she could say. "You can have it anytime you want." *You can have me.*

"Oh, I know." She could hear his arrogant smile in his words.

She was glad she was faced away from him. It made her braver somehow, so she continued. "You've been so busy lately."

"Miss me?" She thought he sounded pleased.

"As much as you missed me." She rocked against his hardness. His cock shifted and swelled. His fingers found the back of her neck, no longer stroking but clamping down on the sensitive points.

"I have a weakness when it comes to you." He pulled out of her and left her side to clean up. When he returned, she was still huddled on the bed, back to him.

He came around the bed and his fingers lifted her chin. "What's wrong?"

She was done bottling her frustration. "Only you would describe it as weakness."

"What would you call it?" No sarcasm, just curiosity.

"I don't know..." His honest expression made her bold. "Affection?"

Her heart pounded through the silent seconds. His hungry gaze dropped to her lips and she felt it like a kiss.

His hands cupped her cheeks, and then he kissed her for real.

"Affection," he agreed. He stroked her hair, petting her like she was an adorable kitten he allowed to sleep on his bed. And her stupid, stupid heart leaped up like he'd declared his love from the rooftops.

"What if we..." Cora's breath hitched but she continued, "what if we just stayed in tonight?" She felt her vulnerability stretched raw, right out there for anyone to see as she asked it. But she didn't take it back. "I— I could make it worth your while." She reached out and placed a hand on the front of his pants, where his cock stirred.

His hand shot down and firmly clasped around her wrist, though, stopping her. She felt her heart sink as he stepped back. He was about to reject her. Again.

"The Orphan is the hottest music act on the East Coast. The press will be there to catch the celebrities attending the concert, and I want them to see you with me. I need you there by my side."

Aha. Of course. He needed Mrs. Ubeli on his arm for a photo op, a distraction to the cameras. Tonight she'd be her husband's arm candy, dressed to dazzle, drawing the camera's eye to the scandalous slit of her dress or her long bare leg exiting the car.

She squeezed her eyes shut to stop a stupid tear from escaping. She legitimized his business, she knew, with her innocent looks and role as the dutiful wife. Like the magician's assistant, she took the focus off him and left him free to whatever quiet business he had in the background.

It was their unspoken arrangement, as contractual as the rest of his business dealings were. She played the role of Mrs. Ubeli and in return he did her the great honor of not killing her and to the best of his ability, pretending she was not a Titan.

But she would never truly be family and she would certainly never be anyone he could ever love. Men like Marcus didn't understand that emotion. They understood power, and in this relationship, he had it and she didn't.

She'd been an idiot yet again, showing even an ounce of weakness by asking him to stay in tonight.

She turned away from him and forced her voice to be steady and cool. "I'll be ready in an hour."

TWO

THE SIDEWALKS around the Elysium club and concert hall were packed with excited concert goers. Marcus's black sedan slid to a stop in front of the back doors, where the crush of people was thicker than at the front entrance.

Cora peered out at the throng. "Marcus," she said nervously.

"It's all right." Marcus leaned forward and gave an order to the driver.

Outside, a few muscle men dressed all in black threaded through the crowd. His Shades. In a matter of seconds, they lined the entryway and were holding back the throng, though it looked like a near thing. Cora had never seen a crowd so big.

Still, amidst the chaos, the paparazzi sensed something was happening as they pulled close and swiveled the cameras' eyes onto the black sedan.

Cora shrank back into the dark cocoon of the car. This was her least favorite part: being stripped and exposed for the cameras. She smoothed her ice blue sheath dress and touched her coifed hair to check it.

"Hey." Marcus cupped her chin and gently turned her head. "You're perfect."

For a moment, his dark eyes held her transfixed. All the thoughts about the noise and mess outside melted away. He frowned slightly and for a second, Cora thought she saw the flicker of something more than obligation and duty in his eyes.

Something thumped the side of the car and she jumped. A roar erupted in the otherwise quiet car as the door on her side opened. Turning with her heart in her throat, she saw Sharo, Marcus's right-hand man, leaning over the car. His large black head filled the window for a moment while he signaled to his boss.

"Stay by my side for a few pictures," Marcus said, his jaw working as he eyed the people swarming around them. "Then go with Sharo. He can handle the crowd and get you safely inside." He pulled out his phone.

The car door opened with another blast of sound. Cora slid out, fighting to keep her dress modest and trying not to flinch at the sudden bright lights. She stepped close to Sharo, whose large body buffered her as much as possible from the light and noise.

Marcus slid out after her and posed for a moment next to the car, six feet of male perfection. Something about his height, his dark eyes and perfect cheekbones under the thick fall of black hair gave him a beautiful intensity. Add in some rumors of a criminal empire, and papers fell over themselves to report on the *Lord of the Underworld*'s fascinating mystique.

Cora took her husband's arm, falling into her role of eye candy. Smiling down at her, Marcus barely seemed to notice the flashing lights or people calling to him. His mask of affable billionaire was firmly in place. She wondered when she'd next see the real Marcus.

"Mr. Ubeli!" a reporter called. "How does it feel to have landed the hottest musical act in an exclusive contract?"

Marcus turned and offered a charming grin, squeezing Cora gently to him. She knew what a great picture the two of them cut, with Marcus's dark good looks and her light hair and pale skin.

"We're very grateful," Marcus was answering. "We want Elysium to showcase only the best."

He'd completely remodeled the venue, inside and out, since they'd come here for the charity ball and auction all those months ago when he'd purchased the fateful theater tickets that would lead to the night ending with a bullet in her guts. Now instead of a venue for conferences and parties, it was one of the hippest clubs and concerts spaces in New Olympus.

A few more questions from the media and Cora felt her fluttering heart calm. Marcus made it look so easy, whether in public or private, he always looked poised and perfect. She was the only one who ever got to see him lose a bit of that perfect control, like she had earlier in the bedroom tonight. A pleasurable tingle skittered down her back even at the memory and she let her lips curve into a satisfied smile. Cameras flashed.

She wasn't as practiced as Marcus at deception and the few times she'd offered fake smiles, the press had commented on it. So she'd taught herself to think of happy things when in front of cameras, even if it meant thinking of Marcus and the memories came with a vicious afterbite.

Marcus looked down as if reading her mind and gave her his own heated version. His hand slid a little lower than her waist.

Cora forced herself to keep her smile but reminded herself it was just for the cameras. Marcus was so drop dead gorgeous when he smiled, but he rarely did it anywhere else other than when there were cameras around.

They were turning as one to go when another person called, "What about reports that The Orphan has connections to the mob in Metropolis?"

Marcus barely let his grin flicker but Cora felt his body tense. He waved for a second and pushed Cora forward. Sharo was immediately at their side, along with several of Marcus's other hand selected bodyguards. The Shades protected the Ubelis and would die on Marcus's command. Or so the rumors went. Dressed all in black, muscles bunched under their suits, they cut menacing figures on the red carpet.

Usually Cora felt uncomfortable with them hanging around, but, as they stepped forward and formed a phalanx around her and Marcus, she was grateful for their protection.

Sharo hovered close, a mountain in a tux. "We need to talk."

"Later. Get her inside," Marcus ordered, and the group moved in perfect formation, Sharo at the back.

"See you at the concert," Marcus told Cora, and handed her off to his trusted second in command.

She glanced back once, right before she went inside, to see her husband standing solid against the mad rush of reporters trying to interview Elysium's owner. Then she— and her black clad corps—were inside.

Sharo's large hand ghosted over her spine as they went down the back hallways, up to the second story to the private lounge.

Cora wondered if she'd see Marcus for the rest of the

night. That's how it went sometimes. She was good for pretty pictures but once he had no more need of her... Cora bit her lip and stiffened her back. No. He didn't have the power to hurt her anymore because she knew the score now.

Still, once they entered the bar area, Cora breathed a sigh of relief. No more false smiles required for a while. There were no cameras up here; Elysium's elite patrons didn't like attention. The ones who paid for access to this private lounge were all business associates of Marcus's.

A few of them were at the bar or in booths, enjoying a quiet drink. Cora recognized a few right away. Santonio, who ran a high-end prostitution ring—he preferred to call them *escorts*—stood talking to Rocco, who controlled all of the distribution business in the Styx, a territory south of the city, near the docks. Another two, Joey and Andy DePetri, were at the bar, arms around women at least ten years younger than them.

It was looking more and more like the concert was a perfect cover for Marcus to gather his capos and discuss business.

Cora ducked into the first booth she came to, hoping they wouldn't notice her. If they saw her, they'd want to pay their respects, and she didn't want to talk to them.

Sharo paused for a moment at the end of her table, surveying the room. The rest of her bodyguards seemed to melt away, although she could see them discreetly stationed near the gold fringed theater curtains that decorated the lounge.

"Sharo," Cora leaned forward. The big man didn't turn but she knew he was listening. He noticed everything. "Was all of that madness for the band tonight?"

The crowd outside had really been something, unlike

anything she'd ever seen before. Elysium might be one of the top clubs in the city but still.

Sharo shrugged. But she didn't expect him to answer. He rarely spoke to her, even though he was Marcus's right hand man.

She relaxed back into her booth, studying him. A wire wrapped around his large bald head, and he wore an expensive platinum watch around one wrist. Like Marcus, he looked flawless and in control even after the mad rush at the door. His tux was perfect; she wondered where he bought it to fit his large frame.

"Nice suit," she said to his back. "You look good."

In answer, he twisted slowly and gazed down at her. Touching his crackling headpiece, he turned and walked away.

Cora sighed. "I need to make friends," she muttered to herself.

Real friends, not the kind who socialized with her out of ambition or fear of her husband's position. Her only real friend was Maeve, two decades her senior, who owned the dog shelter where she volunteered. But it would be great to have more people she felt comfortable around at things like this.

"Mrs. Ubeli," a perky cocktail waitress came by. "The usual?"

"Thank you, Janice." Cora watched the young woman dart away, thinking that the waitress was probably around her age. And how hard would it be to strike up a conversation? And meet her for drinks later? Or go out for a mani/pedi?

Cora tried to imagine asking Marcus if she could have a girl's movie night up at the penthouse. Nope, couldn't picture it.

Meanwhile, the waitress had returned with her glass of wine.

"Are you excited about the concert?"

"Yes." Cora met the young woman's enthusiasm with her own. "Do you know the band?"

"The Orphan?" the waitress practically squealed. "Everyone knows him. He's amazing. Look—" The girl plucked a newspaper off of a nearby stand, and showed Cora the Arts Section.

"Rock God packs Elysium," it read.

Cora smiled. Marcus would be pleased with the free publicity.

"His songs are amazing," Janice kept gushing.

Glancing up, Cora saw a few of the men around the club looking their way, attracted by the girl's excitement. Cora put her hand on the paper and looked pointedly at Janice.

"Thanks," Cora said quietly. "Can I keep this?"

As the waitress left, Cora scanned the article. It was short, just talking about The Orphan's top hits and incipient fame around the country.

Cora buried her head in the paper, hiding her face from the rest of the club to read until the concert started.

"Mayor Pledges Reform as Elections Draw Near" splashed across the front page, with a picture of a handsome blond waving to the crowd. Zeke Sturm. The Op/Ed scoffed at the pre-election speeches, citing broken promises of previous terms. Meanwhile the Style pages were dedicated to articles on the mayor's reign as "most eligible bachelor" with an emphasis on his suave wardrobe. The Gossip pages spun the tale of his latest lover, with a byline listing all his famous liaisons on the side.

"Mayor or Player?" Cora read the title and rolled her

eyes. She tossed the paper onto the table, ready to donate it to the shelter so it could line the bottom of the dog cages. At least the election would be over soon.

"Hey, sweetheart. You're looking beautiful tonight."

Cora frowned up at a tall, stout, balding man in a floor-length fur coat staring straight at her chest. His fat fingers bore a gold ring on each hand.

"Uh, thank you." She glanced around for a bodyguard, but couldn't see one. They probably were out handling the crowd; it looked like they needed all hands on deck. Besides, wasn't she always telling Marcus she would be fine by herself? Well it was true he let her go wherever she wanted in the city, but his Shades were always in the shadows following.

Realizing she had her hand up by her neck in a vulnerable pose, she touched her diamonds lightly and then forced her hand down.

She made herself smile at the man. Was he one of Marcus's business partners? Maybe partner to Santonio or Rocco? If he was, there were too many politics involved for her too tell him to get lost. She would play nice until she was sure.

The man smiled back down at Cora, but it wasn't a nice smile. A lot of Marcus's associates looked at women like that, although they always acted like perfect gentlemen to her when she was on Marcus's arm. They wouldn't dare disrespect her husband like that.

Maybe this gentleman needed a reminder of who she was. "Are you enjoying yourself in our club?" She kept her tone cool and confident.

"Oh, yes, absolutely, toots. In fact," he slapped down a business card in front of her, "I was going to invite you to visit mine."

Cora glanced down at the card and read the purple lettering out loud, "The Orchid House."

"Finest establishment in town." The man grinned and a gold tooth flashed. "In fact, I recommend you visit sometime this week. Preferably around eleven. We're holding auditions."

"Auditions?"

"That's right. Body like yours, you'd make a killing. Guys love the skinny no-tits look nowadays."

Cora stiffened.

"I'm not saying I don't," the man continued, chuckling a little. "Especially with that baby doll face you got."

As he spoke, a skinny redhead wearing a scary amount of eye makeup sauntered up.

"Am I right, Ashley?" The man slid his hand over Ashley's rump and squeezed. In response, the redhead put her arms around him. Her long nails looked vicious as they stroked and smoothed the man's fur coat. She scowled at Cora.

"Anyway, tell the boys AJ sent you. They'll put you to the front of the line." The man winked. Ashley looked like she'd seen a pile of dog vomit in the booth right where Cora was sitting.

Cora could feel her cheeks flushing with embarrass-ment and anger. Who did this man think he was?

But AJ still smiled at her, eyes narrowed as he waited for her reaction. Cora took a deep breath and channeled her Inner Ice Queen.

"Excuse me—" she started to say—she still couldn't help being polite, even in Ice Queen mode—when Hype, in a tux and bright blue hair, ran up to the booth. Together with his twin brother Thane, he managed Elysium, and he more than lived up to his name. Thane did the books took care of the back office while Hype stage managed and, on nights Elysium wasn't booked for a show, played as the House DJ.

"Mrs. Ubeli?" Hype gasped. His blue eyes were wide and frantic under his shocking hair. Both Cora's unwanted visitors stepped aside as Hype leaned in. "Have you seen your husband?"

"No, Hype, why, is something wrong?" Cora rose, relieved to have a familiar face in her corner.

"It's The Orphan. The singer for tonight—he's refusing to play."

"What?" Cora and Ashley said at the same time. The latter immediately looked disgusted that she shared the same thought with Cora.

Meanwhile, AJ was studying Cora with a shrewd look on his face. Cora felt his gaze, and, even though red burned on her cheeks, she refused to look at him.

"He just stopped tuning his guitar and started freaking out. Thane sent me to find help." At this, Hype turned to AJ. "Has he ever done this before?"

AJ shrugged. "He's an artist. He's temperamental."

"You're his manager, for gods' sake." As the blue haired man's voice cracked, it got louder. "Why aren't you in the green room with him?"

Cora's eyes shot back to AJ. He was The Orphan's *manager*?

"Thought I'd meet the locals," AJ said. "Look, I discovered him. I got him here for you. If he doesn't sing, it's on him. Not my problem." AJ reached down to a bowl of bar nuts the waitress had left on Cora's table, took a handful and slapped them into his mouth. His jaws shook a little as he chewed. Cora looked away in disgust.

Hype looked like he was about to explode and Cora took pity on him.

"Ok, calm down," Cora said. "Let's go see Thane." She put a hand on his arm. "We'll figure something out."

Relieved to have a reason to escape, Cora started walking away.

"Nice to meet you, Mrs. Ubeli," AJ called after them, spraying pieces of food onto the carpet.

"What an ass," Hype muttered.

"Who is he, and why is he here?" Cora couldn't keep the anger out of her voice. "A simple band manager wouldn't have dared take the liberties he did. And the things he said—"

Hype glanced at her. "What'd he say to you?"

"He, uh, told me he admired my body." She shook her head in revulsion. "He offered me a job."

"What, really?" Hype looked ill. "Don't tell Mr. U that."

"Why, what does he do?"

"He produces pornos."

"What?" Cora cried out.

"Don't worry," Hype said drily. "Once Marcus finds out he's here, he's going to kill him."

"What? Why?"

"Those two go way back. Before Marcus was—" Hype lowered his voice and intoned solemnly, "Lord of the Underworld."

"Don't let him catch you calling him that." Cora grimaced, but she knew what Hype meant. Before the age of thirty her husband had become a juggernaut in the city of New Olympus, with business on both sides of the law. She knew firsthand how impossible it was to cross him. "So why is AJ here?"

"AJ is like a cockroach; disgusting and indestructible. Careful around him...he's smarter than he looks. Makes good money off his porn business and his club. Hustles on the side. One of his boys had a bloke who owed him a debt, and turns out the bloke was just about to discover the world's newest hot rock star."

"The Orphan."

Hype nodded. "AJ took over the debt and signed the Orphan. We booked the show and *then* found out it came with AJ. Marcus doesn't want him around."

Cora considered this. She couldn't imagine Marcus not getting his way. Although, given the boost The Orphan would give to Elysium, she understood why Marcus compromised.

Cora shook her head. "I think he may have been... testing me." She remembered the intent look in his beady little eyes.

"Testing for Mr. U's weaknesses," Hype nodded. "AJ looks like a slob, but don't underestimate him."

Cora shook her head like she could shake off the encounter. "His companion certainly didn't think much of me."

"Please. I own shirts longer than that skank's dress," Hype cracked.

Cora smiled. Of all Marcus's employees, the blue haired Hype was her favorite. Even when he was acting jittery—which he was about half the time she saw him. The other half he seemed almost too mellow.

Hype slowed abruptly as they turned down a new hall and saw two large men guarding a nondescript door.

The door opened before he could address the guards and Thane, Hype's brother, faced them, solemn faced. Thane wore a grey suit and a pale violet tie, and, other than his clothes and plain brown hair, he looked exactly like his blue haired brother.

Just like the first time she met them, she marveled at how one twin looked like an accountant and the other looked ready for a rave.

The two men stared at each other like they were looking into a mirror at a fun house. Hype seemed even more agitated when juxtaposed with his dignified brother.

"He won't play," Thane stated and Hype started up a fit of cursing.

"What can we do?" Cora interjected.

"Get Mr. Ubeli. Or Sharo—Sharo can threaten to beat his head in."

"Brilliant," said Hype at the same time Cora said, "No!"

She frowned at both brothers. "Can I see him? Maybe I could talk to him."

Thane and Hype exchanged glances that might as well have said, *Couldn't hurt.* Thane led them into the room.

The green room was, in fact, green. Stage hands in black rushed around and more bodyguards in suits stood like statues around the room. Brightly lit mirrors lined one wall; two makeup artists stood at the counters fussing over their supplies. A knot of people were in the corner beside them, looking bored and drinking designer water.

"He's over there." Thane nodded toward the corner.

Cora hesitated, suddenly nervous. "I don't know if I should do this. He has ties to AJ, right? Marcus might not want me to meddle."

Thane blinked. "You met AJ?"

"Back in the lounge. He cornered her," Hype explained. "I practically rescued her. That man never misses an opportunity to make a bad impression."

"I'm just saying, if he's one of Marcus's enemies then maybe I should lay low," Cora said.

Thane scowled at his brother. "You've been talking too much."

"What?" Hype threw his hands up. "You want this concert to happen, right?"

Thane looked at Cora. "We need him to do this, for PR. There's a lot of support in the lounge."

Cora nodded, catching his meaning. Business support. People who came out to see The Orphan in private before the show. People who would owe her husband a favor.

She took a deep breath, because though her husband might always see her as only her mother's daughter, she was determined to make a life for herself here. She would prove herself indispensable and she would start by somehow pulling this off. "Ok. I'll do it."

Smoothing her dress, Cora practiced her model glide all the way to the huddle of people in the corner of the room.

Thane fell into step with her. "Look, he may be rude. He may just ignore us. We've been trying not to strong arm him and risk offending his...artistic sensitivity."

"Thane, I can handle sensitivity. I'm a model, remember? And a woman." She stopped on the edge of the huddle and looked for a way to break through the throng of bodyguards, managers, assistants and groupies.

Thane cleared his throat. "Excuse me, Mrs. Ubeli would like to meet The Orphan."

All eyes turned to her. The groupies looked annoyed. Cora blushed a little, realizing they thought she was just another rich man's escort, in her expensive sheath dress and diamonds.

A path cleared and Cora found herself approaching a young man sitting on a stool in the corner, hunched over a guitar. His blondish hair had fallen into his eyes, his head bent towards his fingers. Other than his extreme concentration, he looked almost normal. He wore jeans and a plain white button-down shirt, and with his unruly hair he looked like a kid made to wear church clothes. Not like a rock god at all.

"Orphan?" Cora made her voice as soft and dulcet as possible. She felt awkward saying it. Everyone put *The* in front of Orphan but surely people didn't address him that way. Apparently it didn't matter how she addressed him because he didn't move or look up either way.

"It's nice to meet you." She searched for something to say. The Orphan still hadn't looked at her, instead remaining focused on his instrument. His fingers moved, ghosting across the neck of the guitar, forming chords, playing soundlessly.

Cora waited a minute, watching him play silently, in his own world. A lock of hair fell away from his face and she tried again. "Is there anything you might need? Some water maybe?"

One of the groupies stepped forward, offering a water bottle. The Orphan ignored it. Cora could hear whispers start to circulate around her.

"Mob boss's wife," she heard someone say, but when she turned all she saw was a circle of blank faces, staring at her. Cora felt her own face stiffen, become a mask. She had to remember she was playing a role, typecast by their judgment.

She always hated being surrounded by people like this —fake, judgmental hangers on who hoped a little fame or power would rub off on them simply by being in proximity to it. Maybe The Orphan hated it too, maybe not. Judging by his closed off body language, she'd say he didn't *love* it... Or maybe he was just really into his music.

Either way, there was no way she could talk to him like this.

"Clear the room." When no one moved, she squared her shoulders and said it in a far louder, no nonsense, do-not-fuck-with-me voice. "*Clear the room.*"

And people started to move. Slowly at first but Cora said to Hype, "Should I go get my husband?" and everyone started scurrying at a much quicker clip after that until just she, Hype, Thane, and The Orphan were alone in the room. She waved out Hype and Thane.

The Orphan finally looked over at her. "You're the club owner's wife, right?"

She nodded.

"You look a lot younger than him," he said thoughtfully.

"He just looks older sometimes," she smiled.

"How old are you?"

"You and I are the same age, I think. Nineteen, right?" She blushed a little under the Orphan's intense scrutiny. He was a good-looking boy.

"You look about sixteen," he laughed and sang a little phrase from a song she recognized, *Sixteen Summers.*

Cora stilled and listened until the Orphan was done. "That's one of your songs?"

He nodded, a genuine smile lighting up his face.

"Wow, I didn't realize you wrote that. They play it all the time on the radio."

"I wrote the lyrics and they bought it for a female artist to sing. That was before I was discovered."

"You sold your song?"

He shrugged. "Practically gave it away, so I could eat and keep on. I just want to make music." He started humming the song again, eyes closed reverently. His fingers flew in a riff on an air guitar and didn't stop until he sang the last chorus.

When he opened his eyes, Cora clapped. She couldn't help it. He looked so charming.

He was oblivious to it, she realized, this light that shone from him. His gift. When he accessed it and shared it freely, he shone like the sun.

"That was amazing."

"Thanks. Wrote it for Iris." His brow furrowed. "I'm waiting for her. I can't go on until she's here. It's a big night."

"She's your girlfriend?"

The Orphan lit up again, smiling impishly. "I have a secret. I'm hoping she'll be my fiancée. I'm gonna propose after the show tonight." His brow pinched. "But don't tell anyone. AJ wouldn't like it."

Cora shook her head. "Your secret is safe with me." She wanted to ask him more about AJ and why he'd taken the sleazy man on as a manager but the door pushed open.

"Christopher?" A tall, lovely young woman pushed forward. Her dark curls were a halo around her head, emphasizing her full lips and beautiful mocha skin. So he had a real name after all.

"Iris," The Orphan, *Chris*, said in the gravelly voice of a hipster singer. He swung his guitar down and the young woman stepped straight into his arms.

Her height put her perfectly face to face with him still on the stool.

"You okay, babe?" Chris searched her eyes, worried lines etching his brow.

Iris nodded. "Always. I'm so sorry I'm late." She wound her arms behind his neck. "I missed you."

"Nothing's right until you're here," he whispered. "It's you and me against the world."

They gazed into each other's eyes with a look of such love and longing...

Cora's breath caught and a pain she couldn't explain clenched her chest. She wanted to look away, to give them privacy, but most of all to shield her eyes from the aching sweetness of their love.

They kissed gently, and Cora did look away but not before seeing the naked intimacy on their faces.

"Ma'am?" the young woman called. Cora glanced back; Chris and Iris were still in a clinch, and Iris was looking back at her. "Can we go backstage now?"

"Yes," Cora managed to say, her throat suddenly dry. "I mean, I think so. I'll check...if you're ready."

"We're ready," Chris said, face lit up. He hadn't taken his eyes off of the lovely Iris, whose smile bloomed easily on her lips.

Cora backed away, signaling Thane, who stepped in.

"That went well." Hype appeared at her elbow, looking way more mellow than when she last saw him. She suspected he'd stepped out and taken something; his blue eyes looked a little glazed. "He'll play?"

"Yes, he was just waiting for—" Cora broke off when the crowd jostled her to the side. The Orphan's entourage moved towards the door.

"Good work, toots." A rough voice made both Cora and Hype turn. AJ stood there smoking a cigar.

"You can't smoke in here. It's a fire hazard," Hype sputtered.

"Beat it, freak." AJ stared the shorter man down. AJ was as broad as he was tall, but his bulk only added to his menace. "I'm here to talk to the lady."

"Mr. Ubeli won't like it."

"Mr. Ubeli doesn't like a lot of stuff I do." AJ gestured with his cigar holding hand, sprinkling bits of ash on the floor. He turned to Cora and she shrank back. He was the last person she felt like dealing with right now. "I'd like to continue our earlier conversation."

"I'd rather not." Cora tried to keep the quiver out of her voice. He was just a man and they were in public. She didn't have to be such a coward. This was her life, she tried to remind herself.

"Oh, I think you do." And AJ slung his arm around her shoulders, steering her towards the door. Cora tried to step away, but he was built like a bear and easily blocked her. She felt panic rising as he bullied her forward.

She could see Hype's wide blue eyes following her worriedly and she tried to halt in her tracks, but AJ's arm caught her and pushed her towards the door with him. *What the—*

She tried to twist away from him but his hands gripped even tighter, hard enough to leave bruises. She was on the verge of freaking out when a voice rolled across the room.

"Get your hands off my wife."

Marcus stood in the doorway, glowering at AJ. As always, Cora felt his presence like a physical thing, a storm front moving into the room. Everyone, including AJ, froze.

"Marcus, man of the hour." AJ grinned at the new arrival. His arm fell away and Cora scuttled to the side.

Marcus put his hand out for her and, gods help her, she went to him. He pulled her close and she sank against his side, "Are you ok?"

"Yes," she lied. She could feel the heat of his anger, but he kept it controlled. She wished she hadn't had to be rescued, least of all by him. She needed to pull away from him if she was ever going to keep her sanity.

But Marcus only put his arm around her shoulder and tucked her more firmly to his side before facing AJ. And it felt so good, so safe in his arms.

The room had mostly cleared. Hype had retreated near the makeup tables and was instructing the people there to take a break and move out. Two of The Orphan's body-guards stood hulking around; Cora guessed they were AJ's men.

The mobster faced Marcus and she realized that if his shoulders weren't so stooped, he'd almost be as tall as her husband. AJ was larger than Marcus, too, and although Marcus had the frame of an athlete, the older man struck an intimidating figure. She felt a little better about not standing up to him. Even now AJ smoked his cigar casually, acting unfazed as he studied Marcus.

"AJ," Marcus finally acknowledged him. "I see you met my wife."

"Beautiful girl you have there, Marcus. Real sweet too." He winked at Cora and she stiffened in shock. Was he trying to imply she'd been flirting with him?

She shuddered in disgust and Marcus's arm around her tightened.

"We'll have to forgive AJ for being so rude," Marcus said to Cora, although he kept his eyes on AJ. "He hasn't been to New Olympus in a while."

AJ lost all interest in Cora as he narrowed his eyes at Marcus. "That's right. A bunch of riffraff showed up. Didn't like the way the neighborhood was going."

"A bunch of your friends moved out at the same time, as I recall. One particular family with two brothers."

"Used to have three brothers." AJ's eyes glittered with

anger, but he controlled it like Marcus. He stuck the cigar in the side of his mouth and spoke around it. "Actually only two moved to Metropolis."

"Ah yes," Marcus's voice held a note of cool satisfaction. "One of the three disappeared during his time here. The one with a twin—what were their names?"

"Karl and Alexander." AJ puffed angrily.

"Karl and Alex. Forgive me, I always get them mixed up." Marcus chuckled. "I don't even remember which one disappeared."

"Karl. Missing, presumed dead."

Dear gods, they were talking about her father. Like she wasn't even here. Like she had nothing at stake in the conversation.

AJ had forgotten his cigar for the moment and Cora stared at its lengthening ash. AJ snatched it out of his mouth. "His brothers Alexander and Ivan send their regards."

Marcus's face split into a scary smile. "He does? How considerate. His widow, too, I assume? How is Demi? Our last meeting was far too short. And you're such a good little errand boy—tell me, when the brothers sent you to spy on me, did they also tell you to bring me my take of your little club? Because that would definitely soften me up. Probably not enough to let my control of the city slip, but your time in exile hasn't made you any smarter."

The mobster flushed so red Cora wondered if he'd explode with anger. The room was empty except for the Ubelis, Hype, and AJ with his two thugs. Cora felt nervous watching the showdown, but Marcus seemed as calm and in control as ever, so she took her cues from him. She was sure her husband's men were just outside the room.

In the meantime, AJ had gotten himself under control

as well. "What, I deliver a musician to you, a show that everyone in the nation is dying for, and I give him to *you*, in an exclusive two week run—and this is how you repay me?" He forced a laugh as if he'd heard a weak attempt at a joke. "You accuse me of spying, of plotting? Marcus, I knew you when you were a boy! I knew your father."

"Don't mention my father in my presence again," Marcus snapped. The two thugs behind AJ shifted and pressed their hands against their weapons as if Marcus's words were actual weapons pointed at them.

Cora held herself perfectly still, recognizing the tension in the room. For a long moment everyone waited for the Lord of the Underworld to break the silence.

"Your bosses have a long memory. So do I," Marcus said softly. "This is my city. I own it. My power is still absolute. You can take that message back."

"I'm here to protect my investment. I'm not leaving—" AJ sputtered.

Marcus held up a hand and AJ fell silent. Marcus spoke in a low voice, but everyone in the room felt its menace.

"I respect the deal we made. You can stay in my city for two weeks. But once The Orphan is gone, you will no longer be welcome in New Olympus."

AJ licked his lips, his hatred for Marcus plain on his face.

"Make your arrangements, AJ," Marcus commanded. "Two weeks and you're out." Marcus started for the door with Cora still on his arm. He guided her forward then looked back over his shoulder at his enemy. "And your club still owes me tribute."

Hype was at the door, opening it for them. Cora and Marcus swept out and Hype followed them, unnaturally quiet. Cora didn't know what to think, but her legs felt a little weak from the entire confrontation.

Outside in the hall, Sharo stood with a knot of black-clad Shades, awaiting their leader.

"You hear that?" Marcus asked Sharo.

The large man nodded. "Two weeks and then kick him out. That really how we're gonna play it?"

"Let him look around before he reports back to Metropolis. Then he can tell Demi and the brothers we're not afraid of them."

"You sure they're behind this?" Sharo asked quietly.

Cora was surprised they were talking so freely in front of her but she was glad, too. She'd been relying on whispers and snatches of conversations she overheard here and there to know what was happening in the war between her family's criminal dynasty and Marcus's.

"It hasn't been so long that they've forgotten what it was like to rule." Marcus jerked his head at the Shades. "Get in there and check on him."

The soldiers immediately left the hall for the green room, to watch over AJ. "The Orphan is a Trojan horse. To get our guard down while AJ looks around. But if we move too early, we'll look nervous. We can't afford to look weak."

"Better play this perfectly," Sharo murmured in a voice deep as a grave. "We've managed to keep it to a few skirmishes between us and the Titans so far. But if this goes bad, it means war." The big man turned and stalked away, pictures on the wall trembling in his wake.

Cora finally took a deep, shuddering breath.

"You okay?" Marcus turned to her. "You shouldn't have had to see that," he murmured.

She was confused when he held her close for a moment, rubbing a soothing hand up her back. Did he mean she shouldn't have had to see it because he was sorry that it might upset her hearing about the ongoing fight between him and her family? Or that she shouldn't have seen it because he didn't think it was any of her business?

"I'm alright."

"I made you late for the concert." He looked concerned and in his arms, Cora felt all her tension drain away. She was tempted, so tempted, to pretend that Marcus was just a handsome businessman who owned a nightclub and concert hall, and she was his wife. To pretend they were a normal couple.

But she was done with all that. She'd glimpsed real love a moment before, on Christopher and Iris's faces. When Marcus gazed at her fondly, she was a beautiful possession. A toy he didn't have to share. It hurt so much, knowing real love wasn't something she could have. Not love like Chris and Iris shared—sweet and fragile and innocent. Marcus didn't understand that sort of sentiment, and if she tried to explain it, he would laugh at her.

She pulled away and crossed her arms over her chest.

A small frown furrowed Marcus's brow but he only said, "Hype will get you to your private box. I'll be there for the second half, after I finish talking to some people."

He didn't wait for a response before handing her over to Hype and leaving in a square of bodyguards. And he didn't look back even once.

THREE

Cora sat in the beautiful box, looking down on the polished wood floor of the stage, waiting for The Orphan's New Olympus debut.

She glanced over at the empty box seat beside her. For a second, she wished Marcus were here with her to see the entire show. But then she shook her head at herself.

It's better this way. Marcus might eventually show, but this was not a date. They weren't that kind of couple and Cora needed every reminder she could get if she was going to get over her ridiculous infatuation with her own husband.

She was distracted from her thoughts as The Orphan came on stage. The crowd immediately started going insane.

Security strained to hold them back from the stage. The Orphan had only just walked out, but already the front of the stage had a mound of roses and lacy underthings.

The Orphan sat on the stool provided, much like his posture backstage. He leaned forward towards the mic. The stage went dark except for a single spotlight shining down over his head.

"This is for Iris," he said in his raspy voice, and the fans started crying out in ecstasy. Cora watched one faint, falling against a security guard who struggled to keep a barrier between the pressing fans and the stage.

Then The Orphan started playing.

And Cora forgot about everything. The concert hall, her complicated relationship with Marcus, even the intermittent cries of fans.

The music.

His *voice*.

It was haunting, full of such longing and...*love*.

He held nothing back. He ripped himself open, right there on the stage for all to see and share. But no, it wasn't for everyone. He didn't look out over the crowd like normal singers did.

It was for her. *Iris*. Every time he looked up, his eyes focused only on one place, and Cora knew it must be where Iris was sitting.

When he sang about stars in her hair and how she was melody made flesh and how Cupid's arrow had pierced his blood and bones—

Cora held herself still even as tears poured down her cheeks. Her body was alive with goosebumps but it was so much more than that. His music transported. It was ecstatic. Transcendent. Soul-shattering.

And it didn't stop until the last guitar chord was struck.

Cora inhaled on a sob, her fingers clenched on the railing, the echo of his voice still ringing through the club.

And then reality crashed down.

The fans, mostly women, were screaming their pleasure. The noise was painful, piercing, and yet Cora still couldn't hear anything but The Orphan's last song ringing in her ears.

. . .

AND IF YOU die before I wake,
   I'll give my soul; it's theirs to take,
   I'll come up to the river gates,
   I'll come and sing the gods to sleep,
   And steal you home for keeps.
   Forever mine.
   Forever love.
   Forever.

CORA SAT BACK WITH A SIGH, feeling as tense and coiled as a guitar string. She wasn't sure she be able to stand if she tried.

The Orphan didn't move from his spot in the center of the stage. He looked perfectly ordinary again.

Until he began playing the encore. Then he transformed again somehow. It was as if his voice transported around the place, making him seem larger than the simply dressed man standing before them.

His voice promised things and caressed the words of the songs. With every passing minute the energy in the room grew higher and higher, until the aching need was a tension no one could ignore.

He finished up another song and the women went mad again. Cora watched one of them start to climb and claw at a security guard, desperate to get on stage.

"I love you," she was screaming. "Please, I need you."

Disturbed, Cora stood up. Her heartbeat was racing. She excused herself past the few of Marcus's associates who shared the box. If they thought anything of her tear-stained face and ruined make-up, they were wise enough not to stare. Her bodyguards were parked in the back, also mesmerized by the song. She slipped past them into the hall.

In the bathroom, Cora breathed deeply, finally letting herself sob outright. The music ran like a current through her and she thought again of how Chris and Iris had looked at one another backstage.

His music was love personified. Every chord he played, every word he's sang...

Why couldn't Marcus love her back?

Love her even a *tenth* of that?

Again she lost her breath because she couldn't believe she'd just admitted it, even in the quiet of her mind. Oh gods, but it was all she wanted.

Still. *Still*, all she wanted was for Marcus to love her back.

He could drape her in all the diamonds from all the world and give her power and freedom and position and a million spa trips—none of it mattered. None of it was what she truly wanted.

All she wanted was the simplest gift. But it was the one that Marcus would never give.

His love.

"Stupid girl," Cora said to her reflection, shuddering with emotion. She hadn't learned a damned thing in all this time.

Marcus used her. Maybe he was nicer to her now than he'd first intended or envisioned. And after saving his life, maybe he felt a little bit indebted to her. But she was still just another cog in the machine of his business. A pretty face for the press.

Only in the privacy of their penthouse did she even get a glimpse of the man behind the mask but she was probably just deluding herself about that, too. What she pretended to herself was intimacy was likely him just using her to meet another of his needs.

He used to fuck that horrible Lucinda woman on the regular, but now Cora was more convenient. She was already always around, so he fucked her instead. But gods, she didn't even know if he was faithful. They'd never made any promises of the sort to one another. And the way he always kept her apart from himself...

He never let her in and he never intended to.

She dropped her head in defeat and for once, allowed the grief in. It was like a death, finally abandoning her hope of ever being loved back.

Long minutes later, she shook her head and looked up at her face in the mirror. Ugh, she was a mess. She couldn't let anybody see her like this. It felt more important than ever to learn the game of pretending to be fine even though nothing was.

She began the arduous process of using endless scraps of tissue to clean up her mascara and was just finishing up when—

One of the stall doors banged open.

What the—? Cora jumped. She hadn't realized there was anyone else in the bathroom. Had they been in the stall the whole time she'd been having her meltdown?

"Hello?" Cora called out, stepping around the corner.

A figure was slumped on the floor just inside the furthest stall.

Cora gasped and ran forward. "Are you okay?"

When there wasn't any response, she moved the door slightly so she could see.

Inside the stall, half sprawled in front of the toilet seat, was a woman. Her dress was black and red, and her long, wicked looking nails were painted to match. It was Ashley, AJ's girl from earlier.

"Oh my—" Cora whispered.

Feeling sick, Cora kneeled down to look at the woman's face. Under the mess of hair, the muscles were slack. Her eyes were open, staring, glazed. She wasn't moving.

Someone in the hall knocked sharply on the door and Cora jumped. Suddenly every detail seemed sharper, clearer. She saw the needle lying on the floor beside the woman's arm.

"Everything ok in there?"

"Sharo," Cora cried out, recognizing the voice. "Help...please."

Seconds later the underboss barged through the door. Cora still crouched, frozen, next to the stall door.

"She's not moving," Cora whimpered. She backed away as the big man approached.

Sharo peered inside the stall and uttered one sharp curse. "Did you touch her?"

"No." Cora couldn't stop staring at Ashley's face. The vacant eyes seemed to follow her, accusing.

Then Sharo stepped in front of Cora, blocking her view. "We need to go." He rumbled, and took her arm. His large body pressed forward, herding her bodily toward the door.

"Wait— What about her—? Is she—?"

"She's dead," Sharo growled and guided Cora firmly out of the bathroom and down the hall. Cora stumbled a little on shaky heels and Sharo almost picked her up, righting her while still moving. "And you can't be seen in there."

A crackle came over Sharo's earpiece and Cora knew he was no longer listening to her. "I've got Mrs. Ubeli. South bathrooms. Yes, sir. Right away."

"What?" she asked. What else could possibly go wrong tonight?

"The fans rushed the stage and the green room. The Orphan barely made it out. I've got to get you out of here, now."

FOUR

"WHAT THE HELL were you thinking wandering away all alone in a crowd like that?" Marcus had managed to hold his tongue until they got back to the penthouse but not for a moment longer.

He'd been dealing with cleanup from the mobbing incident on the car ride back anyway—one woman had been injured in the stampede and when The Orphan caught wind of it, he said he refused to play any more gigs. Thane and Hype were freaking out about it.

But right now Marcus couldn't give a shit about anything other than the beautiful, disobedient woman standing in front of him.

Cora's mouth dropped open as she turned to look back at him right as he closed the front door. "I didn't wander away. I went to the bathroom. And—" Her eyes flashed. "—And I wouldn't have been alone if you'd joined me like you said you would." Her chin went up like part of her wanted to take it back but then she decided not to.

"On. Your. Knees," Marcus ground out through clenched teeth.

Cora looked at Marcus in disbelief. "You've got to be kidding m—"

"Don't make me repeat myself, wife." His voice was so cold it could have iced the North Pole.

But he kept reliving that moment—getting to the balcony where she was supposed to be sitting right as the crowd mobbed the stage.

And he'd had no clue where his own wife was as the violent scene unfolded below him. He'd shouted over his earpiece to all of his Shades but none of them had eyes on her. How the fuck did none of them have eyes on her after the earlier incident with AJ?

How the fuck could you *have left her side after what happened with AJ?* He'd been meeting with his capos about the big shipment due to arrive later this month. It was imperative that they secure the goods and manage distribution instead of the Titans.

But none of it fucking mattered if he lost her.

It had been six torturous minutes before Sharo located her. And when he had, he found her with a dead girl.

Marcus's hands clenched. He needed to regain control and he needed it now.

But Cora only crossed her arms over her chest stubbornly and glared at him.

He didn't miss how her chin quivered the next second, though. He wasn't the only one who'd been shaken by tonight's events. Cora had been the one to discover the girl who'd overdosed—AJ's girl. Because of that asshole, his wife had to look death in the face.

She needed this as much as he did. And he would always give her what she needed. He could quiet her mind and make it all go away—if she would just give herself over to him.

"Bedroom," he ordered.

Her lips tightened but she marched to the bedroom. Good girl. If she'd protested, he'd have turned her over his knee right in the foyer, then made her crawl.

As soon as she stepped into the bedroom, his hands were on her. He stripped her quickly, his cock pressing against his pants as her slender form was revealed. He stepped away to gain some control.

Control. Right. That's what this was about.

He crooked his finger and pointed to the floor. She stepped out of the dress, naked but for her heels and diamonds, but didn't obey any further.

"Knees. Now." It wasn't a request.

Cora tested him for another long moment. But then finally, lips pursed, she sank to her knees in front of him.

The furious rushing noise in his ears quieted, replaced by a different sort of adrenaline. Yes. Hell yes. He'd needed this very badly and he hadn't even realized it.

He regularly claimed his wife's body in the middle of the night. At first he'd tried to stay away and deny his need for her. He couldn't afford any weaknesses and she made him weak. She made him soft when he had to be more ruthless than ever now.

The Titans had pulled back from an all-out street war but now Demi was trying to undercut him with all of his suppliers, willing to take massive losses if it meant driving him out of business. Some were loyal but others, especially foreign players, were loyal only to the dollar.

And the customer didn't care. Why buy product in New Olympus if they could make the hour and a half drive to Metropolis and get it for half the price?

Some even brought it back and tried to resell it in his streets. Ruthless enforcement only went so far when suddenly everyone thought they could make a buck and undercut Marcus's outfit completely. And just like happened every time, when rogue elements tried to step up and seize power, violence ensued.

The Titans didn't have to step one foot in the city and they'd already created chaos.

Controlling supply was the only answer, plus showing people the consequences of fucking with Marcus Ubeli. He'd bring peace and stability back to his city and stomp the Titans out for good this time. But at the moment, he was barely holding his city together.

Which meant he couldn't afford any distractions.

And Cora? He'd never known a greater distraction in his life.

If he could just get control of her, though, and himself too, then maybe everything else would fall into place. Maybe he'd had it all backwards. Maybe true control started at home and worked its way outward, like the concentric circles from a stone tossed in a pond.

Yes, if he could only master control here...

He put his hand on Cora's head, her hair silk soft underneath his fingers.

"You know what to do," he told her. He could and would order her, but this first act would prove her compliance.

Biting her lip, she opened his pants and took him out. Her breath quickened imperceptibly, but he noticed, as he noticed everything about her. He noticed her nipples hardening in her dress. The dreamy cast to her gaze. How she raised her chin, bringing her face alongside his cock, and how she took a deep breath. She swayed a little on her knees as if the scent of him intoxicated her.

His cock throbbed just watching her and she hadn't even touched him yet.

"Kiss it, angel. Show me how much you love this."

A tremor went through her at the word "love" and he hid a smile even knowing it made him a bastard.

She loved him, he knew it. He also knew she wished she didn't. Her love satisfied him in a deep place, even though he didn't love her back. He couldn't. Not if he was going to be the King of the Underworld, the Scourge of the City. They had many names for him. But if there was the one thing the Lord of Night could not afford, it was love.

It was unfair to his sweet Cora. It always had been. If he loved her, he would let her go and tell her to run as far away from him as she could get. Alas, it was just another proof of his black heart.

He would *never* let her go.

She was *his*. Something he would prove again to both of them tonight.

He needed to break apart his lover and remake her into a new creation, a creature born of savage lovemaking, a creature belonging only to him.

Her lips brushed the dark head of his cock, her eyes closed like she was in prayer.

Fitting, because here he was her god.

His hand left her head and cupped her soft cheek. "That's it. That's right. Good girl."

Cora shivered again and put her mouth on him, running her tongue over his turgid length. Slowly savoring.

Her hand came up to stroke his balls. His groin tightened at the sight of her delicate, perfectly manicured fingernails lightly scratching his scrotum.

Her lips worked over him just as he liked it, popping his

head into her mouth and tonguing and sucking the most sensitive spots.

He let her worship, stroking her head and whispering "good girl" over and over. This was a perfect moment, meant to wash the fear and anger of the night away. And it worked. He could rule the world as long as he owned this beautiful woman.

As long as he could have her like this, on her knees.

Looking down at her innocent face taking his cock almost brought him to his. He gathered the hair at the base of her neck and used it like a leash to turn her head this way and that.

He tugged her off his cock and then dragged her up one side of his length and down the other. She nibbled on the head when she came back to it and he pushed her lower so she'd suck on his balls. And suck she did, rolling them one by one in her mouth.

A curse escaped him and Cora's eyes, blue as a summer sky, opened lazily. She gave him a small smile that made his heart soar.

"Suck me," he told her gruffly to hide his reaction. He tugged her hair and she obeyed, letting him slide deep in her mouth, stretching her lips and hitting the back of her throat. Was there any better feeling?

Only one, he decided. The feeling of her cumming around his cock. He might allow that tonight, after he dominated her. After he reminded her of her place.

His hips surged and she gasped around him. He drew out, letting her cough and sputter. Her eyes watered.

"Too much?"

With a little shake of her head, she pushed back onto his cock, determined and straining to take him deeper. *Fuck, that's it.* Her mascara streamed in rivulets with her tears and it was fucking beautiful. Innocence sullied, but only for *him*.

She kept swallowing him down until her nose nearly pressed to the base of his cock. Her tongue fluttered underneath and he lost control.

"Cora," he moaned. Folding, he grabbed her head and kept her there as he sent his cum shooting down her throat and into her belly. He released her as quickly as he could, but she remained on her knees, chest heaving as she sucked in air.

She'd submitted to him fully and pleased him beyond measure. Then why did it feel like she was the one in control?

In a rare moment of weakness, he murmured, "*Sei bellissima. Sono pazzo di te.*" *You're so beautiful. I'm crazy for you.* Her brow wrinkled but he didn't translate. It was bad enough that he'd whispered it aloud in the first place.

Mustering himself, he straightened. With his handkerchief, he gently wiped the mascara stains from her face. "You did well tonight. I never should've left you alone."

She blinked as if shocked by the admission that was close to an apology. "It's fine. I survived."

"You'll never be alone like that again." He'd have Sharo stick to her side if he couldn't escort her personally.

"You don't have to worry about me."

"I do. You're my responsibility. My most treasured possession."

She closed her eyes at that, an expression crossing her face. Not hurt or anger, but longing. Cora might fight, might protest, but deep down she understood his possessiveness. She craved it, even. She was his perfect mate. And she'd been in danger tonight. True danger.

He brushed his fingers over her face. "Were you afraid?"

"A little."

"My business won't touch you." Sudden memories of Chiara gripped him. Finding her body bloodied and broken. No. He would *never* let that happen to Cora. He gripped her chin. "It will never touch you."

"Marcus." She looked up at him, lips shiny, gaze soft and submissive. "You touch me."

He bent, lifted her to the bed, and lay her down. She spread out before him, a sacrifice on an altar.

The diamonds glittered at her ears and wrists and the hollow of her throat. He touched the right earring, enjoying her needy shudder as he fingered her earlobe. The bright jewels winked at him as she moved. She couldn't wear his chains out in public, but she could wear these. She was his and everyone would know it.

"Yes, I touch you. I'm the only one who can. The only one who ever will." He bent over her, rough hands grasping and claiming. He wished he could touch every inch of her at once, hold her in the palm of his hand.

As his fingers penetrated her, he sucked on the tender juncture between her neck and shoulder. Her hands slid up his shoulders and into his hair until he caught her wrists and pinned her.

She quivered under him, eyes wide and pupils blown. He transferred her wrists to one hand and held them above her head. His right hand splayed between her breasts.

"All of this. All of you belongs to me." He needed to know she understood, and that she understood it deep in her bones.

She gave a slight nod. He rewarded her with two fingers

in her pussy, working deep, brushing against the sensitive spot inside her until her hips rose off the bed. Her chest flushed as he watched her orgasm bloom in her. Her eyes went wide, almost shocked, as it peaked, going on and on as he crooked his fingers inside her and tugged. Her feet dug into the bed and her whole body went taut as aftershocks rolled through her.

When it was done, she sagged to the bed. He removed his fingers and thrust them into her mouth. Her mouth softened, accepting him even though he wasn't gentle. Her tongue curled around his wet fingers, licking and lapping, tasting herself.

His cock curled up to the sky, his own orgasm threatening to boil out of him. He'd already cum once and hard, but his cock had forgotten. It throbbed as if her very presence could set him off.

He pulled his fingers out of her mouth.

She was submissive to him. Only to him. And he would keep her safe.

He crawled onto the bed and rose up over her, cock in hand. "Touch your breasts," he ordered. "Cup them. Show them to me."

Cora's slender fingers did as he commanded and he stroked himself faster.

"Your nipples. Pinch them. Harder," he demanded.

She was already rolling her nipples, ripe berries between her fingertips, obeying him like she read his mind. Like they were one—

His climax blasted through him, sending semen spurting over her naked flesh. Growling in pleasure, he marked her with his seed. Without being ordered, Cora stroked her stomach, rubbing the silky essence into her flawless skin. Accepting him.

Her hair spread around her head like a halo. Her body shimmered, pale and beautiful in the low light.

"Angel," he breathed.

It seemed only natural to kneel down at the end of the bed, slide his hands under her shapely thighs to draw her close, and dip his head to her sex to drink of her essence.

After she came once or twice or fifteen times, he rose again and finally fucked her. He fucked her like he owned her because tonight he'd proven again that he did, both to her and to himself.

And he knew that her writhing cries would nourish him through the night and into tomorrow, when he would don his suit like armor and go forth to do battle in the boardroom, in the clubs and street corners he owned—shoring up defenses and strengthening borders until the constant attack from the Titans broke against the unseen walls like a tide.

Tonight though, there was only Cora, the daughter of his enemies, now his in every way.

"*Tu mi appartieni. Per sempre.*" *You belong to me. Forever.*

She sighed as he spoke into her skin. She didn't understand the words of the incantation but the spell still wound around her body nonetheless, binding her to him.

He couldn't tie her to the bed forever, but he could tie her to him with pleasure. With dresses and diamonds, and nights drenched with passion. He couldn't tell her he loved her, but he could keep her safe, locked in a high tower, and give her his body without reserve.

It would be enough. It had to be.

FIVE

Two days after the concert, Cora sat sipping designer bottled water in a robe and watched people backstage at the fashion show. Marcus's friend Armand had just come out with a new line of resort wear, and Cora had been roped into modeling it.

Hair and makeup done, she sat backstage bored out of her mind and half listened to the models' gossip.

"I met the Orphan last night," one of the women was smiling smugly into the mirror. Stunningly beautiful with sky high cheekbones and pouty lips, she was playing with her blonde hair. Her friend, an equally lovely brunette with wide eyes, leaned closer.

"What? Where?"

"At an after party, duh. He was luscious."

"So did you talk to him? What did he say?"

Cora leaned forward too, curious.

"Well, he didn't say much. You know he's refusing to play the rest of his nights? He said he thought it was too dangerous." The model shook her head at the mirror. "I told him he was being silly, and that his art needed to be shared. I think I inspired him."

Cora swigged her water bottle and wondered if she should comment.

"We had a more private conversation after that." Model number one smirked.

"Oh, my, gods," the brunette squealed. Cora rolled her eyes.

"I definitely gave him a few more reasons to stay and fulfill his contract."

Cora decided she'd had enough. "What about his fiancée?" she broke in. Chris would have proposed by now and she knew Iris would say yes. The way those two had looked at each other...

The two models stared at Cora like she was speaking Greek. "You know, the one he writes all the songs to," Cora persisted. "Did he mention her at all?"

"Sweetie, most men don't mention their significant others around me. I guess, around me, they're less significant." The beauty flipped her hair over her shoulder and her eyes went back to the mirror, preening.

Cora wanted to bitch slap the model until the woman made proper eye contact during a conversation. Instead, she jumped up. "I need more water. Do you want anything?" Without waiting for a response, she strode off toward craft services.

She heard the women gossiping about her as she left. They didn't bother to lower their voices.

"I don't know how she got this job at all. I mean, she's fat."

"Her husband landed it for her. He's a crime boss and probably killed someone to get her in."

"Probably."

Cora walked with head held high, her posture perfect, focused straight ahead. She had to stop to let three young fashionistas rush by with a rack of clothes. Another young hair stylist, his hair in a mohawk, caught her eye from his place behind a model's chair. He smiled sympathetically and she grinned back. She recognized him from Armand's spa, Metamorphoses, where she was a regular.

The spread of food at craft services mocked her queasy stomach. She grabbed a bottle of coconut water instead and found a place to sit near the sound system on the outskirts of the activity.

Try as she might, Cora couldn't keep the model's words from bothering her. She didn't care what people called her; it was Marcus she was worried about.

He hadn't come home last night. Since the Orphan debacle at the club several days ago, Cora hadn't seen her husband. She was used to his long business hours. Marcus often went for a late-night swim in the penthouse pool, but at least he'd come home and lie down for a few hours before donning his suit again at dawn.

This morning she woke up beside his untouched pillow. And the papers reported the rumor that The Orphan's concerts would be canceled. Thane officially denied the report but she knew it wasn't making Marcus's job easier.

The night after the concert had been... Cora lifted a hand to her neck just at the memory of it. They hadn't done anything like that for a long time and then two sessions in one night... She felt her face flush.

Out of the corner of her eye, Cora noticed she wasn't sitting alone on the outskirts anymore. A woman all in black had strutted over and slouched against the wall nearby. Her black hair fell around her face in a short, blunt cut. With her faded jeans and her scuffed boots, she looked like a photographer, except she didn't have a camera. Cora wondered for a second whether she was a model; she was pretty enough, though she didn't look happy about it.

Arms crossed and wearing a frown, she surveyed the scene with Cora and moved close enough to comment, "I'm so over these bitches. Cat walk, more like catty-walk."

"Are you a model?" Cora asked politely.

"Please," the woman huffed. "I'm not one of those brainless bimbos. Like I'd be seen trotting my bare ass down a runway. Do I look like an idiot?"

Cora's lips quirked into a smile and then flattened out as she waited for the woman to notice who she was talking to.

"Oh, shit, I'm sorry." The woman realized Cora's catwalk-ready hair and makeup. "Blast, I'm always putting my foot in my mouth." She turned and stuck out her hand. "I'm Olivia."

"Cora." Cora shook Olivia's hand. "Pleased to meet you. So, if you're not modeling, what are you doing here?"

"Favor to Armand. The pretty, bronzed dick head. I did his whole web platform and he wanted me here to make sure I got the vibe right." Olivia went off cursing, calling Armand several more colorful terms while Cora sat silent in shock.

"Are you mad at him?" Cora finally asked.

"Mad at Armand?" Now Olivia seemed shocked. "Not at all. I'm here, aren't I? And I'm going to his party tomorrow. Are you coming?"

"To his party? I don't think I'm invited."

"Ah, of course you are. I'll ask Manny."

"Manny?"

"My pet name for Armand."

Cora reigned in her laugh.

"Oh, I nickname anyone I like. Yours would be easy. Cora Bora."

"So you're a website designer," Cora changed the subject desperately.

"Programmer, hacker. Website design is something I only do for close friends and ex-lovers." Olivia hopped up on the heavy cases for the sound equipment and swung her legs.

"I see." Feeling mischievous, Cora asked, "Which one is Armand?"

"Huh?"

"Which one is Armand—a close friend or ex-lover? Or does a lady not kiss and tell?"

Olivia barked out a laugh. "Oh, honey, I'm no lady. Truth is, he's both."

"Oh?" Cora let her eyebrows rise at this tantalizing gossip.

Olivia shrugged. "It was late, I was working. He called me a genius." A hint of red tinged her cheeks. "That always gets me," Olivia muttered. She shook her head forward so her hair fell over her face.

"Are you blushing?" Cora teased, amused to find a chink in the gruff woman's armor.

"He's a slut, though. Everybody's had him. And we weren't good for each other. We're better as friends."

As if on cue, Armand went by, looking harried yet suave in a grey suit.

"Manny!" Olivia shouted. Everyone backstage paused to stare at her. "Is Cora invited to the party tomorrow?"

"Of course, Olivia. My love. Now please shut up. Makeup!" And he rushed off into the lights.

Olivia chuckled, shaking her head so her short hair fell around her face.

"See, told you. You're invited. Come to the party."

Cora's mouth was gaping open at this point.

"Oh, come on. Do you want me to beg? Ok, I will. Please, come to Armand's party. I need someone there to talk to. No one understands me." Olivia fake pouted.

Cora couldn't help it, she laughed.

Olivia looked slyly out from under her black helmet of hair. "Oh, so the perfect facade does crack."

"You're funny," Cora told her. "I like it."

"Glad to be of service. Are you coming to the party?"

Cora sighed. "I'll ask my husband if we have anything going on."

"Good, clear your schedule. Besides there's a hottie or two there I want you to meet."

"Olivia," Cora gasped. "I'm married."

"Not for you! For me, dumbass." Olivia huffed and blew her hair out of her face. "You can give me tips on how to woo him." She grinned and wiggled her eyebrows.

SIX

MARCUS PROWLED THROUGH THE PENTHOUSE, looking for his wife. They'd lost another shipment to the Titans tonight. Guns this time. Demi was trying to flood his streets with semi-automatics.

Just last week he had to put down a gang that thought to fight his men for territory. Others had the same idea now that the Titans were challenging him so outright, thinking they could take advantage of his distracted focus.

They were wrong. He'd put every last one of them six feet under. But an influx of weapons like this would only further embolden new enemies.

It was just eight at night and he should still be at the office discussing blockades into the city.

Instead he was standing here in the doorway of his master bath. Watching his wife as she toweled off, humming to herself, obviously oblivious to his presence. Steam still filled the air. She must have only just stepped out of the shower.

As she raised her head, she shrieked, seeing his steam-blurred reflection in the mirror.

"Hush, it's just me." Marcus stepped into the room as she wrapped the towel around herself.

"You shocked me," she said, eyes still wide. "I didn't expect you home this early."

"It's almost eight."

"You didn't come home last night. And isn't there a concert at Elysium?"

"Not tonight." Marcus leaned against the sink and watched her, his eyes running up and down her toweled form.

But soon looking wasn't enough. He stepped closer and then his hands closed over her shoulders, sliding down her bare skin and taking the towel with them.

"This is why I come home," he whispered into her ear. "You make me forget all my troubles." It was more than he meant to say but true all the same.

They didn't play today. No, his need was too urgent. He had to be inside his wife so he boosted her up onto the counter, unbuckled and shoved his pants down and then—

He threw his head back as he sank inside her. She was wet for him. Always wet. He reached up and pinched her nipple. Her sharp gasp made him even harder, though he wouldn't have thought that was possible.

This was all he'd been able to think about, all day long. He'd been pissed about the shipment, it was true. He wanted to strangle Demi Titan.

But more than that, he'd wanted to get in his car and break every traffic law to get home and fuck his wife.

He pulled out and then stroked back in and she clenched around him so fucking deliciously. Her body was made for his. There was no other way to describe it. Sex had never been like this before. Like something that felt as necessary as breathing. Every hour of the day he went without being inside her he wanted to make up with two more buried balls deep in her pussy.

Some of his lieutenants were grumbling about his disappearing acts. Sharo had reported that little shit, Angelo, trying to stir the guys up by saying Marcus was pussy whipped by a Titan. Sharo had given the boy a beating he wasn't likely to soon forget for his disrespect. But times were tense and the less time Marcus spent at home, the better.

Frankly, he'd thought it would get better with time. That he'd work his wife out of his system. But like feeding an addiction, it only got worse. Sometimes he fucked her three times a night and then again in the morning...and yet all day he could think only about coming back home and doing this—

He thrust in again, clutching her ass to get the best angle possible, to go deep and also grind against her to make her mewl in pleasure. Her little noises that he was fucking addicted to as well if he was being honest with himself.

"Tesoro mio. Mia moglie." My treasure. My wife.

Her breathy squeaks got higher and higher as he drove her to the edge and everything else fell away. There was only this. Her body. Her nails clawing his scalp and her hips thrusting against his in desperation, she was so close.

Some nights he loved to torture her. To pull back and make her beg. To remind her who exactly was in control.

But right now he just wanted to make her fly and to feel her milking him so he kept pounding away. And when she screamed her orgasm and it echoed off the bathroom tiles, he let go and spilled into her, a king conquering his queen and marking her as his in the most primal way possible.

When it was done, she bowed her head over his shoulder, breath heaving. He ran his fingers down the small bumps of her spine and she shivered. He was still planted inside her and he pulled out and gave another small thrust, groaning at the pleasure she still brought him.

The steam from the mirror had mostly disappeared and he could see their reflections, the beautiful expanse of creamy skin tapering down to the tiniest little petite waste before flaring out again at her womanly hips. And him behind her, dark to her light, brute to her petite beauty.

She looked so tiny. So unbearably breakable. The world would snap her like a twig if he didn't protect her.

He wrapped his arms around her and held her to him, tight. Something in his chest squeezed uncomfortably.

He looked away from the mirror and let go of her, finally sliding out. "I'll let you clean up," he murmured.

For a brief second, she looked up, her huge blue eyes locking on his. Whatever she was thinking, he couldn't read it in her gaze. Except that maybe she wanted something from him. Something he couldn't give.

"Armand is having a party," she said tentatively.

Marcus's brow furrowed. Whatever he'd expected her to say, that wasn't it. "When?"

"Tomorrow night."

"You can't go." He was busy tomorrow night.

Her mouth dropped open and then her eyes flashed. "I wasn't asking for your permission."

"Well you should have been." The city was on the edge of fucking implosion and she wanted to go to a party? Who knew what kind of security would be there and who might sneak in? The wife of Marcus Ubeli would be more than an attractive target for countless enemies.

"I was trying to ask if you wanted to go with me but now I rescind the invitation." She hopped off the vanity and strode out of the bathroom.

Oh no she didn't.

"Don't you walk away from me." He grabbed her elbow and spun her around.

"And don't you fucking touch me without my permission." Her eyes blazed and Marcus's groin tightened. Oh he would have fun teaching her this lesson. She thought she would defy him, on today of all days?

But before he could even begin to chastise her, his damned phone rang. He couldn't afford to miss a single call. Not after all that had been happening.

"What?" he barked after pulling his phone out of his pocket.

"Boss, you gotta come down here," Sharo said. "We already got a lead on a buyer for the semis. Shouldn't talk over the phone but I'll tell you everything when you get here."

Fuck. He felt like throwing the phone against the wall. But no. Control in all things. Control always. Otherwise people got hurt.

He pointed a finger in Cora's face. "You and I will talk later."

She just crossed her arms over her chest and got an even more obstinate expression on her face. Oh yes, he'd enjoy teaching her this lesson very much. It would give him something to look forward to the rest of the very long night he had no doubt was ahead.

But his business kept him out all that night, and the next day, too.

SEVEN

Armand's party was in an enormous brownstone on the corner of two streets. Cora got out of the car, feeling a bit strange walking around in her little purple dress and stilettos without Marcus on her arm.

Her nightlife usually entailed a trip to one of Marcus's restaurants for drinks and greeting her husband's business associates. She felt giddy to be doing something for herself, by herself. And then immediately guilty because Marcus had told her explicitly not to come.

Well, he'd never come home to finish the argument, so she'd decided that meant his point was forfeited.

"Ms. Ubeli, slow down." Her assigned bodyguard exited the car behind her. Cora rolled her eyes.

She'd tried to give him the slip earlier but no such luck. That was fine. She knew security was important and that Marcus also likely already had word of her disobedience... and she couldn't deny the fizzle of excitement that thought sent through her. Which was probably more than a little screwed up. But she'd decided she wasn't thinking about it anymore.

She was here to have fun.

But she slowed when she saw the bouncers at the door.

"Invitation?" one of them rumbled.

"Um, I don't have one. Armand invited me."

The man just stared down at her. "Name?"

"Cora Ubeli," her bodyguard supplied. "Marcus Ubeli's wife."

The bouncer's eyes widened and he stepped aside immediately. Cora ducked her head, waving her hand at his apologies.

Once inside she hissed at the bodyguard, "Can I just keep a low profile for once?"

"Sorry Mrs. Ubeli, just trying to help." The man didn't sound sorry at all.

Cora wished that, for one night, she could just be Cora, country girl from the Midwest, alone in the big city. Of course, that had gotten her in trouble all those months ago. Right around the time she met Marcus.

She sighed. "Just stay over there. I know you have to do your job but everyone here is safe."

A young man with crazy curly hair ran by, holding a smoking bottle of something and screaming, "I've got a bomb!" He bowled into a knot of models who shrieked angrily and swatted at him. The bottle boiled over into a harmless puddle.

Cora closed her eyes. "Ok, that was just poor timing."

The bodyguard grimaced as three guys in suits and large pink wigs went by. "Go have fun." His tone doubted that she would.

Straightening her dress nervously, she turned back to the party. She recognized a bunch of bored-looking models from the fashion show the day before, and made a note to avoid them.

"Hey, bitch!" a cheerful shout caught Cora's attention. Olivia, looking slightly less scruffy in a black spangly top and the same black jeans and scuffed boots, waved her over with a beer in hand. "Come get a drink."

Cora started over and her bodyguard shadowed her. She stopped and addressed him again. "Um, do you mind just waiting over by the wall? I think I'll be safe with her. She's a friend."

The stonewall face was her answer. She sighed and headed over to Olivia, determined to ignore her bodyguard. Halfway there he caught her arm and stopped her.

"Look, Mrs. Ubeli, I want you to have a good time. But I work for your husband. And I answer to him. He's not particularly happy that you're here and ordered me to keep eyes on you at all times."

So he *had* already called Marcus. Cora stared the man down, furious. Marcus thought she needed a babysitter. Even after all this time, Marcus would only allow her the illusion of freedom. He still thought he could tell her where to go and when she could go there. And low and behold if she went anywhere without these ridiculous Shades who always wore sunglasses, even though right now they were inside a house, at night.

Still, she'd catch more flies with honey. She smiled sweetly at the man. "I'll stay out of trouble. I don't want to make your job any harder." She pulled her arm from his grip and joined her friend, shaking her head.

"What's with the entourage?"

"My husband couldn't come. He wanted to make sure I'm safe."

Olivia raised her eyebrows. "You know, while you were strutting your bare ass down the catwalk, I had a chance to look into you. I didn't think Ubeli would ever be an old married guy. And to someone like you."

Cora felt her cheeks tinge, with embarrassment or anger she wasn't sure which. "What do you mean?"

"Oh, Cora Bora, I just put my foot in my mouth again. Ignore it." Olivia handed her a drink with a paper umbrella in it. "Drink up."

Armand flitted by, a model on each arm, one male, one female, both wearing bunny ears. Armand himself had lost the suit jacket and was now in tight grey jeans and a sleeveless purple top. The tips of a black tattoo peeked out on his muscled shoulders.

With his dark eyes and swarthy skin, he could almost be Marcus's younger brother.

"Hey, look, Manny, you match." Olivia sloshed her drink as she pointed towards Cora's purple dress. "Oops."

"Oh, Cora, you gorgeous, gorgeous creature," Armand faced her. "Great work yesterday."

Cora flushed prettily. "Thanks, Armand."

The two models on either side of Armand looked sour.

"I'll be back in a bit, must make the rounds. Come on, bunnies." His entourage turned as one, and Cora could see more of Armand's tattoo across his back. Someday she'd ask to see it all.

"Lucky bastard." Olivia swigged her drink.

"Why do you say that?"

"Armand's amazing." Olivia pointed with her drink again, this time toward the retreating trio. "Dropped out of school to start his own spa. Now he owns twelve, ships product all around the world and has a budding fashion line."

Cora took a tentative sip of her cocktail. "How do you know all this?"

"Wikipedia." Olivia winked over her beer.

"You liar. You know everything."

Olivia shrugged. "Everything interesting."

"What sort of products?"

"Huh?"

"What sort of products does he ship?"

"How the hell should I know? Hair goop of some sort. Do I look like I go to a spa?"

Cora turned towards her. "You could come with me sometime."

"To their mothership?" Olivia watched three models glide by and narrowed her eyes. "I'd sooner die."

"Ok, it's not going to turn you into a bimbo. Unless you want to become one." Cora giggled at the image and then soothed Olivia, "I'm kidding. Just come and get your hair layered." Cora looked at Olivia's silky black locks. "You'd look amazing with a new cut."

"You think so?" Olivia touched her hair uncertainly.

"I know so. My dream job would be giving people makeovers—from hair to shoes."

"Would you go shopping with me?" Olivia asked. "I hate clothes. Seriously, I'd love some help."

"No problem." Cora smiled and clinked her glass against Olivia's. "Just let me know when."

"I'd like everyone's attention, please!" Armand stood on a table next to the drinks, now completely topless except for a furry vest with a tortoiseshell pattern.

"Just don't make me look like that," Olivia motioned towards the man. Cora nodded.

"A toast to a successful new fashion line!"

"To Fortune!" someone else cried, and everyone chimed in. "To Fortune!"

"These are Fortune jeans," Olivia told Cora. "One of the first he designed."

"I'm sure," Cora said, eyeing the faded pair.

"Oh, holy shit, there he is." Olivia grabbed Cora. "See him?"

Cora looked in the direction she was pointing, but all she saw were a few guys in pink wigs laughing with some models. "Where?"

"Right there, dummy! In the corner."

Looking past the more vibrant partygoers, Cora saw two guys standing in the corner, one dressed in a preppy polo shirt and the other in scuffed jeans and a faded t-shirt. Neither looked like they fit in but several models stood around flirting with the one in the polo shirt. Both guys were handsome, but they looked young, like they couldn't be any older than Cora herself.

"Ok, I see two guys. Which one do you mean?"

"Well..." Olivia bit her thumbnail, eyes flicking between the two boys. "That's the thing, I can't decide. They're college roommates, both these wunderkinds working together on some crazy exciting research in medical technology. Save the world kind of shit."

She glanced back at Cora. "I might not look like it but I'm totally a sucker for a hero."

Cora smiled. "So why don't you ask one of them out?"

Olivia's face scrunched. "Well, every time I see them out, they're surrounded by..." She gestured rudely at the flock of bobble-headed women giggling and flicking their hair around the boys.

"The one on the right, Adam Archer," Olivia indicated the blond in the polo shirt, "is the heir to Archer Industries."

Cora let out a low whistle. "Whoa." Archer Industries was one of the wealthiest companies in the *nation*, not just

New Olympus. They were even regularly listed among the top ten wealthiest companies in the world.

"And the one on the left?" Cora asked.

"Logan Wulfe. Boy genius. No one knows anything about his family, but who needs to? He's crazy smart and just look at him. Mmm mmm mmm. All dark and broody."

Cora laughed. "So why don't you ask *him* out?"

As they looked on, one of the models who'd been talking to Adam only moments before threw herself against Logan, arching her back and flipping her blonde hair, pushing her breasts up into his face. Logan's brow wrinkled, his hands hovering in midair as if reluctant to touch what was freely offered.

Again Olivia's face scrunched in amusement. "I dunno. I like the idea of him but I think...he's a little bit...unseasoned for my tastes. These med school types. No time for relationships, but they can name all my body parts...in Latin. I prefer a man with more finesse."

"A better bedside manner?" Cora deadpanned.

"Look at you, making jokes!" Olivia swatted her arm. Cora's pink drink splashed everywhere, mostly right into a redheaded model's path.

"Watch what you're doing! Stupid bitch," the model hissed. Out of the corner of her eye, Cora saw her bodyguard start forward, and she shook her head sternly.

He stopped and leaned back against the wall.

In the meantime, Olivia had jumped up and shouted, "Piss off!"

Everyone at the party turned to stare. Olivia tossed her head, proud to be the center of attention. "Armand! We need music."

"Coming soon, delightful Olivia," Armand called back

from the entryway. "In fact, we have a special guest I'd like to introduce to everyone."

A familiar figure stood next to Armand holding a guitar. Cora recognized The Orphan with just enough time to cover her ears. The excited screams of the women around her immediately followed as the fans rushed The Orphan immediately.

"Ladies, ladies," Armand tried to fend them off. "He's going to sing for you if you'll let him."

In the crush of bodies, Cora's bodyguard looked distracted. But then, the riots The Orphan seemed to generate would be more than any single protector could handle. The room was filled with shrieking, girly chaos, the sort that would strike terror into a man's heart.

Cora jumped up, ready for her opportunity. She waited until the poor bodyguard was pushed into the wall by some rabid models.

"Come on." She grabbed Olivia and dragged her new friend out of the great room, back to where she saw some people disappear. The large kitchen was almost deserted except for some extra bottles of champagne and gorgeous young people in bunny ears opening them or lining serving trays with glasses.

Cora grabbed a filled glass and sipped it. The screams had died down and there were guitar sounds coming from the room they just left. Her bodyguard was probably sifting through the room now, looking for her.

"What's wrong? You don't like his music?"

I like it too much, Cora wanted to say. "We'll never hear it over the screaming."

"I don't know how Armand got him here. He's the hottest thing in this city right now."

"I know. He plays at my husband's club."

"I've been meaning to ask you about that." Olivia swigged champagne straight from the bottle. "How did you meet Mr. Lord of the Underworld?"

Cora winced at the reference to a newspaper article printed two years ago. "Please don't call him that." She set down her empty glass. "It's a long story."

"Cliff notes, please." Olivia's dark eyes glittered over the neck of the bottle.

Cora ran a hand through her hair. How to sum up her intense courtship? "He swept me off my feet. Gave me everything I could ever imagine. It was amazing."

Olivia pressed a new glass into Cora's hand. "Did you know about what he did for a living?"

Cora shook her head. "I didn't find out until later."

"So you didn't target him?"

"What?"

"You didn't find out he was wealthy and seek him out?"

Now the blood rushed to Cora's face as she realized her new friend was accusing her of being a fortune hunter. "No, I didn't know anything about him. He...helped me out of a situation. I knew he was wealthy, but that wasn't why I—" Cora halted.

"Wasn't why you?" Olivia prompted.

"Wasn't why I fell in love with him."

"You love him."

Cora nodded, unable to speak. It was the first time she'd said it out loud after admitting it to herself at the concert the other night. Olivia seemed to accept her further silence on the topic, and gave up her interrogation. In the other room, the song had stopped or was drowned out by clapping and cheers.

"Champagne for everyone!" Armand shouted from the

other room, and the bunny ears dutifully exited the kitchen carrying trays.

Olivia pulled Cora back to the party. The room had cleared out a little; The Orphan was getting a tour of the house with his shrieking entourage. A few models and revelers in pink wigs lounged on the couch, too drunk to sit upright. Cora's assigned bodyguard was nowhere to be seen. He was probably searching the house for his missing charge.

Olivia pushed Cora onto an empty couch and pressed another glass of champagne into her hands.

"Didn't mean to grill you back there." Olivia sat next to her. "I just wanted to know what sort of person you are."

"I understand," Cora said. She realized the woman was apologizing to her.

Olivia shook her short hair and frowned. "I'm too blunt sometimes. But I find it saves time." She turned towards Cora, who was sitting stiffly on the couch. "Here's the deal, Cora. I like you. And I want to be your friend. But I want to know who you are first."

"Okay." Cora nodded. "Do you have any more questions for me?" Cora had wanted a friend, badly, and if Olivia was going to just drop in her lap like this, well, she didn't mind jumping through a few hoops.

"Not right now. And if I ever pry too much, you can tell me to piss off, you know."

Cora grinned.

"Like if I ask you whether you and Marcus would consider a threesome—"

"Olivia! Piss off."

Olivia smiled into her champagne.

"I'm not sure if I should drink this." Cora looked doubtfully at her second glass. "After two glasses I'm pretty much gone."

"Well then bottoms up, babe," Olivia ordered, and then shouted to Armand, who was walking by. "Oi! Cora's a lightweight."

Armand waltzed over, smiling enchantingly. "I'll take good care of you, sweetness."

Cora giggled. "That's what I'm afraid of." She sipped and hiccupped.

"Oo la la," Armand laughed. "Cora, you've stolen my heart."

Olivia kicked Armand to get his attention. "So how'd you swing The Orphan? I thought he was sworn off of performing anywhere."

"Oh, for that we must thank Mrs. Ubeli," Armand grinned. "Or, rather, her intimidating husband." Two servers in bunny ears approached him and pulled him away.

"Well done, Ubeli." Olivia gave Cora a wicked smile. "What do you give your husband when he's good?"

"Olivia," Cora smacked her new friend with a pillow.

Olivia giggled. "Aw, let's make love not war." Olivia leaned in, pretending to try to kiss Cora.

"Oh, my gods, my dreams have come true." Armand was back standing over them, grinning ear to ear. He'd lost his two gorgeous escorts, as well as his faux vest.

Olivia's lips detoured at the last minute and smacked Cora on the cheek. Gods, she'd even used a little tongue!

"Gross," Cora sputtered, swiping at her cheek, and Olivia laughed.

"Later, bitch, I'm going to get more booze." Olivia stalked off towards the kitchen again.

"Just you and me, kid." Armand spread his arms, showing off his not unimpressive chest.

Maybe it was the drink. Maybe it was the freedom she

felt that night. Cora took a chance because she'd always been curious about his tattoo. "Armand, turn around."

Grinning ear to ear, he did.

The tattoo spread over his shoulders—white, angelic feathers, with the tips dripping black ink. The muscles of his back bunched at his shoulders and tapered to his waist. He lifted his arms and his pair of wings seemed to move.

"Oh, wow," Cora reached out but pulled back just short of tracing the edge of a feather. It was so beautifully done. But then he turned and grabbed her hands, pulling her from her seat.

"Come with me, Cora, darling. You must see the view."

She went eagerly. The alcohol had made her warm and the whole night felt like an adventure. And friends. Was she actually starting to have some genuine friendships? With people nearer her own age?

Armand led her through the hall and up an impressive staircase. She could hear people hollering up ahead as they toured the second floor.

"The house was built a century ago. The balcony overlooks the park—you can see all the way to one of the fountains."

"Who lives here?" Cora carefully jogged up the stairs in her stilettos, scurrying to keep up with the fleet-footed Armand.

"A friend," Armand said lightly. They came onto a landing and walked down a long hall, then through a room that led to gigantic French doors. Armand scampered ahead and pushed the doors open with a flourish, revealing a balcony.

"Oh, wow," Cora breathed. The whole city glowed golden before her, spreading beyond the black forest of the park.

"See the fountain?" Armand stepped closer to her and pointed. Cora stood on tiptoe and craned her neck to see. Sure enough, there were lit geysers beyond the trees.

"It's beautiful."

"Yes, it is."

Cora realized that Armand was hovering close to her, and stepped away. Oh. He didn't think— "Thank you for the invite to the party. Maybe next time Marcus can come."

He smiled down at her. "It's good to see you out without him. You two seem stuck together."

"Yes, well, we're married now." She waved her left hand to show off her ring finger. "And I like having quiet nights in." It was true. She'd very much liked last night. Before the arguing, anyway.

"Boring." Armand rolled his eyes. His fingers were busy in his hair, tousling the sexy dark locks, making them stand up as he struck a magazine model pose.

"What's wrong with boring? Maybe I like boring." She shoved him playfully. "I can be boring if I want."

"I didn't mean that. You're anything but boring." Armand's dark eyes caressed her face.

"Whatever." She turned back to look out at the view. "I'm planning on getting out more anyway. Having more fun."

"Good for you. And I'm glad you came out tonight, princess, even if it took Olivia to finally get you past the ogre and out of your tower."

Cora frowned but Armand just babbled on.

"I mean, whenever you come into Double M, all the stylists fight to work on you. You're funny. And you actually have a brain."

"Thanks," Cora laughed. "I think."

Armand waved his hand. "You know what I mean. You're more than just a dumb trophy wife."

"Is that what people think of me?"

"Look, it's no secret what your husband does for a living. A lot of people think it's better him than the family that used to run things." Armand came close to her again, but she was too distracted thinking to notice. *Dumb trophy wife.*

"No one saw Marcus date, much less thought he'd marry. He has too much to hide. And then you show up, all naïve and innocent, a tasty little morsel for the big bad wolf. And he gobbled you right up."

Armand chuckled, right in her face. "But you're smart enough to know what's going on. I mean, you can't just stick your head in the sand, with the big shipment coming in and everything."

Too late Cora tried to hide the question on her face.

Armand leaned over her, his eyes gentle. "He didn't tell you." His hand reached out and stroked her hair back from her face. "Oh, Cora. Naïve, innocent little Cora."

She frowned and grasped him by the wrist. "Don't touch me like that," she glared. The alcohol in her wore away some of her softness. "I don't know what you're trying to say, but—"

"I'm sorry," Armand also drew back from her, his dark hair falling in his face. He seemed to sober up, as if he had shown her more than what he meant to. "I think, I just was drinking and didn't mean it." He darted towards the French doors. "Stay up here as long as you want—I have guests to attend to."

He scuttled down the stairs, leaving Cora rubbing her suddenly aching head. What the hell was that all about? Armand had never acted like that when she visited his spa,

Double M, or Metamorphosis. He'd always been nice, if a little clingy, but she thought that was just his style. Tonight, she would've thought he was hitting on her except for the backhanded compliments.

She shivered in the cool night air. Weird night. First Olivia and then Armand. Maybe they were on something? Maybe she shouldn't come to more parties, just stay home and ask her husband about his mysterious business. Big shipment coming in. It made sense, he was always headed to the area of town called the Styx, southeast near the docks.

So what if her husband didn't share his business with her? She was a commodity to him, not a partner. Besides, maybe she really didn't want to know.

Somewhere in the big house, a crowd of people were whooping loudly. Cora wondered absently where her bodyguard was. Probably searching the corners of this big, dark house.

"Mrs. Ubeli?"

Cora jerked up, arranging her features to be properly contrite. She turned, expecting to see the bodyguard.

The Orphan stood just inside the doors to the balcony. He wore his usual outfit of jeans and a white shirt. His head was bent and his hair was tousled, falling over his eyes.

"Christopher? Where is everybody?"

The singer gestured harshly, as if to hush her. "They're in the movie room. It was dark and I slipped out."

"What are you doing here?"

"Please." He approached her, stumbling a little. Cora backed away, wondering if he was drunk. "You have to help me. No one else will."

Goosebumps ran up her arms. "What's wrong?"

"They took her." His eyes were wild. "Iris. My fiancée.

She went to pack up her apartment and get everything ready. We were going to elope."

"And then she left and didn't come back?" Cora guessed. "Did you have a fight?"

"No. We've fought before, but not...not about this. They took her, so I'd keep playing." He paced a little in front of the French doors, squeezing his hands together.

"Who do you think took her, Chris?" Cora asked, even though she could guess the answer.

"AJ. He wants me to play. He won't let us go. I can't play without her. He's going to kill us both." His voice raised a little.

"Shh, ok. Let me think." Cora shivered as she glanced back at the city. The night suddenly seemed big and terrible. "Can you go to the police?"

"I have to wait forty-eight hours. Besides, they won't let me go anywhere. The only reason I'm at this party is for some publicity thing." The Orphan started pacing again. "They're acting like it's all normal, saying she'll be back soon, that I just need to finish the concert series...but she's not answering her cell phone. She always answers when I call. Or texts back if she can't talk. They took her, I know it."

"I can talk to my husband—"

"No." The Orphan came towards her and Cora took a step back towards the balcony railing. "Please don't. AJ will kill her if he knew Ubeli was involved."

"Chris, then, I'm sorry. I don't know how to help." Cora held up her hands, feeling useless. "Where would I even look?"

The Orphan fumbled in his pocket for something. "The last text she sent me...she was stopping by The Orchid House. She used to work there."

"The Orchid House?" Cora cast about trying to remember where she'd heard the name. *Finest establishment in town,* AJ had said.

"That's AJ's club. I can't go there," she whispered harshly.

"Cora?" a man's voice called up the stairs. Both Cora and Chris's heads jerked in the direction. It was Marcus. Dammit, she thought she'd have a little more time. He'd said he was busy tonight.

"I have to go," she whispered.

"Please." Chris held out a worn picture, old, taken in a photo booth. It was of Chris and beside him, Iris, beautiful with flawless mocha skin and pretty eyes. Iris was laughing. Cora stared at the image. So much happiness waving in front of her. Out of reach.

"She needs help. And I have no one else to go to."

Cora took the picture. Cora had been all alone in the city once, powerless with no one to save her. And then a white knight had come to her rescue. Or so she had thought.

Cora's eyes fell closed and she took a fortifying breath. She wasn't powerless anymore.

"Cora, are you upstairs?" Marcus's deep voice rumbled. Cora looked over her shoulder as he continued to bellow. "Don't make me come up there."

When Cora looked up, Chris had disappeared.

"Wait," she glanced around frantically, holding out the picture, but she was all alone. Stuffing it into her bra, she turned to wind her way back through the rooms and down the stairs, but it was too late.

Marcus stood in the doorway. And he did not look pleased.

EIGHT

"Marcus, I—" Cora started.

"Not another word." His broad shoulders blocked the light. The shadows loomed around him and became part of him, flooding over her and casting her into darkness.

"But I—"

Marcus stalked across the space between them in two strides and then his hand was on her jaw. "Open."

Eyes captured by the dark intensity of his gaze, she obeyed and dropped her mouth open.

He pulled something out of his pocket and then popped two cool little metallic balls with a small thread tying them together into her mouth. Each ball was about an inch in circumference.

"Now suck," he growled darkly into her ear. Obediently she ran her tongue around the gum-ball like metal pieces. Her eyes asked questions but she was too well-trained.

"If memory serves me correctly, I believe I told you that you could not come to this party tonight."

Cora tried to reply in her defense but her response was garbled because of the balls.

"Hush." Marcus lifted a finger to her lips. "Not a single word." And then he held out his hand in front of her mouth.

She let the balls fall onto his palm.

"Marcus, what—"

"I said not a word," he chastised, and by the dark look in his eye, she could tell he meant it. "Turn around. Pull up your dress and lean forward. That's it. Tug your panties down and put your hands on the wall."

As gracefully as she could, she got into position. This is how it always went. He commanded, she obeyed.

The picture of the happy couple burned against her breast as she waited with her bare ass sticking out. She and Marcus played some kinky games, for sure, but never in a strange house with a party raging a floor below. *Was he going to fuck her? Here?*

"So pretty and obedient." Marcus cupped her right ass cheek, fondling it and giving it a light slap. He did the same with the left, landing a slightly harder spank. "At least when I'm here with my hands on you. But you've been a naughty girl, haven't you?"

"I don't look kindly when you put what is mine in danger." His voice dropped lower. Cora shivered, but not in fear. "Spread your legs, angel. I'm going to remind this pussy who it belongs to."

Cora rocked her legs apart. *Oh gods oh gods, he was going to—*

A long finger slid into her slick pussy, slowly probing. She arched her back, already desperate for him. So much for fighting for her independence.

"So wet, baby. Is this for me?" His voice went dark as night. "Or someone else?"

"You," she moaned, pressing her forehead into the wall. "Only you."

His finger continued dipping in and out of her. "Is that so? What were you doing up here all alone, then?"

Cora closed her eyes. *Alone.* He hadn't seen Christopher. He didn't think she was sneaking away for a private assignation.

"I wanted to see Armand's place. I needed a second alone. The party, all the people, it was just..." Marcus added a finger and her voice caught. "A-a lot."

"My sweet, sheltered innocent. My man called me to tell me you ran off. I told him my loving wife wouldn't make so much trouble on purpose. Or put herself so foolishly at risk."

"Please don't punish him. It wasn't his fault."

"I'll punish whomever I wish. And right now...that's you." A gust of air blew against her bare haunches. Cora looked back to see what he was doing but with a stern shake of his head, Marcus ordered her to face front. She didn't have to wait long.

With strong fingers, Marcus pushed the metallic balls up inside her. Cora went to her toes with an indrawn breath. Her pussy clenched automatically, and a ripple went through her as the balls' weight pressed on delicious points inside her.

"There," Marcus said. "These are called Ben Wa balls. You'll keep them in." He pulled her panties up, her dress down, and he smacked her bottom again. Cora cried out as the balls rocked inside her.

"Careful," Marcus warned with what sounded like dark amusement. "You don't want them to fall out."

Slowly, Cora straightened. Her legs tightened, wanting to press together. The balls moved in her wet channel, sending taut waves of pleasure through her. Turning around took an eternity.

With a wicked smirk, Marcus stretched out his hand. "Shall we?" His murmur was all innocence.

"Marcus," she whimpered, grabbing his hand as her knees threatened to give out. "You're not going to make me walk like this... I can't..."

He drew her close, his large body looming over her. His face turned gentle. "It's okay, goddess. I'll be with you every step of the way. You want to please me, don't you?"

Her insides turned liquid, golden honey simmering in her veins. She couldn't resist him like this, the kind and loving husband she wanted. "Yes." Her voice wobbled like her legs.

"Then walk and show me you're learning your lesson," his smile turned cruel along the edges, even as the next moment he added gently, "I got you."

Gripping his hand in both of hers, Cora made her way down the stairs. The balls clanked inside her, but she grew used to their weight. Her panties were soaked.

At the foot of the stairs, a phalanx of bodyguards waited. None of the faces were familiar. Cora raised her chin and ignored them, hoping they wouldn't think too much of her mincing steps and the blush staining her cheeks.

"Easy now," Marcus murmured, wrapping an arm around her as if she was unsteady because she was drunk. He led her through the rooms, slightly emptier of bodies than before. From the sounds of things, the party had moved to the back of the house. Models and servers scattered, quieting and hugging the walls when the Shades entered.

"Mr. Ubeli." Armand pushed through a knot of people by the door, Olivia at his side. Cora made herself smile, praying her body would behave.

"Excellent party," Marcus said to Armand. "Excuse us, we can't stay. My wife isn't feeling well."

Olivia's eyes widened. Armand nodded knowingly. To reassure them, Cora gave a little wave. "Later," she mouthed to Olivia as Marcus steered her towards the door.

Her husband was a perfect gentleman, helping her down the steps and guiding her to the waiting car. As soon as they grew close, however, he pushed her forward and the motion made the balls rock inside her.

"*Oh*," she gasped.

"Easy. We're almost to the car."

She scrambled into the backseat and collapsed, panting. If the balls moved any more inside her, she'd come close to orgasm.

Marcus followed, sitting across from her. He rapped the closed divider to signal to the driver, and leaned back as if to take in a show.

"Sit," he demanded. "Legs apart. Pull up your dress."

Biting back a needy noise, she bared her legs to the thigh.

"Panties off."

"Marcus, I don't think—"

"Do it."

She stripped off the sodden scrap of white lace and spread her knees. Marcus took her in, gaze hooded. He looked at her like a piece of art, an object he owned.

"Rock back and forth on the seat."

She did, and oh— *oh!* The balls rolled inside her. Millimeters that felt like miles. The weight of the balls pressed on all the right spots.

"Marcus, please," she panted. "I'm going to—"

"Stop," he snapped. "You don't cum without permission."

"Do I have permission?"

"No. You deliberately ditched your bodyguard and snuck away into a crowded house full of strangers doing all manner of stupid things. I could kill Armand for inviting The Orphan." He shook his head, his glare dark. "What if there was another riot? What if someone grabbed you?"

"Don't blame Armand."

Marcus leveled his stormy gaze, pinning her to the seat. "I *will* keep you safe, Cora, even if I have to chain you to my side."

And here it was. He protected her, but he didn't love her. He wanted her, yes, but only as an object he could control.

"Chaining me to you won't keep me safe," she blurted. "Remember last time? She put her hand over her stomach, right over the place where she took a bullet. "By your side is a dangerous place to be." She said it under her breath but he heard.

His jaw clenched. The heat of his anger rolled over her, blowing up like a bomb in the car. She could barely breathe.

And then, just like that it disappeared, stuffed away into the fearsome man before her.

"For that outburst," he said in measured tones, his jaw tight, "you won't be cumming for a long time."

He made her rock on the seat and stop whenever she got close. By the end she was gripping the seat edge and keening. Her and her stupid big mouth. Why had she said anything? It wasn't like it changed things. Except now she could cry from being so close to satisfaction but being denied from paradise over and over and over again.

Her head hung down and she panted as the car rolled to a stop.

"We're here."

Here was another high-rise, with a fancy facade and a red carpet lined with camera toting paparazzi. Wait, what?

"Where are we?"

"Donation dinner. I'm introducing the headline speaker."

"What?" Her mouth dropped open. He couldn't be serious. She was a breathless mess and he expected her to face a red carpet?

"Last minute decision. The mayor requested my presence. Of course, I need you by my side."

She gaped at him.

"Dress down," he ordered, sounding almost bored. "Cover yourself."

She reached for her panties but he beat her to them. "I'll keep these." He brought them to his face to sniff before stuffing them in his pocket.

Now there was nothing between her pussy and the air. No safety net if the balls fell out.

"Marcus!"

"You can do it," he said in that gentle, encouraging tone. As if he were a doting husband and not her torturer. "If you're good, I'll let you climax later."

He *was* serious. "But," she gasped, hand going to her hair. "Marcus, I'm all..." She was a sweaty wreck, that's what she was.

Large, gentle hands pulled her worried ones away. Marcus knelt before her, stroking back the flyaways.

"You look beautiful," he told her firmly. He ran a finger along the edge of her dress and her nipples rose in response. "*Perfetto.* Remember, you are mine." And with a kiss that seared her lips, he tugged her out of the car.

In the blinding flashes of the camera, Marcus posed with his arm around her shoulders. He kept holding her as he guided her up the red carpet, playing the doting husband.

Okay, okay, she could do this. *Keep it together. Don't let the vultures see anything is amiss.* And really, it wasn't like anything was. Her husband was screwing with her mind and body, just like always.

Except, oh yeah, if these damn balls fell out on the red carpet, she was pretty sure she'd die from mortification. *Clench.* She squeezed her inner walls even tighter and held her thighs together, all the while trying to put on a natural-looking smile for the cameras.

She leaned into Marcus, keeping her stroll smooth and controlled. If she looked stiffer and more flushed than usual, she could blame her awkwardness on the overwhelming paparazzi.

Thankfully, she and Marcus were a few minutes late so the dinner had already begun. Other than a few nods to people he knew, Marcus didn't leave her or let her go until they found their table. He pulled out her chair and she sank down gratefully. Thank the Fates, the damn balls had stayed in. Marcus tapped her shoulder and headed to the front.

Watching him walk away, Cora felt a pang of desire in spite of herself as her husband ascended the stage. If only he weren't so handsome, his presence so commanding, then maybe she'd have half a chance of withstanding his charms. His dark head bent for a moment to speak to the much shorter man who announced him.

But as it was, when he straightened and surveyed the crowd with a casual authority, he took her breath away. He really was beyond gorgeous, damn him.

"Good evening," his deep voice rolled over the crowd. A few ladies sat up straighter, faces brightening under their thick makeup. Cora felt an undeniable stab of jealousy. *Hands off, he's mine.* She should want him to move on from her, from their marriage bed, but the thought broke her. As much as she loved to hate him, if Marcus left her for another woman... Nausea struck even at the thought.

Marcus's gaze swept the crowd and settled on her. She went still. "I prepared a long and glorious speech to introduce the next speaker, but my wife asked me to keep it short. And I live to keep her happy."

He smiled at her, dimple appearing, and her insides went molten. A blush burned through her cheeks as light laughter swept the room and people turned to look at her. She kept her eyes on Marcus. Like if she just looked long enough she could figure out why, *why*, he had the effect he did on her. Gods, what would it take to rid him from her heart? Because as much as games like tonight might get her off, what was it worth if at the end of the day he still didn't love her—*and never would?*

"Without further ado, it's my great honor to introduce the man of the hour. Our illustrious mayor, ready for a new term: Ezekiel Sturm!"

Cora craned her neck to see the familiar blond head as the mayor incumbent ascended the stage. The man was as handsome as his picture, with a boyish grin that endeared him to everyone so well. He waved to all the cheering people. In the hubbub, Marcus slipped from the stage without shaking the mayor's hand.

Ezekiel Sturm approached the podium like he owned it. Cora tried to distract herself from her maudlin thoughts by focusing on him, intentionally *not* watching Marcus as he walked back to the table.

"Friends, please, call me Zeke. The only person who called me Ezekiel was my mother, gods rest her soul. And she only called me that when I was in trouble." He cut a comical face and shrugged.

The crowd roared. Over the course of his speech, the handsome politician continued making them laugh, until they all were eating out of his hand. Even Cora cracked a reluctant smile.

Sturm covered education, economics, and at one point, crime.

"When I took office, this city was in the grip of the crime families. With the support of the commissioner and our boys in blue, we've made our streets safe."

"Miss me?" Marcus murmured as he took his seat next to Cora. A few people close to their table spared a second to study the two of them. Time to play the part. It was familiar and far easier than dealing with her real emotions. She fixed her face in an adoring expression and fluttered her eyelashes at her husband.

But then, when attention was off them, she hissed, "You didn't have to mention me in front of everyone."

Marcus took her hand and kissed her knuckles. Cora could almost hear the older women in the audience sighing over his chivalry. Still pressing her hand to his mouth, he gave her a wicked smile. "I almost said you preferred Sturm over me, but I figured that was too close to the truth."

Cora pulled her hand back and faced the stage. "I don't even know the mayor. The only reason I'd prefer him is because he doesn't torture me like you do."

She quivered as Marcus tucked her into his side. His fingers ran up and down her arm, stroking lightly, so lightly. She felt the touch right in her ever-tightening core.

"But you love it, don't you? All this torture...you enjoy it."

"I enjoy when it's over," she snapped.

"So will I." The smug promise made her womb convulse. "Now be a good girl and pay attention. The mayor is telling the city how much safer and prosperous it is under his rule. Lies, of course. The only reason New Olympus is still standing and not a smoking hole of ruin is because of *my* rule."

"You should've put that in your speech."

"Next time I will. I'll have you introduce me."

"I'll tell everyone the truth."

"What truth? That I dote on my wife. And give her everything?"

"No." Cora smiled sweetly at nothing, suppressing a shiver as Marcus traced the curve of her ear. "That you're the devil." She almost cringed as she said it. Why was she goading him? Sometimes he liked her to stand up to him, a kitten scratching him with ineffectual claws.

Apparently, tonight was one of those times. He chuckled and stopped his slow, tormenting touch. She was both relieved and disappointed. "I am a devil. I'm not the only one in this city." He nodded to a passing pair of men. "But I am the most powerful. Everyone wants to deal with me. Just like the devil, they come to bargain with me, and leave with everything they desire."

"Except their soul."

"Except that." He smirked.

The mayor finished and Marcus made a show of standing and applauding, slow golf claps that echoed above the rest. The night would continue with entertainment and gentle calls for donations.

Marcus put his hand on Cora's shoulder. "What about you, Cora? Do I own your soul?"

"No," she denied vehemently, praying it wasn't a lie. "Just every other part of me. As you well know."

She waited as Marcus spoke to a few people, mostly men who greeted him loudly and then leaned in to conduct their business in lower tones. Marcus stood beside her chair as he spoke to them. He kept his hand on the back of her neck.

Cora sipped her wine, resting, grateful for the reprieve. Grateful, and anxious. Marcus had only begun and she had a feeling tonight would test her limits. He wouldn't be satisfied until he proved his total domination over her body and senses. Maybe even her soul, like he'd just talked about. He'd leave her with nothing.

And yet...there was a big part of her that couldn't wait to get home. As much as she craved his love, she'd take his dominance. What did that make her?

Leaning forward as if to fix her shoe, she let her hair fall over her breast and slipped the picture Christopher had given her out of her bra and into her clutch. She didn't need to glance at it again; she had it memorized.

Iris had the love Cora wished for, but Cora had Marcus. Arrogant, powerful, frustrating and sexy Marcus. Her husband. She wouldn't trade him for anything, even the remains of her heart. Her dignity. Her soul. He was the devil, indeed.

As if sensing her thoughts on him, Marcus glanced down with a lazy smile. His thumb brushed her cheek. "A few more minutes, Angel."

The people he was talking to spared her a smile. *How lucky,* the women were thinking. *What a doting husband.*

Cora reached up and captured Marcus's rough hand. He squeezed hers and didn't let go. She studied the dark hair dusting his olive skin.

Marcus didn't feel love for her, only obsession, but if she

couldn't have one, she'd take the other. Maybe it could be enough to sustain her?

Her breath quickened when Marcus made his goodbyes and helped her out of her chair. He offered his arm with a sardonic arch of his brow. "Tired?"

"Not really." It would be just like him to take her home and put her to bed without relieving the desire he'd stoked. If he did that, she'd scream. Not that she wouldn't scream if he fucked her. She always lost control when he claimed her. And after the night of tumultuous thinking, she wanted that most of all. She wanted the bliss of being lost in him. For time and space to disappear in only the way that he could provide.

"Good," he purred in her ear. "Because the night isn't over yet." His hand covered hers where it rested on his strong forearm.

"Excuse us," he announced to the cluster of businessmen he'd been speaking to. "I promised my wife a tour of the art gallery."

"I hear it's stunning," a man with silver hair said. "Closed this time of night, though."

"I arranged a late-night viewing. We prefer...privacy."

The men laughed at that, and Marcus led Cora to an elevator. A Shade stepped out of the shadows to hand him something. Marcus muttered something that sounded like, "keep the area secure" before inserting a keycard into a slot above the elevator buttons.

"Where is the art gallery?" Cora asked, her voice calm even as her heart fluttered.

"Upstairs." Her husband straightened, his wide shoulders filling the space. It wasn't just his height and powerful body, but his very presence that dominated the vicinity. "It's a new installation, part of the remodel."

"Let me guess, your businesses had something to do with it."

"Art is a good investment," he said.

"And it's beautiful."

"That too." He turned to her and took her in fully. She pretended to ignore him, facing front, but her body hummed, knowing he was inspecting her as if she was a Degas "little dancer" painting he wanted to purchase.

He hit the emergency button. The elevator stopped with an angry buzz.

And so it begins.

"Marcus," she said breathlessly. His hand came to her neck, thumb stroking a sensitive point. "How's your pussy?" he asked and she closed her eyes. "That bad? Or that good?"

Her pulse pounded under his palm.

"Poor wife. What can I do to make you feel better? Hmmm?" He leaned closer. "Are you wet for me? Let me check."

He sank to his knees, pulling up her dress. Cora gave in and leaned against the elevator wall. She reached for him.

"Hands behind your back," he ordered sharply and leaned forward after she obeyed. Her fingers scrabbled desperately against the metal railing behind her.

"Poor, sweet neglected pussy. I'm here," he crooned, his lips brushing her labia. Cora nearly came then and there. Her head swam as she began to float, her body becoming alight with sensation.

"Marcus...please..."

"You have permission. In fact, I expect you to come. Multiple times. If you don't, I will be very displeased." He punctuated this with a kiss to her sopping slit.

Cora's hands scrabbled on the rail, dying to grab his shoulders and hang on. But no, he'd said to keep her hands behind her back. Obedience equaled pleasure. It was all so simple when they were together like this.

Marcus lifted her right leg and propped it over his shoulder.

"Feel free to scream," he remarked, before diving in. He feasted on her with gusto, nibbling on her lower lips and probing them apart with his tongue.

Her body convulsed and she fought to stay standing on her left leg. Marcus fit his shoulder under her right as he settled himself in and laved up and down her seam.

"Oh— *Oh*— Marcus!" she couldn't help crying out.

Her propped leg opened her further to him, and he used his fingers to part and probe her sex as his tongue fluttered next to her clit.

That was— It was so incredible, she couldn't even—

With a growl, he sank his fingers deep, rubbing her inner wall. Cora went up on tiptoe. *Oh*. The balls inside her pushed further up her channel. Their weight combined with his crooked fingers send shockwaves reverberating through her.

"Cum for me," he commanded, and she did, her legs collapsing as she melted down the wall. Only Marcus's hand on her hip and his shoulder steadied her and kept her upright.

"My wife." He moved up and kissed her. She tasted salt, she tasted herself, and underneath was Marcus. Always Marcus, dominating her lips and mouth while her body pulsed with aftershocks.

His thumb caressed the edge of her jaw and their gazes locked. It was moments like these, when her body and heart were wide open, that she wondered if she'd fallen into a dream. That sweet peace. Like Christopher and Iris had, the kind of forever love that inspired his haunting songs.

Then Marcus shoved his fingers into her mouth.

"I knew when I saw you that you were submissive. You just needed a firm hand."

He pulled his fingers out and wiped them on her dress. The casual degradation made her cheeks burn. So much for sweetness.

"You did well. You've pleased me."

She gritted her teeth.

"What do you say?"

"Thank you."

"Good girl."

Good girl. He was always saying that. Good girl, good girl, good girl. So fucking patronizing. It wasn't something you said to an equal.

But then she wasn't an equal, was she? Not to him. She was a *good lay.* Of course he'd never love her. How could he love his 'good girl', his sex object that got him off when she wasn't being paraded around as his trophy wife.

Earlier tonight she told herself this was enough. That she could be satisfied as long as she had this.

But dammit, didn't she deserve more? Didn't she deserve to be loved? Truly loved? Why was she putting up with these half-measures? Did she really think so little of herself?

She ducked her head away from Marcus. "I...need a moment."

He backed away and hit the elevator button. The smooth ascent began, but Cora's heart remained a few stories down, with the mirage of the caring man her husband could be.

"You all right?" he asked, casually. Not as if he cared. So much wealth and privilege and he couldn't afford to care.

When she remained silent, he called her name. "Cora, answer me."

He wanted her to speak? She'd give him words. "You know, I could've loved you."

He didn't react. His face showed no sign that she'd fired the first shot. "You don't love me?"

"As if I could, after what you've done to me."

"Is that a no?" A hint of a smirk before his expression smoothed. He was calm as a lawyer questioning a witness.

Fucking arrogant man. "No, Marcus, I don't love you. Not anymore. Not like before."

She remembered everything, how much hope she had right up until the wedding night. How he'd held all her happiness in the palm of his hand. How he'd let it fall and then shatter.

"You could've married me, given me the honeymoon of my dreams. You could have told me about your sister. I would've grieved with you. If you had told me the truth and opened up to me, we could've..." Her voice choked off with all the could have beens.

Marcus still watched her with no expression.

"But you chose to punish me." Her voice cracked and she fought for control. "To *break* me."

He reached for her and she wrenched herself away. She wouldn't let tears fall. She wouldn't. "You can have love or you can have revenge. We both know what you chose."

MARCUS LOOKED down at his bride, quivering with the force of her anger and pain.

Blue eyes, the color of a summer sky. Hair a dark

blonde, like wheat fields. Her complexion was pure, peaches and cream, her scent fresh as the country air.

He'd never seen anything like her, not in his city. She stepped off the bus into his world, and he'd known if he didn't take her, claim her for his own, the city would eat her alive.

All that innocence ready to be sullied. He saved her from a long hard fall. He *saved* her.

She should be grateful.

But instead she glared at him, her expression as close to hate as he'd ever seen it.

He loomed over her. "This isn't story time. I'm not a handsome prince. Fairy tales aren't real."

She raised her chin. That vibrant inner strength, the core he couldn't touch. Couldn't break.

"Love is."

"If you believe that you're not truly broken."

She started to shake her head and he grabbed her chin, forcing her to face him. "I will risk everything, even your hate, to keep you safe. To let you live in a world where you believe love is real."

Her expression softened. See, she couldn't hate him. She was too full of goodness. The light in her saved him from the darkness, even when he deserved her hate and earned her loathing, over and over.

"Oh Marcus," she whispered. "What have you become?"

For a moment he wavered. He would tell her he didn't want revenge. That having her was enough, if she would just give herself fully to him—

But no. That was too close to groveling. And he didn't grovel. The facts didn't change whether his face was in her pussy or she was on her knees with his cock down her throat. He owned her.

Body, mind, soul. Heart. End of story.

They were almost to the top floor, but not quite. Good enough. He needed to teach his bride, his *wife*, a lesson.

He stabbed a button. "On second thought, I think we'll take the stairs."

The doors opened and he swept a hand out. "After you."

She took a few trembling steps into the darkness. He'd left the balls inside her. She'd have to tighten her muscles and accept another round of growing arousal. The motion sensor lights blinked on. A museum of white walls and shining wood floors stretched before them, full of statues.

"Run," he ordered her coldly. He could all but hear her heart stutter to a stop.

"Wh-what?"

"Run," Marcus repeated, shrugging out of his jacket. He hung it on a nearby statue and started rolling up his sleeves. "I'm going to chase you. If you reach the other side without dropping the balls..." He arched an eyebrow. "...you get a reward." Then he dropped his voice. "But if you let them fall—"

Her eyelashes fluttered, her breath coming faster. "What if you catch me?"

"If I catch you, I get the reward."

"What's the reward?"

He stared intently into her eyes, which were flitting this way and that before finally settling and focusing on his. "Anything I want."

She gulped.

He'd lied earlier. Some parts of fairy tales *were* real.

Like the big bad wolf hunting down an innocent girl. He was the hunter. She was his prey.

And now she would understand that she would never, ever escape him.

She kicked off her shoes and then took off up the stairs. He leaned on the rail, watching her go. She couldn't quite run. Her ass wiggled back and forth in her attempt to keep her thighs together so the heavy balls would stay inside her. Marcus pulled her panties out from his coat pocket and took a long inhale before finally starting up the stairs himself.

She hazarded a glance over her shoulder and let out a small *yip* when she saw he was following and how quickly and easily he was gaining on her.

Oh he liked this game very much.

She scurried ahead, darting around installations and statue laden pedestals. He paced behind her, a hunter who knew his prey. She left the scent of arousal in her wake.

She reached the end of the room and slipped through the door. He was gaining on her even with his steady, even tread. His legs were longer and she had to take small, mincing steps or risk punishment for losing the balls.

Either that, or she wanted him to catch her. He grinned at the thought. For all her protests, her body recognized its master.

He paused just outside the door, staying in the shadows as he peeked inside. The second room held only a giant staircase, spiraling up several stories to the sky.

A massive chandelier blazed above with each of its crystals twisting slowly so shining patterns danced on the white-gold marble.

There she was, starting up the staircase. She was going slower, gliding from step to step, her face turned to the light.

The brilliant waterfall turned her hair into a glowing halo. Bright and fiercely perfect.

A fist clenched Marcus's heart until he gritted his teeth against the pain. She was so fucking beautiful it hurt.

She is mine, and mine alone. Possessing her completely was the only thing that eased the ache.

He finally came into the room and followed her up the stairs, taking them leisurely two at a time, not rushing but not waiting either.

When he'd closed the distance to less than twenty steps, Cora glanced back and gasped. Her legs slammed together and she grabbed the railing, pausing to regain her control a second before she fled again. Marcus's chuckle echoed around them.

Head bowed, she scurried higher, her steps jerky and panicked. Her fear was so delicious. Especially because he saw her arousal glistening on the pristine stairs.

Near the top floor, he closed the distance to ten steps. In her rush, she must have forgotten to mind the balls. They fell, bouncing and spinning with wet drops flying.

They both froze to listen to them clatter over the white-gold marble, down one step and then another and another, echoing like tinny music around the large chamber. When the noise stopped, Marcus met his wife's wide blue eyes and smiled.

She turned and raced up the final steps, but too late. Marcus sprang and tackled her, his weight driving her to her hands and knees, even as his arm caught her middle and broke her fall.

He eased her down the last inch. Her hands slapped the marble and he tossed up her dress, ripping it in his haste.

He was the victor and he wouldn't waste time in devouring his prize. Her legs parted automatically and he thrust three fingers into her wet center, hooking to find her G spot.

"Scream for me," he ordered and she did, her torso writhing and cunt milking his fingers. "Again." His fingers probed, finishing what the balls started. She was wet, so wet. If he hadn't rolled up his cuffs they'd be soaked.

When she'd convulsed with a second climax, he pushed on her back with his free hand, so her body bowed and her ass propped up right where he wanted it. He knelt a step behind her as she half lay on the landing, legs spread and hindquarters bare, ripe and ready for him.

He almost broke his pants zipper getting it open. His cock throbbed, pointing straight towards the wet heat waiting for it.

The cry she made when he slid into her almost set him off. His balls were tight and ready with a massive amount of cum. He gritted his teeth and took a moment to smooth his hands down her shuddering back.

Then he drove into her, sending her body rocking forward with each thrust. She sobbed and begged for more, her back arched so her ass ground into him. He wound a hand in her hair and made her bow backwards even further. He rode her that way for a while before hooking a hard arm under her helpless body and drawing her up against him, so he could growl in her ear,

"Enough. Enough of fighting me. You'll do what I say because I keep you safe. You'll do what I say because *it is what I say*. You stay pure. Untouched except by me."

His hips slammed into her so hard her body jerked, to make the point. "You are mine and no others. Not even your own."

He wound one of his arms around her until his fingers were at her throat. He squeezed only hard enough that she felt him there. "Your life is in my hands and I have sworn to protect you. And you will fucking *let me*. Do you understand?"

When she didn't say anything except for her moans of pleasure, he shook her again. "Do you understand?"

"Yes!" she cried. "Yes, oh, *Marcus*."

Then she came apart in his arms again, softly keening.

Gods, he needed this woman. His arms clamped around her, holding her tight as if he could merge them into one. When his climax came, it blinded him.

He let them both sink to the floor, one arm around her middle and the other propping them up slightly. Cora lay safe in his arms, her hair spilled over the gleaming stone. They were both bathed in softly spinning light.

He wanted to lie here forever. The fields of paradise couldn't be better than this. Cora's warmth soaked into him, warming him down to his bones. For one long, perfect moment, he closed his eyes and let himself bask in her sunlight.

...

...

...

But...*no*. He couldn't. His place was in the darkness. In the cold. In shadow.

So he gathered himself, drew down her dress, and used a ripped piece to sop up the dripping mess between her legs. He had to help her down the first few steps, until she regained her equilibrium. Halfway down he stopped and pointed to the abandoned Ben Wa balls.

His body still buzzing, he wanted to whisper a sonnet to her.

Instead, he made his voice icy. "Clean up your arousal."

He handed her a handkerchief. Cheeks an adorable

shade of pink, Cora wiped the steps and collected the balls as he towered over her. When he held out his hand for the bundle, she didn't look at him but bit her lip. The sight sent another shot of arousal stabbing through him.

With a hand on her back, he escorted her to the elevator, steadying her when she wobbled. Her dress was torn in the back, the straps slipping down her shoulders, but she was too dazed to notice. She couldn't do anything but lean on him.

If he could keep her in this state, freshly fucked with his cum spilling out of her puffy pussy, gaze hazy and cheeks tinged pleasure-pink, he would. He'd be tempted to sell his businesses, buy the whole Crown Hotel, and take her in a different room night after night after night.

Catching her in his arms, he gave her a kiss.

"Angel," he murmured and she melted into him.

Fuck it. Marcus gave into what he ached to do all night.

He wrapped her in his jacket and carried her the rest of the way, down the elevator, through the building empty of all but his Shades, and out to the car where he held her all the way home.

NINE

"THE ORPHAN SEEMED DESPERATE," Cora told Maeve early the next morning, as they were taking inventory at the shelter's store. Maeve had initially asked about how things were with Marcus—

But Cora just couldn't. Last night... Last night was... She'd thought if she finally got it all out and stopped pretending to be the good little wife...

But her rebellious actions and words had seemed to fire Marcus up even more, if that was possible. She wouldn't have thought so. But that race up the stairwell, and when he caught her— Her entire body flushed hot.

Last night had only proved that nothing had changed. She was just as far under Marcus's thrall as ever.

She'd loved every single thing he did...but that had always been the problem, hadn't it? She *loved*... Whereas Marcus only...what? Amused himself with her? Enjoyed taking his possession out to play with?

And when he tires of you?

No, it was far better to think about other people and *their* problems if she wanted to stay sane. Hence throwing herself into the Iris mystery as soon as she'd gotten to the shelter this morning.

Plus, Chris and Iris really did need her help. And Marcus was wrong. Real love *did* exist. These two proved it was still possible, even in this corrupt, ugly world. It didn't matter that that kind of love would never be Cora's.

"I didn't know what to say when he asked me for help, though. But the more I think about it, the more I know I have to do something."

"A lot of people would say it's not your problem." Maeve swung her red hair over her shoulder, out of the way of her clipboard.

Cora moved down the aisle, counting the bags of dog food and the chic chew toys the shelter sold to raise money for their non-profit. She looked forward to her volunteer time even though it was only two days a week. Though the dogs barked in the back, to her the place seemed peaceful. But any bit of peace was a mirage in the city. She was starting to see that. Marcus had always talked about how this city was barely held back chaos...

Maeve let her work in silence until she came to the end of the aisle and faced Maeve again. Cora thought of the photo booth picture that even now she had in her pocket. Their bright smiles, full of such hope. And love.

"Chris is right. I'm in a position to help. If I don't do it, who else will?" Cora said with sudden certainty.

This city was a bad place to be friendless. And even though The Orphan was worshiped and adored, *Chris*, the man behind the persona, didn't have any true friends. No one else who could help him. He didn't have anyone else in the world on his side, other than the woman he loved.

Maeve didn't look surprised. "So where do you start looking?"

Cora bit her lip as she thought about it. But she always came back to the same conclusion, no matter how distasteful it might be. "The club where Iris worked. I think I'll drop by there today."

Maeve raised an eyebrow. "And what does Marcus say about all of this?"

"I can't tell him." Cora looked away. She was pretty sure Marcus would just tell her to stay out of it and that it was none of her concern. And there was a possibility that... "It's complicated. And anyway, he's busy."

She looked at Maeve for validation. "I was just going to slip away and check around. See if anyone's heard anything. Maybe no one but us needs to know."

Maeve reached out and tugged away Cora's clipboard. "You're done here. Get going, but be safe."

Cora nodded, feeling scared and relieved at the same time. She couldn't even fully explain to herself why she had to do this. Maybe because after last night, she had to show herself Marcus hadn't swallowed up all of her yet—that there would be something left of *her* once he tired of her. She hoped her motives were better than that. She genuinely did want to help Iris and Chris.

Either way, she was doing this. She pulled her apron off over her head and strode toward the back of the shop.

Besides, what Marcus didn't know wouldn't hurt him.

CORA SLIPPED out the back door of the animal shelter, pulling her hair up in a ponytail and tugging a knit hat over it. She never went out this way. The dumpster was out in the parking lot off to the side, so she never had need to use this door.

Still, before she stepped onto the street, she glanced this way and that to make sure Marcus's men weren't around. Usually they dropped her off at the shelter and left, with the unspoken understanding that she stay in the building.

Even if they were hanging around—which they likely were with how twitchy Marcus had been lately—they'd probably be out front. As long as she was back before they came inside to get her at the end of the day, she'd never be missed.

As she loped down the alleyway, she felt a private triumph. This would be her first excursion out in the city all on her own since...she couldn't even remember when. Since before Marcus and that seemed like an eternity now, like a different life.

She cut across to a side street, then took the bus part of the way and walked the last bit down a street lined with shops. Finally she came to a nice covered entryway with black pillars. "The Orchid House" was inscribed in purple letters over the door. It looked like a restaurant.

She bit her lip and glanced around. The chances of her running into AJ were high. He owned the club. But if she stood here for much longer, she'd definitely look out of place. But she'd forgotten—until now—that AJ had told her to attend auditions at eleven.

A glance at her phone showed that it was around ten now.

She took a deep breath. It would be fine. She'd be in and out before anyone noticed. Well, she *hoped* she would be.

Or she could be smart and get the hell out of here right now.

She pulled the old picture out of her pocket. Iris smiled back at her, so innocent and carefree.

"This is the dumbest thing I've ever done," she hissed

under her breath to Iris's picture before pocketing it and pushing into the club.

A dark narrow hallway led to a coat check area. From there the room opened up into a lushly decorated restaurant, with a bar on one side and leather armchairs facing a stage. And she couldn't miss the two poles going from ceiling to floor on the stage.

She gulped, hard. If she was caught, how exactly was she going to explain to Marcus why she had showed up to a strip club at ten in the morning on a Tuesday?

She almost turned around and left. At least she'd tried.

"Hey, honey," a friendly voice called.

Busted, Cora peered into the gloom.

A young man stood behind the bar, wiping glasses dry. "You're too early. Auditions don't start until eleven."

"Sorry. Um, I'm looking for someone who works here?" Cora called.

The man leaned against the bar. He was gangly but good-looking, with longish blond hair ending in curls around his face. "What's your friend's name, honey?"

"Iris."

"Is that her real name or stage name?"

Uhhhhh...good question? Cora's mouth was suddenly as dry as dirt. She swallowed several times. The young man cocked his head and gave her a dazzling smile. He seemed amused by her discomfort.

Fumbling inside her pockets, Cora approached and laid the picture of Iris and Chris down on the polished surface.

The young man studied it, then shook his head. "I don't know her. You sure she used to work here?"

Cora tried to recall what Chris had said. "I think so. She's missing and I'm looking for her, for a friend." She stopped abruptly, wondering how much to share.

"If you wait a minute, Anna might be able to help you. She's worked here longer. She might recognize your friend."

Cora nodded her gratitude.

"You can sit if you want. Anna should be right out."

"Uh, I don't know." Cora turned and stopped, distracted by the posters on the far wall. Most were of women in provocative poses, poorly disguised as gaudy art. "I don't have much time."

"You sure you're not going to audition?" The bar boy was still smiling at her, now overtly appraising her body. When Cora caught his eye again, he winked.

"Don't be shy, sugar. Everyone's nervous their first time." He nodded towards the stage and Cora turned back, walking slowly to one of the chairs to sit.

She saw smoke curling out from the corner of the stage.

"Um." She glanced over at the bartender. He was watching it too and seemed unconcerned. For a second Cora listened hard, until she could hear the click of a fog machine in the background. She relaxed and turned back to face front.

The mist kept creeping over the black stage, thickening until it was at least a foot deep.

Then a song started playing, violins plucking on beat.

A figure slowly appeared in the mist. The arms appeared first and then the face of a young woman, her big brown eyes staring right into Cora's. She was petite and curvy, her figure clad only in black hot pants and a white skintight top. She came out of the fog, moving swiftly to grab a pole.

She twirled slowly, her feet swishing through the smoke. She landed and twisted, spinning gracefully and then soaring around the pole again, somehow hooking her legs so her hands were free.

She peeled the white shirt off provocatively, baring a sexy midriff. Then she smiled at her audience of two. She turned her back to them, then glanced back over one sexy shoulder as her booty swayed wildly. She reached up and loosened her long, glossy hair, letting it pour over her.

The song ended and wow. Just...wow. Cora had never seen anybody move like that, so unconsciously raw and feminine and sexy. A clapping sound from the left caught her attention; the bar boy was grinning as he gave a standing ovation.

The dancer disappeared and the smoke machines sputtered to a stop. In a minute the woman reappeared, hair tied back again, shirt tucked into wide legged black pants. She looked perfectly normal, like the girl next door.

"Bravo," the youth at the bar clapped his approval. "Looks great, Anna."

"Thanks, Paul." The woman had a high-pitched, breathy voice. "Everything's working perfectly. This is going to be my best show ever." She giggled, a gorgeous, delighted sound.

"Hey, this lady's here to see you." Paul waved to Cora.

Anna kept her sweet smile as she approached Cora. "Can I help you?"

As she came closer, Cora caught her breath. Anna was beautiful. Wide brown eyes surrounded by thick black lashes and perfectly bronzed skin—the woman wasn't wearing a touch of makeup and she was lovelier than any model Cora had ever seen.

"Are you here to apply for a job?" Anna asked, smiling broadly. She was several inches shorter than Cora, if more curvy. Even her plain clothes couldn't hide her sexy figure.

Cora realized she'd been staring. "Um, no, sorry." She

shook herself. "I'm looking for a friend who works here. Her name is Iris."

Anna's smile switched off. Her dark brown eyes became assessing. She obviously knew something about Iris.

"I just need to talk to her," Cora pleaded, lowering her voice. "She's missing and her fiancé is worried."

"I haven't seen Iris in a while," Anna said. "She used to work here but I think she left when she got engaged." She hesitated, glancing at the bar hand as if she didn't want to say more in front of him. "Paul? I'm going to head out for a bit and then I'll be back."

"You're on at two. Though I might need a dance or two before because the others are always late."

"I'm sure it will all work out." Anna smiled enchantingly.

"Did you get everything you needed?" Paul asked Cora.

Cora blinked and nodded. "Um, I need to go actually."

"I'll walk you out," Anna added in her breathy voice. "Just let me grab my purse."

The petite woman ran behind the bar and grabbed her things. She came back, sliding on large dark sunglasses that swallowed up her face. The hoodie pulled over her hair took care of hiding the rest.

"Come on." Anna grabbed Cora's hand and pulled her out of the club.

They ended up on the street. Which was where Anna rounded on her, her voice sounding more normally pitched and less sex kitten.

"Look, I'm going to ask this once," Anna demanded, "and I want the truth. Are you one of AJ's girls?"

Cora blinked in the bright light, surprised by this turn of events. "Um, no."

Anna put her sunglasses up so she could gaze straight into Cora's eyes. "Are you working for him?"

"N-no," Cora blurted as the shorter woman got in her face.

"Then how do you know Iris?"

"I know her fiancé. The Orphan. He's a singer and doing a show at—" She stopped when she realized she shouldn't say 'My husband's club.'

"I know who The Orphan is. Everybody does."

Faced with those striking brown eyes, Cora wanted to tell the truth. "Okay, well, his real name is Chris. I met him backstage and then later at a party. Iris is his fiancée and she's been missing since yesterday. He wanted me to help ask around until the police can get involved."

Anna's eyes narrowed, weighing Cora in the balance.

"Chris asked me to come look for her. He's not allowed to leave to look himself. Something about his contract. The guys he's working with aren't the best types..." Cora trailed off.

She couldn't imagine how that sounded. Right, a famous guy she'd met a couple times at a party had asked her to look into his missing fiancée. She probably sounded nuts.

For a moment Anna just studied her face. Cora shifted from foot to foot, ducking her head nervously when someone drove past. AJ could walk up at any moment. They were still far too close to the club for Cora's comfort. But crazy or not, she couldn't just let this go. Anna obviously knew something about Iris.

"Look, I'm not here to pry. Or cause trouble. I can give you my number, and if you find anything out, just call me, ok?" Cora fumbled in her pocket and took out the little notebook she carried. She handed Anna a slip with her number scribbled on it.

Anna took it, and Cora started to walk away. If the woman didn't trust her enough to talk to her, there was nothing Cora could do.

"Wait," Anna called. Cora stopped and looked back.

Huddled in the hoodie and sunglasses too large for her face, Anna seemed almost childlike. "Why would you help Iris?"

Cora took a deep breath. She'd wondered that herself, all the way from the shelter to The Orchid House.

You and me against the world, Chris had said. The lovers in the green room, gazing into each other's eyes like they were the only people alive.

"She and Chris were going to elope." Cora took out the picture again and held it up so Anna could see it. "I want to help them. It means something, to have a love like they have. It's special and precious. But it's not..." Cora shook her head as she tried to find the words. "It's not just that. It's... I could *be* her."

She met Anna's eyes, trying to be as honest as possible. "When I first came to the city, I needed someone to watch out for me." She paused again. Marcus's face flashed in her mind but she shook it away. He'd been her savior all right. With a vengeance. "Right now, I think Iris needs help, too. Sometimes that's all it takes, one person willing to help. It can change everything." Not always for the better, but that was neither here nor there.

The dancer's eyes bored into her, piercing her skin. Cora wished she hadn't said so much, so awkwardly. She was ready to bolt, leave the area and find another way, when Anna spoke.

"I can tell you about Iris," Anna said. "But not here."

TEN

Anna led Cora to a shop around the corner.

Part coffee shop and part bookstore, the restaurant had nice private booths with high backs. Anna slid into one. "This is my favorite place to get a Buddha bowl. And they do a nice vegan lasagna. Plus espresso to die for."

"I'll have what you're having." Cora smiled at her, glad she was letting her guard down.

Anna ordered without looking at the menu. After the waitress got them waters and a pot of green tea, Anna settled in and studied Cora's face.

"I recognize you from somewhere."

"I sometimes work as a model," Cora admitted. She was nervous about giving too much of her identity away but thought it was best. She wanted this beautiful woman to trust her, but revealing she was the wife of Marcus Ubeli... Some things were better left unsaid. "You may have seen me in a magazine."

"Maybe," Anna said softly. She poured the tea and cupped her hands around her mug, eyes still on Cora.

"How long have you worked at The Orchid House?"

Anna smiled absently. "Awhile."

Cora paused. "Should I not ask questions about it? Is that rude?"

Anna laughed her delightful laugh. "It's not rude, not unless you're going to be rude."

"Why would I be rude?"

"Most people like to judge."

"Well, I don't. I mean, I won't. I don't like looking down on people." Cora felt her cheeks heat. Why did she always get so tongue-tied around people she admired? "Anyway, your dance was amazing."

A smile curved Anna's lips. "Well, thank you. I don't mind talking about my dancing. I've been doing it about four years now."

"Wow."

"Yeah." Anna gazed into her mug, a fond look on her face. "I love it, actually."

"I'd love to see your act." It was the truth. Cora had never seen anyone move with such sensuous grace. An image of Marcus, naked and prowling toward her, popped into her head. Okay, she'd never seen a *woman* move with such sensuous grace.

"You should come back, then. Don't come alone. Come with a man. And I'll make sure to mark you two, so none of the other girls fight over you. Although not many of them approach couples; they don't know how to market to them."

Cora could never go back to AJ's club, as nice as it would be to see Anna's act, and she certainly couldn't imagine asking Marcus to go with her. Still, she was curious. "Market to them?" she asked after the waitress had put down their meals and coffees and walked away.

Anna pulled off her glasses and unzipped her hoodie to expose a fair bit of cleavage, then she grabbed her coffee and pulled out her phone. She smiled sinfully at the camera, the coffee at her lips and snapped a selfie.

Then she zipped the hoodie back up and shoved a forkful in her mouth before her fingers were dancing over the buttons on her phone. She spoke around a mouthful. "It's all about marketing yourself these days. Online and in person. It's a business. If I dance, I get tips. If I dance well, people want more. And then I upsell. Champagne room. VIP section. Private lap dances."

Cora digested this, picking at her food. The Buddha Bowl was a meal in a giant bowl. The turquoise ceramic dish held spinach, kale, chunks of avocado, and some brown grain Cora couldn't identify.

"Quinoa," Anna explained. "It's good for you. Try it."

Cora did and found it was good. "So," she continued after a few bites, "Iris worked with you?"

Anna chewed for a bit before answering. "Iris was a dancer. She did parties, too, and another side business. That's probably where she met The Orphan."

"What side business?"

"She was an escort."

Cora thought back to some of the events she'd been on Marcus's arm, surrounded by other couples. Some of the men had women with them that looked out of place. Too young and gorgeous for their partners. "Like, going out and being a date at parties?"

"Sometimes. I've done the arm-candy-for-hire thing. But there's also a side of it that happens in private, in a hotel room."

"Oh." Cora blinked.

"It's alright," Anna laughed, "It's a pretty good gig. You can work for an agency or on your own."

"So have you ever...?"

Anna just smiled in answer. Cora was torn between wanting to apologize for prying and wanting to ask a million more questions. She blurted out the most pressing one. "Why are you telling me all this? I mean, you just met me."

"You're honest. And you seem like someone who wants to help. Which is kinda rare. And you don't seem like a creeper. I mean, you're my age and you could easily be working alongside me. And, I guess, I don't know, I like the idea of someone looking out for one of us."

Cora nodded. "So any ideas on how to find Iris?"

"Iris and I worked for the same agency. They aren't the problem here. They were fine. They screened clients and I felt safer working with them than anyone else. But Iris was caught up in much deeper stuff. She hung out with a bad crowd."

Cora fell silent, trying to piece things together.

Anna put her elbows on the table and leaned in. "A few months ago, Iris stopped dancing. But she was still caught up in the life—she came to the club a couple of times. I thought for a second that she was a sugar baby—"

"What's that?"

"A lady who gets an allowance from a man to regularly escort him, or be with him."

"Her sugar daddy."

"Exactly. So Iris was hanging around one of the guys who came to the club a lot. I thought she was getting an allowance, maybe good enough to keep her from dancing or being with any other men."

Anna's voice dropped to a whisper. "But I don't think

that's what happened. I think Iris was in trouble, and this man was holding something over her. And then suddenly she was with Chris." Anna shrugged. "I saw her once. She seemed happy with him. She told me she was out of the life."

The waitress took their bowls away, and Cora realized how long they'd been sitting there.

"Thank you for telling me all this."

"Happy to help," Anna said.

They stood up to go but had only walked a few steps when Anna pulled out her phone again, this time aiming it not at herself, but at an artful bit of stained glass in one of the windows nearby. She frowned and moved the phone around to different positions before finally snapping the shot.

"But be careful," she looked back Cora's way. "The guy Iris was with before Chris, he's bad news. I've seen girls get caught up with him before and then disappear. I think he runs a ring or something."

"A ring?"

"Trafficking. Really scary stuff. Maybe guns and drugs, too. His name's AJ."

"AJ?" Cora said his name slowly. "Are you sure?"

Anna paused as several people passed by, then leaned in. "Have you heard of him?"

Cora thought of the concert, Marcus's tense standoff with AJ, and the girl, Ashley, dead on the bathroom floor.

"I met him. At a concert." She shivered. "He gave me the creeps."

"He's definitely creepy."

"I heard he owns The Orchid House."

Anna nodded, grimacing. "He's involved somehow. He

hasn't been around for a long time. I wish he'd stayed away. If he hangs around much more I'll probably end up quitting."

"You thought I was one of his girls."

"You're his type. Well, one of his types. I don't know, I just try to avoid him." Anna re-donned her large sunglasses and put the hood up over her hair. "He wants me to star in a porno. I mean, I wouldn't mind it, but not with him producing."

Cora followed her new friend out of the restaurant, wondering at Anna's incognito look. Right outside, Anna pulled out her camera phone again. Before Cora realized exactly what she was doing, Anna had lifted her phone and snapped a picture of Cora herself.

"Please don't put that up on social media," Cora said. Marcus might freak out.

But Anna just dropped the phone with a smile. "Don't worry, I won't. That one's just for me. I like taking pictures of beautiful things."

Oh. Cora felt her cheeks redden but Anna was already walking, so Cora hurried to catch up with her.

They rounded the corner and a man came out of an alley and fell into stride beside Anna.

"Hey, Annie," he said.

Cora gripped her purse tighter and looked around. They were on the sidewalk of a wide thoroughfare but for once, there were no Shades to call for if this guy made trouble. She hadn't realized until now how much she'd begun to rely on them. And take them for granted.

Anna didn't seem fussed or worried, though, but she did pick up her pace. Cora kept up with her, ready to run if the situation called for it.

"Pete." Her voice lost all of its sultry qualities. "Don't call me that."

The man grinned and rubbed his chin where a three-o-clock shadow was already appearing. His stubble was grey and matched his closely shaven head. "Call you what, Anna Banana?"

Anna growled and looked over at Cora. "Don't talk to him. Ignore him and he'll go away."

"I'm really a nice guy. Here to help. Protect the weak." He flashed a badge. He was a *cop*? "Gather little orchids up and take them back to their house."

"Well, we're no shrinking violets, so get lost."

"Huh," he guffawed, shoving his hands back into his pockets. He looked around her towards Cora. "Who are you? You look familiar." The cop frowned, and Cora wished she had large sunglasses and a hoodie to hide behind, too.

"She's a friend, Pete. Back off. You'll get the info."

"Get it to me and I won't crash your little party tonight. I know what goes on in the back rooms of that place."

"Legal lap dances." Anna almost sounded bored. "You have nothing."

"Oh, and the side business in the hotel room afterwards?"

"Time spent between consenting adults. Don't be a dick, Peter. I know my rights."

"Careful, tiny dancer. And lovely friend, if you ever need to call on the boys in blue..." He shoved a card towards Cora and, for lack of knowing what else to do, she took it and dropped it in her purse.

The man stopped abruptly at the corner of the block facing The Orchid House. Anna and Cora continued walking briskly. He seemed like he wanted to say more but simply watched them go.

"Oh my gods," Cora breathed in relief once they were on the steps of The Orchid House.

"I know. He's a dick but he's harmless."

"What was he talking about?"

Anna shrugged. "Just something I'm helping him with." She rolled her eyes towards the door as if to say, *Anyone could be listening.* "Hey, I'll dig around and let you know. Come visit me again?"

Oh. Cora glanced behind Anna at The Orchid House. She'd gotten lucky today but did she really dare push it? If Anna called with news about Iris, they could meet somewhere else again, like at the little restaurant. All she said though, was, "Sure."

Cora had actually really enjoyed spending time with Anna and adding her to her fledgling group of friends would be kind of great.

"Ok, come soon."

Cora waved and started to walk away when a thought struck her. "Anna," she called. "What's your stage name?"

Anna's smile this time was mysterious, enticing. "Come to the show and find out."

CORA WALKED BACK to the shelter slowly. She'd seen AJ's club and met the charming Anna. Talk about beauty and beast. She wondered if she should've warned Anna, telling her to get away from AJ.

He had to be behind Iris's kidnapping. He was acting as the Orphan's manager. He needed the singer so he could do his business in New Olympus.

Maeve took one look at her and sat her on the couch in the office with a mug of steaming tea.

"How did it go?"

The whole story came out. The older woman listened without moving a muscle.

"I don't like this. I don't like that you were there alone. Take someone next time."

"I don't intend on there being a next time. Anna's great but AJ's too dangerous."

"And Anna? Do you trust her?"

"What do you mean?" Cora frowned.

"It's possible she was throwing you off the scent."

Cora thought for a moment and conjured up Anna's sweet, honest face. "I don't think she was lying."

"She was very quick to open up to someone she'd just met."

"I think she recognized that I didn't have an agenda. She was friendly, sure...but she's friendly as part of her profession. And maybe she does have an agenda of her own, but she's still worried about her co-worker. She told me she was glad that someone cared about Iris."

Maeve's mouth moved into a small smile. "Well, you state your case for your new friend quite well. I think this excursion was good for you."

"How do you mean?"

"You seem to have a lot of strength to tap into when you're working on behalf of others. But what about for yourself?"

Cora jerked her head in a quick little no. "I just—"

"You have more energy now talking about helping these women than in the past few months combined. It's like you've come alive." Maeve frowned. "I've been worried about you."

Cora was about to start babbling about how she was fine, how everything was *fine*, when Maeve continued.

"And I want to ask something else, but I'm afraid you'll get upset at me."

Cora shook her head. "I'd never get upset with you for asking a question. You're my closest friend." It was the truth, age difference be damned.

Still Maeve hesitated a moment, but then she finally asked, "Why are you coming to me with all of this instead of going to your husband?"

The question hit Cora like a load of concrete, but Maeve didn't notice. "Is it possibly because you think he might be involved? In the girl's kidnapping?"

Cora shot off the couch and paced away. An immediate denial was on her lips but she didn't voice it. She couldn't. Because...Maeve had just said out loud one of her deepest fears.

Nobody knew better than her just how ruthless Marcus could be. Especially when he felt like he needed to be in control. Having AJ, an obvious enemy, as The Orphan's manager might have thrown him. So he could have sought out the upper hand to regain control over his investment by pinching Chris's pressure point—Iris.

It didn't fit with the Code he supposedly lived by... But then again, that had been his *father's* Code. Marcus had made it very clear that everything had changed the moment the Titans killed his sister, Chiara.

"I've upset you. I'm sorry," Maeve said.

"No, no. It's fine." Cora flashed a smile that both of them knew was fake. "It's okay." Her phone beeped with an incoming text and she pulled it from her purse.

It was from Marcus and had all of two words: Home. Now.

What had crawled up his ass now? Then she bit her lip. Had he somehow found out about her excursion to The

Orchid House? "I have to get going anyway." She walked over and gave Maeve a long hug.

Maeve rose too, and started walking her out.

"Good, get some fresh air. The next hour of my life is going to be giving this puppy a bath. Meet Brutus. I'll need a few hours at the spa afterwards." Maeve pointed to a large grey dog lying in a cage. Cora stopped to stare.

"That's a *puppy*?"

Maeve chuckled. "Few months old. His mother was a Great Dane and got out when she was in heat. Breeder dumped the pup on a family that couldn't keep him when they realized how big he was going to get."

"What did the mom breed with, a horse? Look at his paws—he's going to be huge." Cora dropped to her knees and reached her hand through the bar to pet the puppy. He immediately raised his paw up as if to "shake."

"Is he trained?" Cora shook the gigantic paw.

"I've been working on it." Maeve smiled as she watched the two. "He just seems to like you. Want to help?"

"I'd love to." The mutt was rolling over now, ears flopping. Cora laughed. Her phone buzzed again and she stood reluctantly. "I've gotta run."

On the way out, she checked her texts. She had some older ones she hadn't seen yet. One from Armand, thanking her for doing the show and coming to the party. One was under a name she didn't remember programming in: 'Goldwringer': Hey, bitch! It's Olivia. Let me know when you want to party again.

Cora smiled and texted back polite replies. While she did, two more texts came in.

She scrolled down; they were from Marcus.

Are you on your way yet?

Don't ignore me unless you want the consequences.

It was wrong, so very wrong that she thought about not texting back just to see what these *consequences* might be.

But then she thought of Maeve's words and her fingers were flying over her phone screen. Leaving now.

Sharo was waiting outside with the car.

ELEVEN

"WHAT THE HELL is taking so long?" Marcus barked into his phone.

Sharo's cool voice responded back. "The fans are mobbing the bottom of the building. Security and cops are trying to hold them back from the lobby. I've arranged with Marco, Stan, and Lorenzo to head the team guiding Mrs. Ubeli into the building from the southeast entrance. We are approaching now."

"I'll meet you there," Marcus said, thumbing the phone closed and jamming it in his pocket. His jaw clenched. How did the fucking vultures even learn The Orphan was here? But no, he knew the answer the second he asked it.

AJ. He was trying to put pressure on them and see how they'd react. Force their connections out into the open. The sooner that bastard was six feet under, the better. But keeping The Orphan playing shows was important, too, and not just because of ticket sales. Mobs needed appeasement. Even the ancient Romans knew that.

It was the off-season for the Spartans, the New

Olympians favorite sports team, and Marcus needed the people distracted.

Look over here at the shiny, sparkling attraction—instead of seeing what I'm actually doing under the table in the dark. Keeping the people amused and happy was one of the first lessons Marcus had learned as unofficial king. He could keep them safe and drugs mostly off their streets and the gambling halls and prostitution rings regulated.

But it was a mistake to forget that people always wanted a little bit of sin.

Try to clean up the drugs completely and the city became combustible. The one and only time he'd tried, he'd nearly lost his crown to an upstart gang who took it as an opportunity to try to usurp him. He'd taken the little shit down easily enough and learned the lesson. He eased up on the drug trade, deciding it was enough to keep it out of schools. Consenting adults could do whatever the fuck they wanted.

But with The Orphan had come AJ, and that was one nasty surprise Marcus could do without. He was handling the situation, but he didn't like it. Not one damn bit.

The elevator opened to chaos on the lobby floor. Cops were everywhere, questioning people and checking their IDs before letting them up to their hotel rooms. Outside, the blues and reds of police lights flashed. And the roar of the crowd outside. Marcus's hands unconsciously closed into fists.

AJ had set the mob on his home by moving The Orphan here, to a private floor. The fans found out, no doubt tipped off by AJ himself. And now he and his wife would be stuck in this mess any time they wanted to come or go.

Marcus turned on his heel and headed for the Southeast entrance. It was around the back of the building, near the gym and should be less crowded. By the time he got there, Lorenzo and Stan were already ushering Cora through the doors. She looked harried but not scared. His strong, beautiful wife. For a moment, all he could see was her. So fucking beautiful even after working with smelly animals all day.

"What's going on?" she asked.

Her question immediately brought back Marcus's sour mood. "The Orphan moved in," he snapped.

"He's here? Don't they have to ask you before they do that sort of thing? Move in such a high-profile client?"

Marcus's eyebrows went up. "I'm flattered you think my sway extends so far, but no." He glared as they rounded the corner to the main lobby. "If I had any say, this debacle would never have happened."

Cora looked confused. "But don't you own the hotel?"

Marcus laughed out loud at that. "What gave you that idea?"

Her mouth dropped open. "I don't know, I just assumed... Since you live in the penthouse suite permanently. After a while I guess I thought this was just another of your businesses."

"No, I don't own the Crown."

Her brow furrowed. "Then why do you live here? You own so much real estate in the city."

Marcus smiled at that because this was one of his favorite triumphs. "A man owed my father a favor; I called it in. He owns the hotel, but the penthouse is mine for as long as I want. And as long as I live here, he'll never forget what he owed my family."

He chuckled grimly. "He hates me. Wishes he could throw me out, but he can't without everyone knowing he goes back on his word. But whenever he thinks of his pride and joy of a hotel, he grinds his teeth because he thinks of me, living in the penthouse he designed for himself."

Cora looked appalled but Marcus would never apologize for who he was. Like everything in his life, Marcus's residence sent a message.

And now his castle was under siege. His bad mood came thundering back. Especially when two police officers came toward him like they intended to question *his* credentials.

Marcus immediately locked eyes with his man, who came forward and cut the other two off at the pass. Good.

When he looked back to Cora, he saw her watching the whole exchange with curious eyes.

"Upstairs," he commanded her. He'd intended another long, slow night of reminding his wife exactly where her place was in their marriage—underneath him—but dammit, he was letting her get underneath his skin again.

He'd been spending time with her when he needed to be focused on the business at hand.

The shipment.

Nothing could go wrong this time. The mob would be appeased for only so long by side shows. If everything went as planned, then he would have the monopoly on the next hottest commodity the crowd would be slathering over. Which meant crushing the Titans and bleeding them dry of every tyrant's greatest source of power—money.

"Lorenzo will keep watch outside the door while I'm gone until they get this mess settled. I have to go out." Marcus's features hardened as he looked around. No more distractions, not until the shipment had been delivered and distribution was going smoothly.

He turned away from his wife. "I've got business to attend to tonight."

TWELVE

The next morning after a restless night, Cora met Olivia for a shopping excursion.

Cora had almost cancelled their plans, except her new friend had been so excited when she'd promised. And Marcus wasn't home when she woke up. He'd stayed out all night again. Doing his *business*, whatever that was. Or whomever. The thought was acid in Cora's brain.

And it wasn't like she had any more leads on Iris. She thought about calling the police. "Excuse me, I'd like to report a missing person. I have a picture of her but we've never met. Oh, and please don't tell my husband I'm asking; his men might have abducted her."

Sure. That would go over well.

Cora was waiting on the curb, deep in thought, when a latte appeared in front of her face. Olivia stood grinning at her.

"Oh, you're an angel." Cora took the proffered cup and sipped it. Perfect. "Thank you."

"Least I could do, considering the Herculean task before us."

"Shopping?"

Olivia grimaced. "I hate clothes. If I ever move somewhere warm, I'm not going to wear them."

Cora sputtered a little. "That should go over well at work."

"It's my company." Olivia sipped a coffee of her own. "They'll get over it."

Cora paused. "Wait, you own your own company?"

"Aurum? Yeah, it's mine."

"Aurum? Like the mobile apps and devices?"

"Yep."

"Holy crap." Cora stared at the shorter woman drinking coffee in faded black jeans and a turtleneck.

"What?"

"I've read about you, in the papers. You're like a super genius." Aurum was one of the fastest growing companies in New Olympus.

"Told you," Olivia said smugly.

"You were at Armand's show, doing his website?"

"I like to get out among the commoners once and awhile." Olivia shrugged. "Besides, I love Fortune jeans. They're pretty much all I wear."

"Well, we're going to change that."

"Bring it on."

As they started walking, Olivia's eyes immediately shot to Sharo, large and hulking in a black suit, who'd started following them. Cora's shadow for the day.

"Ignore him," Cora whispered.

Olivia just raised an eyebrow. "Not sure I want to. That man is one hunk of gorgeous beefsteak."

Cora laughed out loud at Sharo being described that way, then shook her head.

Cora started with the shop she used to always walk by

her first weeks in the city. Back then she could only gaze longingly but it had become one of her favorite haunts after marrying Marcus. Olivia followed her around obediently, only fussing when the shop manager approached. "Back off. I'm with her."

Cora's head flew up to see the manager's startled face. She always helped Cora and she was actually really nice. "Sorry," Cora mouthed and hurried to get Olivia into a dressing room.

In the next few hours, Cora kept Olivia busy trying on new outfits. Olivia didn't want anything but black, and the color suited her all right so Cora went with it, picking out different fabrics to lend a little richness to Olivia's mono-chromatic look.

"This looks like crap," Olivia announced, pointing at a display of dresses. The shop manager's eyebrows shot up to her hairline.

"Time for the dressing room," Cora sang, pushing her friend inside the room and shutting the door behind her. Cora continued looking and flipped a few clothes over the door, ignoring Olivia's muffled curses from inside.

"She's...prickly," Cora told the manager. "I'll take care of her."

As the clothes mounded up beside the register in a "To Buy" pile, the manager's expression changed.

"She owns a really successful company," Cora told the manager and cashier. "The tech company working on the phone you can fold in half."

"Oh wow," the cashier breathed.

"Perhaps you'd like to open a personal shopper's account? That way you can conduct in-office sessions for your client."

"That's a great idea," Cora said as Olivia's voice rang

out in the back of the store—"This is crap!"—accompanied by gasps from the store personnel.

"Ring up everything," Cora instructed, and ran to rescue the poor saleswomen from Olivia's blunt barrage.

In the end Olivia paid without comment, and the entire store's staff sighed in relief when Cora pushed her friend out the door.

They lunched at a popular curry house.

"Well, that wasn't as bad as I thought it would be."

Cora smiled quietly into her mango lassi.

"Seriously, after the fashion show and party, I'm surprised I didn't wind up getting fitted for bunny ears."

Cora nearly choked, remembering Armand's arm candy at the party. "Oh, that's the next stop," she teased. "I'm just giving you a break before more torture."

"That's what you think. All I have to do is call that giant you call a bodyguard over and he'll be ready to carry you away if you push me."

Cora stilled. "You mean Sharo?" He was sitting in the corner far enough away to give them their privacy but he was far too big to be unobtrusive in the busy restaurant.

Olivia shrugged. "Is that his name? Who is he anyway?"

"Just one of my husband's colleagues," Cora said, gnawing on her lip.

"He doesn't look like a colleague, looks more like a... I don't know. A wise guy or something." Olivia laughed and for once Cora wished her new friend wasn't so blunt.

Cora honestly didn't know what to say, and it seemed impossible to talk about her husband's business here, in a restaurant, in broad daylight. This was why she didn't have friends. She hadn't realized it until now. They'd ask uncomfortable questions and she'd retreat into the safety of her husband's penthouse.

Olivia pushed around her rice, obviously noting Cora's silence. "So, what's the deal—I can't imagine you get into too much trouble." Olivia was studying her; Cora could almost see her calculating how much to pry.

Time for a topic change. And, considering what Olivia did for a living...

Cora hesitated, then put her drink down. "Olivia, if you suspected someone was missing, and you needed to look for them without anyone else knowing, how would you do it?"

"Ping their phone," Olivia answered immediately, her eyes lighting up. "There's technology that allows you to pinpoint a device. Like a trace."

"Is it legal?"

"Not really. But where's the fun in that?"

The rest of the lunch turned into a technology lesson. Olivia showed Cora some of her hacks and some of her company's apps. Cora's phone got an update and a few new downloads, with Olivia's promise to show Cora how to use them.

"Thanks for all the help, I really appreciate it." If Cora could get a hold of Iris's phone number, then maybe she could figure out this phone pinging thing and get another lead. Once she found out where Iris was being held, she could send the cops in. Marcus never had to know she was involved and Iris would be safe.

"No problem." The bill came by and Cora reached for it, but Olivia grabbed her hand. "Cora, you'd tell me if you were in trouble?"

Cora nodded.

"I know we just met but...I'd like to help."

Cora bit her lip but then took a chance. Like Anna, Olivia seemed genuine. "I may need to take you up on that."

"Anytime, bitch," Olivia said affectionately. "Except for the shopping part."

Cora laughed. "I guess I can't convince you to visit one more shop, then, for shoes?"

"Hell, no. I'm more interested in your other...project."

"I'll keep you posted," Cora promised. "And will hopefully have something to you soon."

An idea was budding, but first Cora needed to get home. Cora hugged Olivia goodbye and then signaled Sharo she was ready to leave.

THIRTEEN

BACK AT THE CROWN, Cora pressed the up button to the private floor on the elevator and punched in the code. The police had the horde of fans well in control outside, finally, and once Sharo saw her get in the elevator, he didn't follow. He'd gotten a call right before, so she guessed that Marcus needed him more than she did.

She'd gotten used to living in the high-end hotel, in the section that was more of a palace of suites. Who owned the hotel? Who had owed Marcus's father the favor?

She shook her head. She had more important fish to fry. Like getting Iris's phone number.

She had to go see Chris. And he now stayed in a suite one floor below where she lived. A private floor that required a key, just like her floor. The same key worked for the top floor with the pool...so maybe she'd luck out?

Cora held her breath until the door slid open to the requested floor. *Yes.* Her intuition had been right. The key worked for the Orphan's floor, too.

The door to the private floor opened and she walked in. A hallway held a series of doors that must lead to suites. Two thugs lounged on either side of the nearest doors.

Surprisingly low security, considering the night before. Something was up. Was Marcus involved? He'd been so upset about the invasion into their privacy last night. He might not own the Crown but his power and influence everywhere throughout the city was undeniable.

The men stood up and came to attention as she approached. AJ's men. Gods, Cora hoped their boss wasn't anywhere nearby.

"Hey, lady, you need to leave." One of the men held out a meaty hand to stop her from going further down the hall.

Taking a deep breath, she channeled her inner Ice Queen. She wore nice jeans and a sweater along with a string of pearls around her neck. They probably thought she was just another hotel guest. Maybe some rabid fan.

Cora looked at them coolly, her chin notched up. "Do you recognize me?"

"Woman, you could be the queen of England, you can't be here."

"I'm Mrs. Ubeli. As in, Marcus Ubeli's wife."

The two men didn't budge.

"I'm here to see Christopher. My husband wants me to make sure he's comfortable."

"No one gets in. Boss's orders." The larger one folded his arms across his chest.

"Just go tell him I'm here to see him." Cora tried to channel Marcus's authority. "If he doesn't want to see me, I'll leave."

The one with his arms folded leaned forward, getting into her space. "We don't take orders from you."

Cora didn't back down, she just lifted an eyebrow as if to say, *oh really?* A classic Marcus move.

"Wait," the other said, looking a little nervous. "Let me check something." He went inside the room, closing the door behind him.

The other stared hard at her. She ignored him. The types Marcus associated with usually studied her like she was a threat or a piece of meat. When he finally looked away and leaned against the wall, she memorized his face, from the blunt features to the little gold ring in his ear.

Meanwhile, the other guard came back out, holding his phone like he'd just taken a call. "He wants to talk to you. Says he knows ya."

Cora started forward and the thug with the earring put his arm out to stop her. "Wait," he started but she cut him off.

"Touch me and my husband will hear about it." The two men stiffened. "You two have been nothing but perfect gentlemen so far," she continued, with a sweeter tone. "I'll only be a minute."

She flashed a smile. The first guard settled back on his heels. The one with the earring looked like he wanted to kill her.

"Only a minute," she sang as she entered the apartment. And stopped.

The room was trashed. A room service cart lay on its side at her feet. The food from the tray was all over the ground. In the suite itself, a chair lay on its side, leading her eye to the brocade curtains hanging askew on their rod.

Across from the bedroom, lovely white and gold wall-paper was stained with ribbons of red liquid, as if someone had picked up wine delivered on the cart and thrown it. The rest of the room's décor, with Victorian chairs, was largely untouched, but it was shocking, this scene of obvious violence.

Cora was about to call out Chris's name to ask if he was all right when the guard with the little earring stuck his head in and laughed, not a nice sound. "He's temperamental."

Cora swallowed, and didn't let them see her flinch. She wouldn't show weakness to them.

She turned and stepped carefully, hearing broken glass under her boots. The doorway to the bedroom gaped.

"Chris?" she finally called. "It's Cora. Marcus Ubeli's wife."

A slight noise drew her to investigate. Once her eyes adjusted to the dim light, she saw Chris's curly head jutting over the bedcovers.

"Chris, are you ok? Did something happen?"

"It was me." The rock star's voice came weakly. "I did it."

"You did this?" She picked her way carefully into the room, stopping at the foot of the bed. Gods, he looked terrible. His hair was dirty. The room stank. She didn't know when he'd last showered but it couldn't have been recently.

He drew a raspy breath. "She left me. She didn't love me anymore. They showed me a note she wrote. I sort of freaked out and...trashed the place."

Cora squinted at him. "They showed you a note? What did they say?"

"They said they went to look for her." He stretched a hand over to the bedside table, knocking another bottle onto the floor. Cora darted forward to help him. Grunting softly, as if the movements were painful, he handed her his phone.

Cora turned it to see the picture. A woman lay sleeping, her face wan on the dirty pillow. Iris. Even Cora understood what the needle in her arm meant.

"She's using again. She doesn't want me anymore."

"This is your proof?" She held it up. "Who took this picture?"

"One of AJ's men."

"Men like the assholes outside?" Cora could feel the rage welling up inside her. An innocent woman, drawn into this net. She worked over the phone, forwarding herself the picture, then going to Iris's contact information and forwarding that too.

Something had to be done. It couldn't be a coincidence that a woman disappeared when her fiancé was threatening to break a multi-million-dollar contract.

After seeing that picture... This wasn't Marcus. Maybe he would have kidnapped Iris to put pressure on Chris, but he never would have put her in a dank hellhole or pumped her full of drugs. No, this was all AJ.

"Chris, it's been long enough. We need to go to the police. She's in trouble."

"I threatened and they told me to try it. They said she'll end up in jail, or worse." He stared up at the ceiling, eyes bloodshot. "I can't do anything. I can't help her."

Drawing in a harsh breath, Cora let the phone fall. She turned, went to the window, and drew back the curtains in a violent move.

Chris cried out but she felt no sympathy for him.

"Enough. Get up. If you ever loved her, get out of bed and start acting like an adult."

"She left me—"

"I don't care! She's in trouble and someone needs to find her." Cora took another deep breath and said firmly, "I've already started looking and have some leads."

"You won't find anything. If they took her and got her using again, she'll never be back."

"Then I'm going to find her and give her that option. If

you could, would you help her? Get her to rehab or whatever?"

Chris was sitting up now. He nodded. "Of course. I love her."

"Then get up out of bed and start acting like it. Practice or something. Your job is to play." She drew herself up, trying to show confidence she didn't feel. "I'll take care of the rest."

The two guards outside the Orphan's room jumped when the door swung open. Cora stalked out.

"Call the maid." She looked them in the eye. "This place needs to be cleaned up, even if you take The Orphan to another room while they do it. And order him a decent meal."

With that, she swept out into the hall.

FOURTEEN

Back in the penthouse, the afternoon sun slanted thickly over the living room. Cora dropped her purse and worked busily over her cell, sending Olivia Iris's phone info to trace.

Goldwringer replied: Cool! Give me five.

Relaxing back on the couch, Cora allowed herself a satisfied smile. They were one step closer to finding Iris.

She raised her head when she heard the front door open. Strange. Marcus was never home this early, not lately anyway. But this was good. He wasn't the one who took Iris. Maybe it was time to talk to him, to lay it all out on the table and ask for his help.

Standing, she squared her shoulders. Even if Marcus had business reasons he shouldn't cross AJ, she was going to convince him. What was a business matter against a person's life?

"Marcus? I thought you were out on business tonight..." she started to say, then gasped.

AJ's frame filled the doorway. The man looked larger than when she saw him at the club; his bald head shone in the sunlight. The rest of him was dressed simply in a long trench coat, a grey shadow on his unshaven face. His beady black eyes were fixed on her, assessing.

Shit, what should she do? How had he even gotten in? She must've left the penthouse unlocked when she returned from seeing Chris. The only people who could even access their home needed a special key to work the elevator. But duh, she'd just proved the same key worked on all the private floors. And as Chris's manager, obviously AJ would have access to the same key.

"What are you doing here?" Fear made her voice sharp.

AJ sauntered into the room, looking around like an investor surveying a potential property. Cora stiffened her spine so she wouldn't shrink away. One thing the Underworld taught her: if you cowered, they thought you were prey.

Still, she was glad there was a couch between her and the approaching gangster.

"You shouldn't be here. Marcus won't like it."

"Nice place." AJ strolled forward, taking in the view. His stoop took inches off his height, but also gave his movements a predatory look. Like a bear, sniffing outside its lair.

AJ stopped to study a white statue of a bearded man capturing a fleeing woman. Walking around it to view it, he rubbed his jaw. "You pick this out?" He squinted at her, then at a small but exquisite replica of a statue, a copy of the first one.

"My husband." Cora's voice was clipped. "And he'll be home any minute."

AJ turned from the statue to face her. The deep lines around his mouth bent into a smile. "You know, for a woman stepping out on her man, you sure invoke his name a lot."

What the hell was he— "What are you talking about?"

"You think I wouldn't find out about your little visit to my pet singer?" The man started walking towards her. "I thought I'd hide him here, keep him from the fucking fans. Freaky rabid bitches."

AJ smiled. He kept walking forward, closing in on her. Cora backed up despite herself. "Well, now we have a new story for the paparazzi: Ubeli's wife doing The Orphan. Little Miss Innocent spreads her legs."

"How dare you?" Cora snapped. She'd had enough. She stood up to him, not backing down any more. Her five feet eight inches put her almost at his grizzled chin. "When I tell Marcus—"

"You were in his bedroom," AJ spit back at her. His breath was foul on her face. "There are cameras on the hall."

Cora froze as what he said sunk in.

AJ watched her face closely. "Tell me, little girl. What's Marcus going to think?"

What *would* Marcus think? There was no trust between them, not now. Still, she refused to give this disgusting man an inch.

But AJ took advantage of her momentary silence to reach out and capture a lock of her light hair.

"So, gorgeous," he twisted the strands between two fat fingers. "What will you give me to keep your little tryst from your husband?"

Cora jerked back. AJ let her move away, watching her go with glittering eyes.

"That's right, baby, think about it. Then think of how to convince me." His eyes swept up and down her figure.

She felt dirty just being in the same room as him.

"You can't threaten me," she said, trying again to

channel some of Marcus's authority. It came out sounding petulant. A child refusing to go to her room.

She cleared her throat and tried again. "I know what you did. I'm telling Marcus—you kidnapped an innocent woman to threaten her fiancé."

AJ stared at her, then his shoulders started to move. A strange, heaving sound came from his barrel chest. Cora watched nervously, thinking he was having a fit.

Then she realized the man was laughing at her.

AJ's mouth gaped, showing his gold tooth. "Are you kidding me? That's your threat?" The man's jowls shook with mirth. "I'm going to tell," he mocked her voice. "Pretty, stupid slut. You think your husband doesn't know I took Iris? Ubeli ordered it."

Cora felt his words like a blow. "No," she whispered.

"That's right, little girl. And if you ever push me, I'll tell him exactly where you were this afternoon. And what do you think he'll want me to do with his cheating whore of a wife?"

Squeezing her fists, Cora let his words wash over her. She was still stuck on the thought that Marcus ordered Iris's kidnapping. But he hated AJ. Didn't he? He'd never work with him...

But he already was, wasn't he? To book The Orphan. If Marcus had wanted Iris gone and ordered AJ to do it, he wouldn't have had control over AJ's methods. But Marcus was all about control. So did that mean AJ was ly—

"Maybe I'll be the one who gets to punish you," AJ continued, smirking. "You might even like it."

Fighting back furious tears, Cora watched the man move to the liquor cabinet. "Hell, half of Ubeli's men must be gagging for you. We'll get a movie camera; make it a best-seller. The black giant would be first in line. I know I'd pay to watch you choke on him." He chuckled as he poured himself a drink.

A rushing sound filled Cora's ears; she couldn't find her voice to talk or scream.

"I'm just saying, if Daddy ever don't satisfy—Uncle AJ is here."

"Get out." Cora's voice came out strangled.

He raised the glass to her and then downed it. She watched him, fists balled. She'd never hated anyone so much in her life. "Get the *fuck* out of my house right this second."

AJ took his sweet time moving to the door. "Pleasure visiting you, *Mrs. Ubeli*." He spoke her name with a sneer. "Hope to do it again real soon."

Cora shivered with anger and fear.

He was almost outside when he turned. "Oh, and we're moving your boy, so no more little visits. Although, if you do come down—" His hand slipped down to his crotch crudely. "Uncle AJ will be ready."

Cora wanted to kick him where he was so rudely gesturing. With her pointiest heels.

"It'll be our secret." He winked at her.

Cora waited until she was sure he was gone before collapsing on the couch, still shaking with fury. *Ubeli ordered it.* She mopped her face with a hand, ordering herself to get it together.

He was lying about Marcus. Right?

One thing she was sure about, she was going to free Iris from AJ. Then she would find a way to make him pay. *Pretty, stupid slut.*

Her phone buzzed. She looked down and opened Olivia's text, then clicked on the highlighted address. The link took her into a map, where a light blinked, signaling the location of Iris's phone.

Cora took a deep breath. She knew exactly where Iris was. Or, at least where her phone was. And it was time to finally do something about it.

FIFTEEN

MIDAFTERNOON THE NEXT DAY, Cora took a little walk into the park. No bodyguards with her. She'd given them the slip again after they dropped her off at the shelter earlier that day. She'd been worried about what she would say to Marcus or how to act with him once he got home last night...but he never came home.

Whatever Marcus was up to had him working day and night. Either that or he was avoiding her. Which was probably for the best right now, all things considered.

She flopped down on a bench and checked her messages. Nothing.

A shadow fell over her, and she squinted at Pete the cop. He took a seat next to her on the far side of the bench. His posture was relaxed, but his eyes swept the path and park area around them.

"I have to say, you're the last person I expected to hear from." Pete looked her over. "I nearly dropped my phone when I got your message last night. I looked into you. Married to the biggest crime lord in the city." He let out a low whistle.

Cora spoke without looking at him. Anyone watching would see a young woman resting from her jog and a man on lunch break. "I want to be clear. I'm not ratting on my husband."

"Oh, you made that clear." Pete sat up and rummaged in his pocket, taking out a cigarette and lighter. "I heard about your little visit down to the station two weeks after the wedding. Wouldn't flip even though the feds were offering you witness protection." He lit the cigarette and puffed on it.

"The offer wasn't real," Cora said stiffly. "It was a test." And if it hadn't been, she'd still have made the same decisions. There was no point dwelling on the past.

"Well, you passed anyway. Not sure what that says about you. The type of woman you are." He squinted at her through his smoke.

She waved the cloud away. "I'm loyal. And anyway, I'm not here to talk about my husband."

"No? Then why the hell did you call me?" He glanced around warily. "You playing some sort of game?"

At the cop's raised voice, a grey shadow lying on the ground next to Cora raised its large head. Brutus, the Great Dane *puppy*, got to his feet, coming around the bench to stand in front of Cora, between her and the cop.

"Gods, what is that thing?" Peter coughed and scooted further down the bench.

Cora reached out a hand and scratched the dog's ears. "Great Dane mixed with something. I took him from the shelter to stretch his legs." She raised her hand and the dog leaned happily toward her, begging for more.

"I thought he was a boulder." He watched as she praised the Dane, and got him to lie back down to chew a toy. "So Ubeli lets you wander around alone?"

"My husband's men are too busy to be babysitting me."
The lie fell easily from her lips. But she realized it was the
wrong one when Peter's eyes lit up.

"Busy, huh? What has their attention?"

Cora took a deep breath. "That's not why we're here.
I'm actually trying to find a missing person. The singer at
my husband's club—The Orphan. His fiancée disappeared
late Saturday."

Pete shrugged. "So have him go to the station, file a
report."

"It's more complicated than that." Cora rushed to fill in
the details about the tragic couple and her and Olivia's
search. She pulled out Iris's picture and laid it on the bench
for him to see, along with the shot she'd forwarded from
Chris's phone of Iris. "We think a man named AJ is behind
it. We tracked her phone. She's in his club, or well at least
her phone is. And she's in trouble."

Glancing down at the picture, Pete grunted. "Yeah, I
heard of AJ. Used to run a few corners in this city. Got
flushed out with the old crowd. Now he's back."

"The old crowd?"

"Gods, your husband don't tell you anything? The
Titan brothers. There were three of them, or maybe it used
to be three? I think one of them got axed back in the day?"
He frowned as he thought. "They owned this town before
your husband did. Some think they're trying to get back in.
They say that this AJ is the first advance."

The wind picked up, and Cora wished she'd worn
something other than a cashmere cardigan. Even in the sun,
she felt the chill. "So, can you help find Iris?"

Pete snubbed out his cigarette on the concrete by his
feet. "Look, miss, this just isn't my line of work. Find a
missing junkie? You don't even know if she wants to be

found. Maybe she wanted to leave this Orphan fellow and go back to scoring."

"She didn't want to leave him. And AJ's a snake. He—"

Pete cut her off. "But I guess I *could* tail this AJ guy a little. But I'm not doing anything without getting a favor back. This is small time stuff you're asking here. I'm going to need something in return. Something juicy. And I wanna know why you're not taking this to your husband."

Cora didn't answer, staring down at the picture of Iris.

"You think Ubeli's involved," Pete deduced. "That's why you're sneaking around."

"I'm not—"

"You called up a cop and asked for a meet. How's that going to look to your husband? Or anyone who runs with him?"

This sounded too close to what AJ had said to her. "Marcus knows I'm loyal."

The cop rubbed his head and jaw again, not listening. "Hell, I'm probably a marked man just for meeting with you."

Something inside her snapped. "Then why'd you chase me down and give me your card?" Cora rounded on him. "You know what—forget it. I thought you had a pair. An innocent woman is in trouble."

She snatched up Iris's picture and waved it in his surprised face. "You're supposed to be a—I don't know—a protector of the city. Instead you just want a big bust to make your career. And use whoever you can to make it."

She turned away from the cop's surprised face and stuffed the picture back in her purse. "Look for someone else to hand you my husband's head on a silver platter. And anyway, he's done more to protect people in this city than you ever will—"

"You really think that, you pampered princess?" Pete rose to his feet, towering over her. She tugged at Brutus's leash and the big dog leapt up, pushing between them.

The cop retreated, but kept talking, his face twisted with anger. He shouted after Cora as she hurried away, Brutus in tow. "You're just like the rest of them, with your money and your secrets. You people think you're gods and goddesses, better than us. Untouchable by us mere mortals. Well, you know what? We're going to bring you down."

She strode away, head down, as his rant hit her back like ineffective bullets.

And when she got home, her fingers flew to open her contacts. She hesitated a moment, then dialed.

Armand answered the phone. "Cora?" Surprise was in his tone.

"Hey," she said lightly. "Are you busy?"

"Just about to leave the spa—why?"

"I need a favor." She bit her lip and remembered how the designer had hovered over her at the party. If she'd read his body language right, he'd be up for helping her. She only hoped she wasn't opening herself up to too much trouble.

"Sure—you ok?"

"I'm fine. I just—I promised a friend of mine I'd help her out and go see her show tonight. Marcus is working late and I wondered if you'd go with me."

"Uh, sure. If it's cool with your husband, I'm free. What's the show?"

"Well, that's why I'm asking you to go. It's a tiny bit out of my norm." She rose and pulled AJ's card from her purse. "I need you to take me to a strip club."

SIXTEEN

Two hours later, Armand glanced out of the taxi cab in front of The Orchid House and frowned at the sign.

"Cora, as happy as I am to visit this fine establishment, are you sure this is a good idea?"

"Relax. It's just to help out a friend." It wasn't even a lie. Cora grabbed her purse and made to get out of the cab but Armand caught her arm.

"I don't think Marcus is going to like this."

"What he doesn't know won't hurt him. Besides, he'll just think it's cute."

"He thinks you're cute. He'll just kill me," Armand muttered.

"He's not going to kill you." Cora shook his hand off.

"You're right, he'll get the big guy to do it."

"Sharo's not going to hurt you, either. I won't let him. Now come on."

She swung her legs out of the car and immediately regretted wearing a miniskirt. She'd gone for maximum vamp style, hoping to lower the chances of her being recognized. Black mini skirt, black spangly top, and black high heels: she looked a little like a goth princess. Add to that thick smoky eye makeup and a black wig she convinced Armand to loan her (and help affix to her head) and she was sure she'd be totally under the radar.

"This is insane." Armand checked his hair in the cab's rear-view mirror one last time and then exited the cab. He wore a grey suit and white shirt with a skinny black tie. With his mussed hair and her thin black clad figure, they looked like two kids playing dress up.

"Just follow my lead and I won't let you do anything dumb. I mean, other than this entire venture." Armand stuck out his arm to escort Cora in. "I haven't been this reluctant to visit a strip club since...ever."

Cora looked around as they walked in. The Orchid House looked much classier at night. The bar had cool purple lighting, and there were actual flowers placed on pedestals near the walls.

As soon as they were inside, Armand seemed to relax. He charmed the hostess and kept his hand on Cora's back as they took a booth near the stage. He flirted with the waitress when she came to take their order, batting his long black eyelashes almost as much as the woman batted her mascara-laden ones.

"What are you doing?" Cora asked once the waitress left, walking on air.

"Just chillin.'" Armand smiled when the waitress returned with a bottle of champagne. "Be cool."

Cora sat back in the deep chair but she couldn't relax. She couldn't stop scanning the room, glancing at the faces all around them to make sure she didn't see anyone she knew. Especially AJ. But mostly all she saw was men in suits, and a few couples.

Armand handed her a glass of champagne and leaned

close. "Don't look around so much. Some people here don't want to be recognized, either."

"You seem pretty comfortable," she whispered back.

Armand shrugged. "I'd like it better if you'd tell me what's really going on."

Cora paused with her champagne glass halfway to her lips. "What do you mean?"

"You're acting funny. For one, you called me and asked me out. To a strip club. Without your husband. Are you two doing ok?"

Did he think she'd asked him here because she— Unable to find her voice, Cora just stared into Armand's dark eyes.

He sighed. "Look, Cora, I'm happy to help. That's what friends do. But it'd be nice to know what I'm getting into."

"It's not what you think," she blurted. "That is, I don't know what you're thinking exactly, but Marcus and I are fine." Okay, that was a giant lie, but she wasn't going to even start getting into that with Armand. That wasn't why they were here. "I just need to help...a friend."

"And Marcus isn't involved?"

She hesitated.

"Right, well when we get out of here, we're going to talk about it. Like I said, I want to help you, but I don't want trouble."

Crap. Maybe it wasn't fair to ask him to help her. She'd never fully understood the nature of Marcus's and Armand's business relationship. The last thing she wanted was for Armand to end up getting burned because of her.

"I understand." Cora said softly.

Armand turned to her and took her hand. "It's not only that we're friends. Marcus and I are business partners.

Without him, I never could've gotten Double M off the ground."

Cora nodded, thinking about Metamorphoses, Armand's spa. It was opening its third location soon.

Okay, if she was going to keep asking him to help her, he deserved an explanation. She leaned in and was about to explain when she noticed the fog starting to roll over the stage.

"Ladies and gentleman," a voice came over the loud speaker, "We are proud to present: *Venus.*"

A trance-like humming filled the room, a woman's breathy voice. The fog piled up on the stage as the music intensified, building with drums. Subtle lights revealed a pool of water shimmering under the mist.

Anna emerged slowly from the water, a wet cloth clinging to her body, leaving it covered and at the same time fully on display. Rising from the mist, she looked like a primordial goddess; her curves evoking a millennia of raw, potent desire.

"Wow," Armand breathed.

The music went low until there were only drums beating. Beating deep into the brain. Anna smiled at the crowd, pirouetted slowly, and let the cloth peel away.

Underneath she wore a gold bikini, stretched tight over her flawless figure. The audience murmured their appreciation as Anna floated to the pole for her dance routine.

Cora glanced over at Armand; he had his mouth open and was almost drooling.

Anna's dance was less acrobatic this time and much more sensual. Her hips made love to the air, and every man in the room felt it right in their groin. Anna gyrated slowly and Cora couldn't help mentally filing the move away for later. She needed all the help she could get to manage Marcus.

People were throwing money but Anna danced over it like she didn't notice.

The stage went dark and the cheering went on for a while. When the lights came up, Anna stood there transformed, now wearing a glittering red dress with a plunging neckline. As an old tune came on, she started to sing in her sweet baby voice.

The crowd went crazy.

"That's my friend," Cora whispered to Armand. The svelte young designer looked so mesmerized; it was almost comical. He took a gulp of champagne and poured some on himself without even noticing.

"Armand," Cora called, and he blinked. She looked pointedly at his suit. "I didn't know you had a drinking problem."

Grabbing a napkin, he hurriedly blotted the liquid, then gulped more champagne.

"Oh my gods," he said hoarsely, then cleared his throat. "Uh, she's incredible. How did you meet?"

"Long story." Cora smiled up at Anna as she vamped with the mike. "She's helping me with some charity work."

The song ended and other ladies came on stage.

Anna descended to dance and flirt with her patrons.

Cora wasn't sure if Anna recognized her until Anna winked at her. She came slowly over and leaned over Cora as if she might kiss her.

"We need to talk," Cora whispered, then indicated Armand with a slight jerk of her head. "Alone."

Anna nodded, looking deep into Cora's eyes as part of the act. "Just follow my lead."

Anna moved to Armand, swaying over him. He held his

hands over her hips like he wanted to touch her, but she gathered them, and pulled until he came up out of his chair. He followed her obediently on stage as the announcer spoke again. "Please welcome onstage a special guest, here on his birthday!"

Cora sat up, wondering what was going on. The women had set a chair onstage; they tied Armand to it and took turns grinding on him. The crowd whooped.

Armand's face held a look of goofy pleasure and he didn't even protest that it wasn't his birthday.

Then two of the dancers climbed up, straddled his head as they faced one another and started rocking back and forth.

Eyes fixed to the debauchery on stage, Cora almost didn't notice Anna signaling her to come around the stage to a side door.

Grabbing her purse, Cora rose and loped to Anna. The audience was transfixed on Armand's plight onstage. The women had climbed off of Armand and now were untying him and forcing him down onto his hands and knees. One of them was unfastening his belt.

"Time for his birthday spanking—"

Anna pulled Cora into the hall and shut the door, cutting off the raucous laughter.

"Um," Cora began.

"Can't talk here," Anna whispered and drew her through gauzy curtains and then a door marked *VIP*.

"Is that your boyfriend? He's a handsome one." Anna motioned Cora inside the dimly lit room.

"No, just a friend." Cora entered and stood in the center of the lush surroundings. "And, uh, I'm just curious. What are they going to do with him?"

"Oh, don't worry, he'll love it. It's part of the fun."

Cora wondered how much the fun had to do with Armand getting lashed with his own belt. "Ok."

"They won't hurt him." Anna giggled. "Much. So, what have you found out about Iris?"

Cora caught her up to date, explaining Olivia's cell-phone trick. "Iris has to be here—or was here at some point, and left her phone. Have you seen or heard anything about her?"

Anna shook her head. "Maybe one of AJ's guys has it. They've been crawling around here lately." She shuddered. "Although, it's possible she was here…"

Anna broke off when they heard voices in the hall. The sounds grew louder as people stopped just outside the door.

"Shoot—someone has a customer."

Anna rushed to the back of the champagne room and Cora hurried after. Crap. The last thing she needed was to get caught here. Anna had just said that AJ's guys were crawling the place. And she couldn't tell where on earth Anna was taking her.

But as the voices grew louder Anna drew back one of the curtains covering the wall to reveal…a wall. But then Anna leaned down and pushed on the crown molding and with a slight *creeeeeeeak*, a panel of the wall slid aside. A hidden door. Thank the Fates.

As Cora crowded behind her, Anna stepped into the dark passageway beyond. It was totally black. No lights at all.

Cora couldn't help hesitating on the threshold, but Anna pushed her into the hidden corridor and tugged the door shut after them. It clicked back into place just in time, too, because the next moment they could hear voices muffled in the champagne room.

"Where are we?" Cora breathed, the barest whisper.

She fumbled in her purse and fired up her cellphone flashlight, raising it so she could see more of the narrow hall. It stretched in both directions, just barely wide enough for the two of them. Cora put her hand to the opposite wall and felt the cold brick.

"This place used to be a speakeasy," Anna whispered. "I think this leads to a secret room in the back. I haven't explored it much. Too creepy. And with AJ's guys everywhere the past few days, I haven't really been able to sneak away."

"You think they could be keeping Iris here?"

"We could look." Anna's voice was quiet but held an undercurrent of excitement.

Cora kept the light high. "Which way?"

SEVENTEEN

A FEW MINUTES LATER, Cora's arm ached from holding up her cellphone light. And she was battling claustrophobia. It was *really* tight in here.

The passage had narrowed even further and she couldn't be sure because her sense of direction was a bit turned around, but she felt like the floor was sloping down. Like they were headed to a basement or lower floor.

"Are you sure you don't need to be back onstage?" Cora called quietly to Anna. Anna plunged ahead confidently, almost like she was enjoying this.

"Don't worry," Anna waved a hand. "They'll think I'm back in the VIP room with a customer. If we happen to get caught, I'll tell them you wanted a lap dance and we got carried away."

"Yeah, snooping around in dark creepy basements always turns me on," Cora joked feebly.

"You'd be surprised what people like." Anna stopped in her tracks as the narrow passageway broke out into a larger room. Cora huddled close to her.

"What now?" Cora's voice wavered a little. The place

was spooky, with a low ceiling that was barely six feet tall. At five feet eight inches, Cora felt like stooping. Dust and cobwebs hung from the beams. Real cheery place. Cora shivered.

"Over there." Anna pointed out a small door. They crept forward together, huddling in the small pool of light. Cora's eyes kept skittering all around the room. Her phone better not run out of battery, that was all she was saying. She didn't dare check, though. Iris could be only a room away and she couldn't let her fears stop her now. Just please, gods, no rats. Please no rats.

They made it across the room but the door was stuck. Anna took the cellphone and Cora pushed at it. The thought of being stuck down here in the old air gave her a burst of strength, and she forced it open with her shoulder, staggering forward when it opened suddenly.

The room was tiny. Little more than a closet.

And it was empty.

"Damn," Anna cursed softly. "I really hoped we would find her."

"But look, is that a bed?" Cora pushed through the door and stepped into the small room, nose twitching at the stale air. Anna followed and pointed the cell phone flashlight at the floor. They both looked at the pallet and ratty blanket stuffed inside the tiny space.

"Do you think..." Anna began but then trailed off as Cora knelt down and pushed her hand up between the wall and the pallet.

Holy shit, was that a—

Cora came away holding a cellphone in a bright pink case. "It's Iris's. I'll bet anything. They kept her down there, I'm sure of it." But Iris herself was long gone. Still, this was one more clue.

When Anna said, "Let's get out of here," Cora was only too happy to agree.

They were back in the dark passageway when Cora caught Anna's hand. "Wait, slow down."

Cora held the pink phone between them and tried turning it on. It was dead. Cora cursed and took her purse back from Anna, sliding the new phone in there.

"Do you think—" Anna started, her voice grim.

Cora shook her head and cut her off before she could voice it out loud. "I don't think AJ would harm her, yet." Other than a needle in her arm. "He still needs her as leverage over her fiancé." She said it for Anna as much as for herself.

Anna nodded and threaded her fingers with Cora's again. "Come on."

They started back through the tight space, holding hands. It seemed like it took forever. But gods, all Cora could see was that tiny closet and the pathetic pallet on the ground. Iris must've been so scared. And if they locked her in there without light? A shiver went through Cora that shook her down to her bones. She clutched tighter onto her phone.

But no, AJ still needed Iris. They could still save her. How much had they missed her by? A day? Hours?

When they reached the secret door to the VIP room, Anna's fingers gave her a squeeze before pulling a latch and pushing the door open slowly.

They both waited a beat, listening. For a moment there was nothing but silence. Cora's shoulders sagged in relief. She might just get away with this after all.

Then someone inside moaned and both Anna and Cora froze, hearing the sounds of two people kissing and panting. Anna looked at Cora and Cora made a face.

Someone was having a good time in the VIP room.

"Come on," Anna mouthed, and Cora shook her head. Since they were stuck anyway, Cora picked a few more spider webs out of Anna's hair. Anna held still and after a minute Cora had gotten them all. Cora felt like a nervous wreck but Anna looked completely composed, barely a hair out of place.

Cora looked down at her own cobweb-streaked dress and grimaced. She swiped at them and held still as Anna checked her wig.

After they were both set aright, Anna mouthed, "*Ready?*"

Not hardly, but she still let Anna tug her into the room and close the door behind them. They were behind the curtain and the champagne room lovers hadn't yet noticed to them. Granted, they were otherwise engaged, the man moaning a little.

"You like that, baby?" a woman's voice purred. "Takes the edge right off."

Anna peeped out from behind the curtain.

Cora pulled on her shoulder. "*No*," she mouthed, but Anna shook her off and stepped into the room. What was she *doing*? Did she not get how dangerous this all was?

Cora peered out after her. A dancer was moving over a male client, wearing nothing but a thong, as she giggled and let his hands roam all over her curvy body.

Anna strode confidently past them to the champagne bucket on its stand. She popped open a bottle and started pouring glasses.

"Oh, Anna, I didn't hear you come in," the other dancer said, glancing up. "He was looking for you."

"I'll take over." Anna nodded and the other dancer immediately vacated her spot.

"Come join us, baby." The man sounded woozy, reaching for the retreating dancer.

Wait, Cora recognize that voice.

Armand?

She yanked the curtain aside more abruptly to get a better look. And yep, it was Armand. He was lounging on the plush loveseat, his hair messy and his shirt half unbuttoned. His belt was gone.

"I'm coming," Anna said sweetly, pouring champagne.

Cora came out from the curtain and put her hands on her hips, frowning down at Armand. He looked totally wasted.

"Cora?" His eyes blinked lazily. "Where'd you come from?"

Cora rolled her eyes, accepting a glass of champagne from Anna and taking a gulp to steady her nerves. She was officially ready for this night to be over.

Anna's wide eyes over the glass said it all.

Reaching in her purse, Cora pulled out the pink cellphone. "It's definitely dead," she said, still pressing buttons.

"It's a clue." Anna came over with wet wipes, and started cleaning up Cora's dress better. In the light of the room, the dust smudges were still apparent.

Armand hiccupped on the couch.

Cora ignored him and tried to piece together what had happened. "So her cellphone died but she figured Chris would know about this place and would look for her here. So she leaves it behind. But that means she was alert enough to leave it."

Cora paced a few steps and stopped and spun back to Anna. "And there must be a message on it, or something. Otherwise why would she leave it behind?"

"You guys wanna play?" Armand interrupted. They

both looked down at him. Gods, his eyes were glazed and his pupils were huge. What the hell had he taken?

Anna shifted her gaze back to Cora. "What are you going to do now?"

"Get him out of here." Cora frowned at her drunken friend. "Regroup. See if I can get anything off this phone."

"What do you want me to do?"

Cora started to answer, when she heard a raised voice in the corridor. A very angry voice.

Cora's eyes shot to Anna's. They both recognized it.

AJ. It sounded like AJ.

Anna darted to the door. Cora ran to Armand.

"Come on, we have to go," Cora hissed, pulling at his arms.

"Don't wanna." He grinned up at her, catching her hands playfully. Cora squawked in surprise as he pulled her down on top of him.

"Cora, you always smell so nice." He nuzzled her neck until she pushed herself away. "You're my dream girl."

Behind them, Anna was standing at the door. It opened and Anna shoved her body into the crack, posing provocatively in her sexy red dress.

"Looking for some fun?" she purred.

"Get out here; they want you on stage again."

Cora stiffened. Definitely AJ's voice.

"Sounds great, big boy." Anna arched her back and slid her arm up the door frame so she was blocking the room from AJ's view. "I'll just help these two finish up, then—"

Anna's body jerked forward and she let out a soft cry. Someone had manhandled her into the hall.

Cora jerked her face away from the door to hide it. She hurriedly slipped her purse off her shoulder and stuffed it behind a cushion.

"I said now," AJ was growling. Anna didn't reply. Cora could hear the door swing open.

Whirling back to Armand, Cora straddled him. She tugged down her shirt until her bra covered breasts popped out. Armand's face fell forward into her chest and she let her hair fall across her cheeks.

She could hear AJ's heavy breathing as he stood in the door watching them. Armand moaned suddenly and Cora, afraid he'd call out her name, drew his head back and smashed her lips against his.

Armand's eyes popped wide open. Cora stared back into his, trying to communicate her panic to him.

"Make sure you get the money, sweetheart, before you go all the way," AJ muttered from the door before closing it.

Cora heard the knob click and she sagged, then scrambled back.

Armand was breathing heavily. "Uhh, Cor—"

She leaped forward, plastering both her hands over his mouth. "Just shut up for a minute," she whispered harshly and listened for sounds of AJ bursting back in.

When nothing happened, she relaxed the pressure on Armand's face, but kept her hands against his mouth. His bushy eyebrows were raised in surprise, his eyes shifting wildly.

"I'll explain everything later," she whispered. "Right now we have to get out of here."

"Ok." Armand's words were muffled under her hands. She snatched them away and wiped them off on her skirt.

Ok, think, *think*. AJ was outside; he wouldn't expect them to be done anytime soon. Not if he thought she was one of his girls. She could wait a while but he might come back any minute to check on them.

Someone banged into their door as they moved down the hall and she jumped.

"We're going out a different way," she said, grabbing her purse and pulling Armand to his feet. He stumbled forward and it was enough for her to drag him behind the curtain.

She opened the door and took a left, moving forward in the dark, the opposite direction she and Anna had gone earlier. Anna said this way led to an exit and they just had to find it.

Cora didn't care about the dark this time. AJ was far more terrifying than some stupid rats. If he caught her, she'd be at his mercy, on his turf, and neither Marcus nor any of his men even knew where she was.

"What the hell?" Armand mumbled at her back.

"Keep moving," she whispered hurriedly. She finally turned on her phone's flashlight again. The long narrow hallway stretched out in front of them, and there were a couple of doors ahead. She headed toward the one at the very end. They'd go out the back way and hope no one was watching that exit. If they were, she didn't know what she'd do.

They came to a doorway and Cora listened at the heavy wood. She didn't hear anything. Ok, this had to be the back exit.

She turned the doorknob and pushed the door open.

"Hey! Who's there?"

Oh shit! Not an exit, not an exit!

Cora nearly climbed onto Armand's back, she pushed him back so forcefully down the narrow passage.

"Go, go, go," she hissed. Armand lost his footing and bounced a little off the brick wall. Cora almost got tangled up in him but somehow they managed to move forward.

"Hey, you can't be in here!" The lights hit on her back

as the door behind them opened before adrenaline kicked in and gave her some speed and Armand some focus back. They surged forward, running into the darkness of the hall, Cora continuously pushing Armand forward.

"Where are we going?" Armand asked, sounding more sober as they turned a corner.

"Just keep moving," Cora bit out frantically. "The door should be up here."

Tiny lights from around the crack of a door up ahead gave her hope. The hall had widened enough for her to move past Armand, and she nearly clawed at the next door handle they saw.

It had to be this one. It was really stuck, though, like it was rarely used. She backed up and charged it wildly, only barely hearing Armand protest feebly behind her, "Wait. I think that's the—"

The door burst open and Cora staggered forward, out from behind a curtain and right onto The Orchid stage.

Anna had slipped off the dress and was in the gold bikini, gyrating with her ass towards the audience. Her head flew up and she stared at Cora in shock.

Whirling back the way she'd come, Cora only managed to slam her body into Armand. He toppled over and she went down under him.

"Well, if it isn't the birthday boy, back for more," she heard Anna adlib. Cora pressed her face into Armand's shoulder to hide it and think of what to do.

"And it looks like he got lucky," Anna announced.

A few appreciative whoops rose up from the crowd. Cora wrapped her arms around Armand and desperately hooked a bare leg around his waist.

Armand looked completely dazed. "Cora, what the *hell* is going on?"

"Just go with it," Cora pleaded. "We need to get out of here."

~

"SO THEN WHAT HAPPENED?" Olivia demanded. She sat at her computer desk, sorting through chargers that would match Iris's phone.

Cora shook her head, causing the faded black sweatshirt she'd borrowed from Olivia to slide off one pale shoulder. "Then Anna got the lights to go down and got us off stage. We left out the front." She flopped backwards on Olivia's couch, still unable to believe they'd all gotten out in one piece.

Olivia shook her head. "A night at a strip club and you don't take me. I thought we were friends!"

"Keep it down," Armand groaned.

Cora glanced at him where he lay on the couch, an ice pack held to his head. On the taxi ride to Olivia's, he'd admitted to taking some pills from the first dancer they'd found him with—something to help with the pain of his rump. Mixed with champagne, they'd messed him up and then given him a big ol' headache.

Cora felt no sympathy.

"So, you still have no idea where this Iris girl is?" Olivia had found a charger and was now working on one of her many computers. She had a whole wall of her tiny loft dedicated to electronics.

"No, and I'm out of leads besides the phone. Well, except for AJ. But I can't just follow him around."

"Think maybe it's time to get your husband involved?" Armand asked.

She closed her eyes and tried to envision it. What

would Marcus say if she took it all to him? What would he *do*?

He'd definitely put Cora on lockdown for defying him and going places without his bodyguards.

But would he do anything to help Iris? That was the question. There was still a chance he had a part in the kidnapping. Cora didn't want to believe it, but she hadn't wanted to believe things of Marcus in the past and they'd turned out to be true.

Cora shook her head. She couldn't risk putting her belief in Marcus again and not just because she didn't think her heart could bear another disappointment. If he locked her away again, then who was there to help Iris? She'd be just another disappeared girl in a city that didn't care. "No, I'm not taking this to him. I need to figure it out myself." She yanked on her braids, unravelling them roughly.

She noticed Armand and Olivia were both staring at her.

But then Armand was nodding. "She's right," he said. "Marcus has other things to take care of right now."

"Right, he's busy," Cora agreed, filing away Armand's insight for later. What did he know about Marcus's late nights and the business that kept him away all hours lately?

"How do we even know Iris had her phone with her when she was supposedly abducted?" Armand asked Cora.

"She's a twenty something year old woman. We sleep with our phones."

"Especially when they're on vibrate," Olivia muttered, clicking her mouse.

Armand perked up.

Cora cleared her throat. "Anything on the cellphone yet?"

"Well, it's charging. I'll work on it tonight and as soon as

I hack it I'll let you know." Olivia's fingers flew over her keyboard.

"I'm staying here." Armand sagged back onto the cushions. "Let me know if I can help any more. Especially if your friend Anna is involved."

Olivia and Cora both rolled their eyes.

"Well, my ride's here." Cora stood the moment after her ride service app pinged. "I gotta go. Let me know as soon as you get anything."

Sharo had sounded grouchy over the phone earlier when she told him she was staying late at the shelter to help Maeve take inventory. Cora had been surprised at how easily the lie rolled off her tongue. She was getting better at it.

"You're not really going to try to tail AJ, are you?" Olivia asked, pulling out a drawer and rummaging in it.

"Let me sleep on it."

Cora might be determined, but she liked to think she wasn't stupid. Today's activities aside. But tailing AJ? That might tread into TSTL territory. Cora was still unconsciously playing with her hair, letting it pouf out in a corn silk cloud.

"Wait," Olivia held out a hand. "Give me your phone."

Cora's brow wrinkled as Olivia clipped a black case over her device. "What is that?"

"It's called a Wasp. It's a stun gun that looks like a cellphone case. New prototype. The next one will be smaller, but this works pretty well." Olivia grimaced as she fitted her hand around the bulky thing. "Here, watch."

She showed Cora how to uncover the two tiny metal teeth that delivered the shock, then slide a button to activate the stun gun. It was all but invisible against the casing of the phone.

"Holy crap, Olivia, are you sure?"

"Absolutely. It's still in beta testing, so you'd be doing me a favor if you use it and let me know how it works."

Feeling bad ass, Cora took her phone and pressed the case's "on" button. A buzzing sound filled the apartment.

"Six hundred and fifty volts. It'll knock a grown man on his ass." Olivia grinned at the thought. "Come here, Armand, let's try it out."

"Pass," he called from the couch. "I've been beaten enough by beautiful women tonight."

EIGHTEEN

CORA ROUNDED the corner to arrive at the shelter and saw Sharo standing on the curb, glaring at the door. She halted in her tracks. Well crap.

Cora eyed her husband's second in command. Well, no point putting off the inevitable. She straightened and moved forward towards Sharo, who had spotted her.

"Where have you been?" Sharo asked as she approached. She didn't answer, but stepped through the door he opened for her.

Inside Maeve came forward, hands outstretched apologetically. "Cora, I'm sorry, I told him you were just on a quick walk..."

"It's ok." Cora turned back to Sharo, who was still by the door.

"Get in the car."

Shrugging her purse higher on her arm, she obeyed.

"Where's Marcus?" she asked, once they both had slid in, her in the back, Sharo up with the driver.

"Mr. Ubeli has been tied up in a business deal. It's

important. He sent me to check on you when you didn't return his message."

Cora pulled out her phone and checked her voicemail. A new one was there. She sighed.

"I didn't hear it ring. It was an accident." She'd put it on silent before entering the club earlier. She put it away, shaking her head. "You don't have to babysit me, Sharo. I'm a grown woman. I can take care of myself."

"Stop the car," Sharo told the driver. Cora's heart thumped faster as the car slowed to a stop and the big man turned around in his seat to address her.

"You were out walking the streets. Alone. You don't need Marcus to tell you how fucking stupid that is."

Cora cringed. Usually Marcus and his men kept the language clean around her.

"There's trouble coming and we've been dealing with it." From Cora's family. Sharo didn't have to say it. "But until it's blown over, you're going to need to act like a fucking adult and use some common sense."

Something flared inside Cora, a little spark of anger. She was sick of people talking to her like she was a little girl.

"Sharo, I was fine, I was just walking—"

"It's fine until one of our enemies pulls up, kidnaps you, and rapes you with a knife until you bleed out for us to find you. You think being a Titan will save you?" He gave an ugly scoff. "I've seen what these animals can do. In their minds, you've chosen the enemy's bed. They won't take mercy on you."

Cora's breath left her. Her spine pressed deep to the car seat as she met Sharo's angry gaze. How many men had seen this face just before dying?

"If you don't want to be treated like a naïve little girl, stop acting like one," Sharo growled. "I'm going to get you to the penthouse, and you're going to sit tight until Marcus comes home and takes you to dinner. Because he's been neck deep in shit all week and he wants a nice night out with his wife."

Unable to find her voice, Cora jerked her head *yes*.

Stone-faced, Sharo turned around and the car moved on.

Cora sat quiet, but somewhere, deep inside, her anger started to boil. *Stay on the farm, Cora. Don't talk back. Mother knows best.* Then Marcus. Now even Sharo. Meanwhile the Irises and Ashleys of the world were disposable. Throw them out with last week's trash. Who would fight for them if not another woman? Who would even fucking *care*?

She got it, okay? The world was ugly and dark and people were only looking to use one another. But she wanted to believe in something more. She wanted to believe in a world where love meant something and good was real, even if it didn't always triumph like the storybooks said. It was still worth fighting for.

It was still worth fighting for, dammit.

HOURS LATER, Cora stepped off the elevator, dressed for dinner. Her bodyguard stood off to her left, a constant shadow. Marcus was in a meeting already at the restaurant and was sending his car to pick her up. Following orders, she was to wait for his driver in the lobby.

"Can I wait at the bar?" she asked her bodyguard. He nodded and she stalked towards it. Two guys in designer polo shirts watched her pass, taking in her long legs, put on display perfectly by her short peach-colored cocktail dress. She'd let her hair down and curled the ends so it bounced around her face like a movie star's. Her makeup played up both her blue eyes and red, red lips.

Sharo wanted her to grow up, she'd show him. Marcus, too.

She paused as she entered the posh hotel restaurant and pulled out her phone to check it.

Any luck? she texted Olivia.

No answer. She'd called Anna and Armand back too, but gotten only voicemail. The phone would turn up something. It had to.

"White wine, please," she ordered at the bar. She was about to hop on the bar stool when a familiar snigger caught her ear.

She turned to see a couple sitting at the bar. And her breath caught.

There was AJ in his long fur coat, gulping down oysters. One of his thugs stood nearby. The man and her own bodyguard exchanged nods.

Cora felt cold chills up and down her spine as she stared at the mobster. He sat there, so smug and carefree while he caused all this misery.

Cora's chest went hot with sudden rage. Probably in part because when she'd seen him earlier today, she'd been so terrified. She hated that he had that power over her, over any of them. She put her hand to her chest to steady herself.

"Ah, Mrs. Ubeli. Looking lovely tonight." The bastard raised his drink to toast her. His eyes glittered. "Going out? Your husband's a lucky man."

Cora ignored his gold-toothed grin. "Say, Cora, have you met my little friend? She's about your age." He turned and touched the arm of a woman who sat beside him, very straight and stiff, staring ahead.

Her face was hidden behind her brunette hair but her

red dress left little to the imagination, cut short on her thighs and even then, open on one side almost up to her waist.

Cora recognized that tight dancer's body poured into an hourglass shape. *But no. No, it can't be. Please—*

AJ turned to grab the woman's arm and she turned, her hair swinging back from her sculpted face.

Anna.

Before she could stop herself, Cora was up and moving in their direction. Out of the corner of her eye she saw her bodyguard following and halted. "Where's the ladies' room?" she asked a passing server.

By the time Cora had gotten directions, she was sure Anna would notice her trajectory towards the back of the room and follow. Her mind was racing. What the hell was Anna doing there with AJ?

Cora paced for several minutes in the fancy bathroom seating area, waiting for her new friend. Had AJ figured out they'd been snooping around at the strip club? How much did he know?

Cora whirled around as the doors opened and Anna finally walked in.

"Anna, what's going on? Why are you here with AJ?" Cora's voice cut off when she saw the furious look on Anna's face.

"How dare you," Anna said. "Like you even care."

Whatever words Cora had been about to say died on her lips.

"Cora *Ubeli*," Anna ground out her last name. "You think I wouldn't find out? Your husband is the biggest mobster in Olympus."

Under all her makeup, Anna looked tired, but her brown eyes flashed. Cora wasn't the only one who was fed up. "I should've guessed it when you showed up at The Orchid House. You weren't there to help. You just needed more soldiers in your war."

"Anna, no, I—"

"Don't." Anna held up her hand. "I trusted you. I needed to get away from AJ, not sucked into a vendetta between him and his biggest enemy—your husband."

Gods, no, that was the last thing Cora wanted. But how could she even begin to explain—

"Don't worry, he didn't recognize you. It was your friend you brought with you—the designer. You think AJ doesn't know his whole business is a front for your husband's drug trade?"

Cora drew in a shocked breath. *That* was why Armand and Marcus were so close?

Cora shook her head. "Anna, I swear I didn't know AJ would recognize Armand. You have to believe me."

"AJ hates your husband," Anna hissed. "He knows everything about him. And now he thinks I have an in with Armand somehow. He's looking for weakness. I should point him straight to you."

All of Cora's air left her lungs.

"Don't worry," Anna said bitterly. "I won't sell you out. I have standards."

"Gods, Anna, I never wanted to drag you into this. I'm sorry. I'll get you out of it, I swear—"

"You've done enough." Then Anna's face fell, her expression going bleak. "You should know, AJ will do whatever it takes to hurt your husband. We're both just collateral damage." Anna took a step back. "AJ says he'll be taking me back to Metropolis to star in some movies. He owns me now."

"I'm sorry. I'll figure something out," Cora babbled. She

didn't know how, but she had to fix this. "I'll come for you."

Tears glistening in her eyes, Anna shook her head. "They call me a whore. But you spread your legs for a monster. I never want to see you again." And with that, she left.

Cora let herself sag into a chair. Anna's words had hurt, but worse than the accusation of betrayal was the look of terror in her eyes.

He owns me now.

Lowering her head into her hands, Cora tried to think it through. Had she just made everything worse?

The question was, was AJ *still* working for the Titans (aka her mom)? Or was he branching out on his own now that there was unrest among the power players?

Either way, it amounted to the same thing. AJ was just a power-hungry pimp. And he wanted to expand his borders beyond Metropolis. He'd needed an in to New Olympus.

Her mind worked through it, clinging to the facts and trying to work out the bigger picture now that she had even more puzzle pieces.

AJ was looking for Marcus's weaknesses when he came to town, that was for sure.

He found the Orphan and the Orphan's weakness—Iris. So he kidnapped her to control The Orphan. Then he could use The Orphan to dick around with Marcus. But what did that really get AJ besides giving Marcus a headache and a publicity hit when The Orphan refused to play Marcus's club?

No, it had to be about something bigger.

What about that mysterious shipment she kept hearing about? The way people whispered about it, it sounded like a game changer.

It was drugs. It had to be. And now that she knew that

Armand's businesses were a front for Marcus... AJ wanted a way to get access, so he took Anna.

So what now?

"Come on, think," she whispered furiously. *Pretty, stupid slut.*

At least all this meant Marcus couldn't be behind Iris's disappearance. AJ had thrown that out there to manipulate her, just like he was using Iris, and now Anna.

What would he do when Anna and Iris no longer helped him get what he wanted?

Cora felt cold, very cold inside.

A rap on the door startled her. "You okay in there, Mrs. Ubeli?" Cora's bodyguard called.

"Coming," she said, rising.

Enough was enough. The cops wouldn't help. She couldn't tail AJ; she'd only get herself hurt.

No matter the consequences to herself, Marcus was Iris's and now Anna's only hope. He had the resources to take on someone like AJ. His Shades could find out where AJ was holding Iris.

Cora checked the mirror and straightened her dress, making sure she looked perfect.

Yes, it was time to talk to her husband.

He would hear her out or he wouldn't. He'd lock her up again for breaking his rules and going out on her own or he wouldn't. He'd either help Iris and Anna or...

She turned for the door.

Looked like she was still a stupid girl after all because even after everything, hope pulsed in her heart like a beacon that Marcus would listen, that Marcus would care, and that Marcus would be willing to help.

Otherwise, she didn't know what options Anna or Iris might have left.

NINETEEN

"We'll see you tonight at eight, full dark," Sharo said as the meeting with Philip Waters came to a close. For once everything was working out the way it was supposed to.

Marcus, Waters, and Sharo stood in the back of Giuseppe's, a restaurant Marcus's father had loved. Marcus could remember playing hide and seek in this little room behind the kitchens with Chiara when he was little. Now he made war plans here. Speaking of.

"No reason your workers need to wait until then," Marcus added, addressing Philip. "The docks will be clear. Your men won't have any trouble."

"I appreciate your thought for detail, Mr. Ubeli," Philip said. He was a tall black man, also bald. But that was where the similarities between he and Sharo ended. Where Sharo was large and built like a tank, Philip was slender, and quick to smile with his mouth full of bright white teeth.

He was whip smart and the power Marcus held over New Olympus's Underworld, Philip held over the Eastern seaboard's black-market shipping lanes. Nothing came in that didn't go through him. He'd had a relationship with

Marcus's father and now for many years with Marcus himself.

Marcus knew he preferred working with those he knew and trusted. At the same time, Philip was a businessman and the bottom line couldn't be ignored. But Marcus had been fighting long and hard for this deal and now that the shipment was finally here, Philip had agreed to sell exclusively to him.

Two and a half tons of a new designer party drug, supposed to be more benign then coke but with an equal rush. When Marcus had control over it, his hold on the city would be secure.

"See you tonight," Marcus said, shaking Philip's hand. Philip nodded and then headed out down the back hall, the way he'd come in.

Marcus looked to Sharo and spoke in a low voice. "Get these troops out of here. I want everyone but Tony ready for distribution. Tell the capos."

"Consider it done," Sharo said, and then he too moved down the hall.

As Marcus moved out of the bathroom and into the kitchen, Giuseppe pushed through the swinging door that led into the main restaurant. "Your beautiful wife is here. I've settled her in the back booth and gotten her started with a glass of wine."

Marcus nodded, unsettled by the small leap of pleasure in his chest at knowing she was near. He'd been avoiding her, it was true. Cowardly? Maybe. Or maybe just efficient.

He'd needed to focus on the shipment and getting everything prepared so he could make the best case possible to Waters. And in the end, it had worked out. He'd secured the contract.

And apparently his wife had taken his neglect as indulgence to disobey his rules. When Sharo had phoned earlier letting him know she'd snuck away from the shelter, Marcus had been beyond livid. He'd almost walked out on the meeting with Philip before they begun, the meeting that had been a month in the making, before Sharo finally called back and said he had her.

Marcus pushed through the door to the restaurant, easily locating Cora in the booth separated in a small room at the back.

The place was full, but only a few of the tables at the front held normal couples. Towards the back, a line of his Shades sat hulking at the little tables. Marcus had taken all precautions to make sure the meet went off smoothly, including surrounding himself with his soldiers.

The restaurant had old world charm with mahogany paneled wainscoting and dark leather booths. Marcus slid into the booth seat across from his wife.

Her wide eyes blinked up at him and even though he'd been about to immediately rip into her for ditching her guard, for a moment he was frozen, mesmerized by her beauty. Red lipstick highlighted her kissable lips and as always, her blue eyes entranced.

"Hey," she said softly, then swallowed like she was just as affected by him as he was by her. Good. She better be. It was his one comfort in all of this.

And suddenly he couldn't stand not having his hands on her. "Come here," he commanded.

Her eyebrows went up. "Where?"

He gestured to the booth seat beside him.

Her eyes narrowed. "Why?"

"Now."

She let out a small huff but scooted off her side of the bench and moved over to his side. She left about two feet between herself and Marcus and he let out a small growl of impatience.

Then he moved over, hooked an arm around her shoulders, and cemented her body tight against his. And the fist that had been clenched around his lungs ever since Sharo called earlier finally released. He hadn't even realized until this moment that he carried the tension around for all these hours. And it pissed him off that she could still affect him this way.

He squeezed her shoulder. "I hear you've been a bad girl."

Her head swung towards him. "Let me guess. You're going to punish me for it." Her eyes held a challenge. Like she dared him.

The wolf inside Marcus growled. "You'd like that, wouldn't you? I haven't played with you for a while so you decided to get my attention, is that it?"

With a gasp of disgust, she pulled away, or at least tried to. Marcus wasn't letting her go anywhere.

Her eyes flashed at him. "I'm not a toy you can take off the shelf and play with whenever you feel bored. I'm more than that." She squirmed out of his grasp. "And to think, I wanted to talk to you about something real. Something that's actually important."

She'd pulled her body away from his and he didn't like it. He didn't like it at all.

"Being reckless and putting yourself in danger is something I have to address," he spoke through his teeth. "But yes, wife, we are going to talk about it and deal with it." He scooted close to her, halving the distance between them. "And then you're going to tell me everything going through that head of yours."

"Because you own me?" She glared up at him.

His pants tightened as he went rock hard. Just like he always did when she challenged him. He caught her cheek and chin with his hand, forcing her gaze to lock with his. "Yes. Because you belong to me."

Her mouth dropped open but no words came out. That delectable little fucking mouth. He wanted to do a thousand debauched and filthy things to that mouth.

Right now, though, a mere kiss would have to suffice because he couldn't stand another moment without devouring her.

As he dropped his lips to hers, though, the room erupted with gunfire.

TWENTY

MARCUS WRENCHED Cora to the floor. She moved in slow motion, in shock, not realizing what was going on. As glass smashed and people screamed over the deafening reports, they hunkered down under the table, his body sheltering hers as the gunfire continued.

Cora didn't know when the sharp racket stopped. Her ears rang.

Marcus already had his phone out and was speaking into it. "Shots fired at Giuseppe's. Tony should've been out front. We need backup." He crouched beside the table, barely a hair out of place.

Cora pushed up from the floor as her husband pocketed his cellphone. His other hand was fitted around a gun.

The weapon brought the world into focus.

"You ok?" he was asking. She read his lips and nodded. A minute ago they'd been sitting at the table. He was about to kiss her and then— And then—

"Sit tight. I'll be right back."

Slowly, she started to hear the sounds in the restaurant:

the dazed, pained din of shocked patrons. Some crying, a few screams.

Weirdly, Cora's teeth started chattering, but her body became light and loose, untethered from the moment.

Her thoughts swirled. *I've never been shot at before.* No, wait, that wasn't right. Her mom had shot at her. Well, at Marcus, but the bullet had hit her. Still she didn't remember that gunshot being as loud as these were. So loud. Was this what Marcus's life was usually like? But... It would be his enemies shooting. So that meant... Her own family, right? Did her mom know she was here? Did they want her dead, too?

Before the whole world started to crash down again, Marcus returned. "Come on." His face was cold and chiseled even as he held out his left hand to help her up.

They left through the back kitchen, hurrying past a shrieking Giuseppe and his panicking workers to escape into an alley. A black sedan rolled up and Marcus opened the door, climbing in behind Cora.

"What do we know?" he barked at the driver.

"All other Shades were out of range but Tony's on their tail. He saw them pull in, and called for backup. They took off right after firing the warning shots."

"Firing into a restaurant where I'm eating with my wife —that's more than a warning. That's asking for war," Marcus bit out. "Get Sharo on the phone."

War. She'd known somewhere in the back of her head that things were escalating between her family and Marcus. But war? She was being naïve and stupid again. Really it was shocking that it'd had been put off for this long.

It had been easier to dig her head in the sand, though, and fight for something tangible. To fight for Iris.

But here it was. Her husband sat across from her,

calling out orders with a gun in his hand. Rocco, Santonio, Joey and Andy DePetri—they weren't kist rough-looking men who were nice to her when Marcus met with them at the Chariot. They were warriors and her husband was their general.

People *died* at their hands. Just like people had probably died tonight, simply for being in the wrong place at the wrong time: standing between the gunmen and their target: Marcus and her, the Ubelis, rulers of the Underworld.

We're just collateral damage.

The adrenaline hit Cora's stomach. She doubled over and retched onto the car floor.

And then Marcus's hands were there, holding back her hair and offering her his handkerchief to wipe her mouth.

"You're ok, baby," his voice was clipped but his hand was soothing on her back.

The driver talked over his shoulder. "Sharo's online, says Tony lost the trail. But it's looking like it isn't Waters."

She heard all the words but barely registered them. The voices sounded muted and far away, like she was under-water and separate from everything that was happening.

"Put him on," Marcus ordered, sitting forward, one hand still on Cora's back even as she curled up into the car seat, trying to make herself as small as possible.

"Where the fuck is Waters?"

"Back to the ship," came Sharo's voice over the speakers. "He's not coming back."

"If he crossed us, I swear to the gods—"

"Not him. I was with him the whole time. You think this is Metropolis?"

Marcus breathed hard out his nose. "Has to be. And they know about the shipment. Must be an inside man."

"AJ." Even over the phone, Sharo's menace was clear, a

tangible hate. Cora couldn't believe she'd ever thought for a minute AJ was their associate.

"We move on him now, it's all-out war," Marcus said. "The Titans will move in to protect him. We'll lose Waters, the shipment, the deal, everything."

"What do you want to do?" Sharo asked.

Cora watched her husband control himself and take his emotions in hand, shutting them down. Always so controlled. How did he do that? She wanted it so desperately right now, to not be able to feel anything.

"Ignore AJ," Marcus fired orders into the phone. "We'll deal with him later. Meet can't happen tonight. We prep the street, tell Waters we need more time."

"Needs to be soon," Sharo answered. "Waters wants the deal, but he's not a patient man."

"Tomorrow then. I'll tell our man with the force and he'll keep the docks swept."

"We get this done and then we start making plans to visit our friends in Metropolis." Her husband's voice hardened, and Cora could feel cold rage rolling off him.

"Any word from Tony on the scum who did this?"

"He lost them. But they fired on sacred ground. We'll make them pay."

Oh gods. Cora leaned forward then, whispering, "Giuseppe and the people there—are they ok?"

Marcus's eyes cut to her.

"Yeah, Sharo, you hear that? Make sure the Shades are standing by to see how we can help these people, ok?"

Cora sagged back. She didn't have anything left. Nothing left. She was used up. Wrung dry. *Collateral damage.*

Marcus hung up the phone.

"Never again," he said, staring at the road in front of them. "Never again."

"Where to, Mr. Ubeli?" the driver asked quietly.

"Take us to the Estate," Marcus ordered.

TWENTY-ONE

CORA WAS TREMBLING as Marcus led her inside the Estate. Fucking shaking so hard, he could all but hear her teeth clacking. And it wasn't from the cold.

She was scared. Scared out of her wits. They'd shot at her. Opened fire with no care for who might be nearby—

Marcus clenched his jaw as it all flashed again before his eyes. The eruption of gunfire, a sound you never forgot after you heard it once. Shoving Cora down under the table, not knowing whether she'd been hit or not—fuck, he needed a drink. Or to shoot something. But no, dammit, both of those things would take him away from his wife's side and he wasn't letting her out of his sight.

"We're going upstairs," he barked as soon as they were inside. Useless to say, really, since he was all but dragging Cora up the stairs already. His men had already checked the residence when they first arrived and he'd ordered them to stay outside on perimeter duty for the night.

Cora didn't say anything or talk back. That wasn't like her. Neither was passively letting Marcus move her around like a doll as they got to the master suite. But she didn't give a moment's protest when he led her straight into the bathroom.

And she washed her face like he instructed and brushed her teeth without a single word. What the fuck? Where had his spitfire gone?

"Cora, look at me." He grabbed both her cheeks once they were done in the bathroom and tried to force her to look at him. She stared at the floor.

"Look at me," he demanded again.

When her eyes finally moved sluggishly up to meet his, they lacked their usual shine.

"Stop it or I'm going to take you over my knee."

No response. Not the usual flare of her nostrils or widening of her eyes. Her face was as blank as a painted doll's.

"Cora. Cora." He wanted to shake her but he didn't trust himself. He was feeling too many things. He'd gone so long without feeling anything and then now for everything to rain down on him all at once, coming at him from all directions—

He gripped Cora's hair at the nape of her neck and wrapped his arm around her waist, crushing her body to his. Willing her to wake the fuck up.

He crashed his lips down on hers.

She was still unresponsive. Limp in his arms. Pale and cold and lifeless like some dead thing.

"Gods damn it! Cora." He pushed her up against the wall and pressed his lips to hers again. But for once in his life, he didn't demand. He didn't force his way in.

He coaxed.

He teased.

He prayed at the altar of her lips.

He closed his eyes and kissed her. *Come back to me.*

Come back to me. Please. He didn't know if he was entreating Cora or the gods.

Because what he was really begging for was forgiveness.

None of this was ever supposed to touch her. He promised to keep her safe.

He'd promised and he'd failed her. Just like Chiara.

No. He shook his head. No. Not his Cora. He wouldn't lose her. He fucking refused. He'd never let her go. The gods and Fates be damned.

He pressed his body more firmly against her so that she was pressed tight, trapped between him and the wall. He'd shield her until the day she died. Which would be a long fucking time from now.

And yes, he was hard. He was hard whenever she was near. Even now. If he thought it would bring her back to him, he'd bury himself balls deep right this second. But he couldn't be sure it wouldn't do more damage.

So instead, he took her wrists and pinned them to the wall above her head. He stepped even closer into her, crouching slightly so that his face was beside hers.

"Do you feel that?" he demanded. "Your heartbeat is right next to mine. Because we're both fucking alive. People died back at that diner but it wasn't you and it wasn't me."

Her brow scrunched, the first sign of life he'd seen since before the shooting began.

He brought a hand between them and clutched her cheek roughly. "That's right. You are alive and I'm not letting you go anywhere."

"Because you own me?" Finally, a spark lit in her eyes. "Tell the truth. I'm just as expendable as any of those people back there. Except, I forgot. I'm still of use to you. Or maybe not so much anymore. I can't be much of a pawn to hold over the Titans if they were willing to kill me tonight just to get to you."

He let her talk only because she was finally showing signs of life again, but every single word out of her mouth only pissed him off more.

"Expendable?" He couldn't keep the incredulity out of his voice.

But either she didn't hear it or she pretended not to. "Collateral damage," she said. "We're all just collateral damage to you. Nothing matters but your agenda. You don't care about anyone or anything."

His hips thrust forward at her insolence, his rock-hard cock jutting rudely against her thigh. Her body shifted to cradle him between her hips. His cock snug against her sex.

Her eyes flew open, apparently just realizing what she'd done at the same time he did.

He smirked down at her. "Your body knows who you belong to."

Fury lit up her eyes but his head was already descending, taking that lush mouth. Taming it.

Or at least he tried. She bit his lip and yanked her arms down from where he held them above her head and started pummeling him with them. Well, as much as a kitten could pummel a lion.

He easily caught her wrists again and pinned them above her head. She screamed out a roar of such fury and frustration, the Shades outside would surely hear and wonder what the hell was going on in here.

But Marcus didn't care if they heard. He didn't care about anything except the furious, bright, and shining goddess in his arms.

He could have lost her. He'd barely found her and he could have fucking *lost* her.

It was just like four months ago when she'd been on that gurney being wheeled into surgery except worse. Because now he'd had four more months of knowing her, four more months of coming home to find her sweet body in his bed, always so hot and receptive to him. Four more months of her whip smart intelligent eyes on him, challenging him, not letting him get away with any of his shit, and he—

"I love you."

It was out of his mouth before he even registered what he was saying.

Cora froze and stopped struggling, blinking up at him in confusion.

But Marcus wasn't confused, not anymore. "I love you, goddess."

He felt like laughing, it was such a weight off his chest, finally admitting what he'd struggled for so long to deny. He'd loved her a long time now. So long he couldn't remember what not loving her felt like.

Cora shook her head back and forth, her brow scrunching. "No. You just want to use me. I heard you. The night I woke up from the coma. I heard you and Sharo."

Fuck.

He let go of her arms and instead cupped her cheeks again. Gently this time. "I'm an ass. I don't know what all you heard that night but I've been a coward. For a long time now. Ever since I met you, you've made me feel—"

He shook his head. "You're different from anyone I've ever met. *I'm* different when I'm with you. I thought it was weakness."

Her huge blue eyes searched his back and forth like she was terrified to believe what he was saying. He'd fucked this up so badly but he'd make it up to her.

"But it's not weakness." He narrowed his eyes and

brought his forehead close to hers, needing her to understand. It was also clear now. "You're my strength. You wash me clean. Without you, I'm nothing. None of this means *anything* without you. I *love* you."

"Stop saying that," Cora whispered.

Marcus shook his head. "Never. I love you."

Fat tears rolled down Cora's cheeks. "Don't say it unless you mean it. Please. Don't—" her voice choked off, head shaking back and forth. "Don't—"

"I love you. I love you. I love—"

His words cut off when Cora threw her arms around his neck and smashed her mouth against his.

Drinking in her kiss, he scooped her up and strode into the bedroom. He lay her down on the bed and draped himself over her. "Goddess," he smiled against her mouth.

"Now," she panted breathlessly, squirming under him, tugging up her dress. He helped, tearing the fabric and palming her sweet pussy. Gods, she was wet.

"This is mine," he reminded her. She nodded so frantically he chuckled. "As long as you remember who you belong to." With his thumb, he rubbed her favorite spot, to the upper left of her clit and her body spasmed, her gaze going hazy.

"That's my girl," he murmured, brushing the sweet spot over and over until she trembled. "Let it come, let go for me, that's it—"

Her breath rushed out and pink flared in her cheeks as a soft climax took her. Her hands grabbed his shoulders and pulled him in for an eager kiss.

He indulged her, rubbing his face against hers, leaving her cheeks red from his rough stubble. He loved marking her. Later, he'd rub his face between her thighs and leave her chafed and aching so tomorrow, she'd remember him.

Now he had to be inside her. His fingers fumbled with his zipper.

They both moaned as he breached her soft entrance. Her inner walls kissed along his cock. When his thumb found her clit again, teasing another climax, her pussy squeezed him so tight he grew light-headed.

Cora twined her arms around his shoulders, tugging him close. "Say it again," she whispered as if afraid the moment would shatter.

"I love you."

Her happy gasp nearly sent him over the edge. He rose up to one elbow, hitching her long leg over his hip so he could drive deep. Her head flew back but her own hips rose up to meet each thrust.

Marcus growled, pulling his cock almost all the way out to slam into her slick wetness again. As he bottomed out, he ground against her entire pelvic cradle until her juices coated his lower stomach. Then he pulled out and slammed home again.

"*Oooh*," Cora moaned, her face scrunching. He stilled.

"Did I hurt you?" Each thrust went so deep, his cock bumped her cervix.

She shook her head and wound her legs tighter around his back. "More."

Fingers clawed into the bed, Marcus drove in his wife's welcoming body, pounding her into the bed. Cora's nails raked his shoulders, her feet digging into the muscles of his back.

"Marcus, I'm—"

"Come for me, baby." She detonated with a series of soft cries, her cheeks and chest blooming pink roses. He nuzzled her a moment before pistoning his hips faster, driving towards his own climax. His limbs and torso tightened, a bow ready to let loose the arrows of his seed.

When he came, his world shook apart, focused on the sweet, smiling face of his beautiful wife.

"Angel," he brushed his lips over hers, kissing every inch of her mouth. Gods, he wanted to live inside her. He could tie her up forever and fuck her every hour and it wouldn't be enough. Never enough.

With a groan, he separated from her. Her pussy was as pink and swollen as her well-kissed mouth.

"I meant to be gentle," he muttered.

"It's all right." Her fingers trailed along his shoulders, soothing the scratches her nails had left. "I'll take you as you are."

"Because you love me." He rolled to his side so he could cup her cheek.

"Yes." Her breath hitched.

"Even when you didn't want to." He smiled as he traced her lips. He didn't deny the swell of pride. She'd given her love even when he hadn't deserved it.

"Yes." Her eyes grew shadowed and he leaned in to taste her.

"Never again. I won't hurt you. I'm gonna take care of you."

She winced and he cursed himself. He'd made that promise before. "It'll be different this time. I'm gonna keep you safe, protect you from everything—"

"Even yourself?" she added with a wry smile. She was too smart. She saw right through him, to the monster he was.

She loved him anyway. The depth of his feeling made his heart thud to a stop. He'd do anything for this woman. Even die for her.

"Yes. I won't let the darkness touch you, Cora."

With a small, hesitant hand, she reached up to stroke the dark hair from his brow. "You can't keep it away," she murmured. "It's a part of you." She sighed, her gaze slipping away. "It's a part of me now, too."

"You're made of light, angel. Summertime and everything good." He buried his nose in her hair. She even smelled like sunshine. "Your light will drive the darkness away."

"Maybe." She pulled back and palmed his cheek, her blue eyes searching his. "Just love me. It'll be enough."

In response, he turned her away from him so he could hold her to his chest. Her head rested over his heartbeat.

Later, he'd clean her up and go down on her. Go slowly, make her scream. But right now, he wanted to hold her. His dick was hard again, straining, but he'd wait. He had the rest of the night to be inside her.

The rest of the night, and the rest of their lives.

TWENTY-TWO

HOURS LATER, Cora awoke with the sounds of gunshots ringing in her ears. She sat up in bed, gripping the empty sheets beside her until her dream—of bullets crashing into the restaurant—faded away.

Cora looked around, confused for a second not to be in her bed at the penthouse. But then the rest of it came crashing in.

I love you.

Three little words with the power to break her. Or remake her. She pulled the silk sheet up to her chest and crossed her arms over her knees.

He loved her. He loved her back.

She smiled silly and looked around but Marcus wasn't anywhere in the large master suite and she didn't hear him in the ensuite bathroom either. And then her chest tightened with fear. Would he take it back? What if it was just another cruel game to him?

All of a sudden she could barely breathe. She threw the sheet back and jumped to her feet, grabbing a robe and all but running out of the room. She had to find him. She had to know if it was real or not.

She'd just pulled open the bedroom door when she heard angry voices coming from somewhere in the house.

Frowning, she followed the sounds down the hall. She and Marcus always stayed in the master suite on the second floor. Most of the house had been closed up for over a decade, the furniture under blankets like ghosts from another time.

The voice was coming from somewhere near the front door. She paused at the landing above the stairwell, pulling her robe more tightly around her and listening hard.

"We had a deal." The words echoed around the foyer's cathedral ceiling and came right to her ears. It was a man and she'd swear she recognized the voice from somewhere. "I've done my part. Given you land rights, re-zoned the docks. Turned a blind eye to the scum building up on every corner in the Styx."

Holding her breath, Cora crept around the corner. Marcus's dark head came into view. He stood with Sharo at his back, facing two other men who'd come with the noisy guest, a handsome blond man who looked familiar. Cora couldn't put her finger on where she'd seen him before. He was shorter than Marcus, but he stood in the center of the foyer with a posture that said he was used to dominating conversations.

"I kept you clean," the blond said. "You've stayed in power. But everything you've built on is mine. I laid the foundation. I control it. I can take it away."

Who dared talk to Marcus this way?

Beside Marcus, Sharo shifted slowly. Cora's breath caught. Sharo was large enough to take all three of them down. And here, on twenty acres of private land, who would ever find out what happened? Was she actually afraid for the blond man and his two bodyguards? She couldn't tell. So much had happened today, she could barely sort through one thing before another was being thrown her way.

"I understand your concern." Marcus's voice came low and level. "At the same time, I can't help but be offended by what you imply."

"I'm not implying," the blond man said, taking a step forward and getting right in Marcus's face. Gods, did the man have a death wish? "I'm telling you. I've done my part. I expect you to deliver. I don't expect a restaurant to be shot up the very night I'm pointing out my strong stance on crime."

Cora's eyes flew open and her hand shot to her mouth to cover her gasp. It was the mayor. Storm or Strum or something. No, *Sturm*. Zeke Sturm, she remembered now. She'd seen him talk at the charity dinner. He and Marcus worked together? The golden boy mayor and the city's biggest crime lord?

"It's being handled," Sharo rumbled.

"My ex-wife's hairdresser could handle this better," Sturm snapped right back. "We're looking at war. Now? On the eve of the election?"

Cora backed further into the shadows, wanting to know more about how he was connected to Marcus.

"What I want to know if you'll make good on the promises you've made over the years." The mayor jabbed a finger towards Marcus. Cora sucked in a breath. She'd never seen anyone talk to Marcus like that.

"The reporter vultures are circling. They'll say I look soft on crime. The vote is in less than a week. You move on your enemies now, this whole election goes down in a hail of gunfire. You say you control the streets? Then control them."

"Mr. Sturm, you're upset. You're not seeing the big picture." Cora recognized that voice. The quieter and more still Marcus became, the more dangerous and calculating he was.

"Big picture, my ass. Here's the big picture: Tuesday, I lose, and the Titan brothers are back in town with the circus. Then we can stand around and talk about the picture, because we'll both be out of it."

Marcus paused before answering, using silence to his effect. It worked. By the time he spoke, Sturm looked a little less sure of himself. "Because of your status, and our partnership, I am going to overlook your disrespect. But I will tell you. This is the last time you come to my house and make demands of me."

"Believe me, Ubeli, I don't intend to be seen with you ever again," Sturm returned. "Our partnership works because you run your thing and I run mine. But I'm a man who does what it takes to prove to people I intend to return on their investment. And to do that, I need votes."

"You'll have them. Tuesday," Marcus said in the deep, final tones of an executioner. "Sharo will see you out."

Sturm opened his mouth, but seemed to have run out of words. Instead he glared up at Marcus.

"We'll be in touch," Marcus said, and his voice held a note of finality.

Sharo moved forward then, herding the three towards the door.

Before Cora could move back towards the bedroom, her husband turned his head and pinned her with his eyes.

Cora saw many things in that gaze.

A very dangerous man.

A predator.

Her husband who loved her.

It *had* been real. She could see it even now in his eyes, though the meeting with Sturm had obviously angered him.

He looked at her like he wanted to eat her up but also like...like he loved her.

Her breath caught. And maybe her heart skipped a beat or two as he started up the stairs towards her.

All she knew was that if he loved her, if he *really* loved her, then she would give him the world. She would be his world.

And she would start by soothing the beast. She smiled saucily down at him and let her robe hang open.

He growled in reaction and started taking the stairs two at a time. "I won't take it easy on you."

She arched an eyebrow. "Who says I want you to?"

But as he closed the distance between them, she retreated up the steps.

"You should run," he warned and she whirled, her robe flying behind her. She made it down the hall and almost to the bedroom before he slammed into her, his weight carrying her forward to trap her between him and the door. She struggled and he caught her arms behind her, pushing her against the unyielding wood.

"Got you," he growled in her ear. "You didn't run fast enough."

Her heart pounded against the door. "I wanted you to catch me."

He turned her roughly. She looked straight in his eyes, full of feral possession, and she smiled.

"Oh, goddess. You were made for me." His mouth slammed onto hers, lips hard enough to bruise.

She pushed up to her tiptoes and hooked an arm behind

his head, meeting his kiss. His hand found the doorknob. They stumbled together into the bedroom, Marcus recovering first. His hand clamped on the back of her neck, marching her to the bed.

"You've been a naughty girl." He shoved her down, face first and held her there, cheek to coverlet.

"Yes," she breathed as he shucked off her robe. "Punish me?"

"Oh, I will." He slapped her ass hard enough to shock the breath from her. "Floating through the house wearing almost nothing, flaunting that body just out of reach..."

"Do you think your guest saw?"

"You better hope he didn't. Not him, not the Shades. No one gets to see this but me." His fingers swept over her pussy and she quivered, yelping when he followed the gentle touch with a sharp smack.

"Not even Sharo?"

Marcus growled. "You have a thing for Sharo?"

"No...he's just so...big." She bit her lip at her brazenness. Her nipples pressed into the bed.

"I'll show you big." Twining his hand in her hair, Marcus wrenched her up and forced her to her knees. His cock bobbed in her face. "Suck."

She reached for him and he grabbed her hands, shackling them with his. "Just your mouth. You know better than that."

"I'm naughty," she whispered, eyelashes fluttering. "Remember?"

"I'll teach you to be good."

"Teach me, Daddy," she mouthed over his head, and his eyes turned black.

Gripping her hair, he slid into her mouth. He thrust his hips, each time pushing a little deeper. His cock bumped the entrance to her throat and she coughed, eyes watering. He eased out only a moment before doing it again. He choked her on his cock over and over but the hand on her head turned gentle.

"That's it, good girl. There's a good girl." He no longer held back her hands. When she cupped her breasts and rolled her nipples between a thumb and forefinger, he murmured his approval. "Touch yourself. Show Daddy what you like."

She shivered, rivulets of pleasure running through her. Tears streamed down her cheeks as he invaded her mouth, but she loved every second. The taste and the smell of him. His wiry hair scratching her face as he made her throat him. Her pussy throbbed like a second heart.

She gasped when he pulled her off and tugged her to her feet. "Up. Onto the bed."

She scurried to her hands and knees with her ass upturned, just the way he liked. Since their first night together, he'd trained her and now she didn't dare disobey. Especially since she didn't want to.

"So precious." His fingers penetrated her, teasing her slippery folds, finding the mind-melting spots inside her pussy that made her weak. He pressed between her shoulder blades and she folded, head down, ass up, back bent to offer her glistening center. If she was lucky, he'd only tease her a moment before he made her cum...

A gust of air told her he'd walked away. *Noooooo.* But she knew better than to move. She didn't ease the strain of her back, or slip a hand between her thighs. He'd punish her for sure and she might never earn her release.

"Good girl." Marcus was back, palming her ass, squeezing the cheeks, holding her open. She held still, knowing better than to squirm underneath his gaze. She didn't protest as he parted her most secret places and examined her. She hoped he liked what he saw...

A condescending smack on the side of her thigh, a small chuckle. "You're so ready for me. Needy. Does my pretty pussy miss me?"

"Always," she whispered against the coverlet.

"Does it want me to touch it, make it feel good?"

"Yes...please... Marcus, I need..."

Another smack. "I'm not talking about you. I'm talking about your pussy."

Cora clenched her teeth, holding back a whimper. He knew just want to say to humiliate her, to make her burn...

"What about the other parts of you, hmm? Do they feel neglected?"

What was he talking about? His finger left a wet trail up between her ass cheeks and she knew.

"No," she moaned, catching herself too late.

"Yes," Marcus said, pressing a firm finger to her clenching asshole. "It's time." He stroked her bottom a moment. "You belong to me. All of you. It's time I claim this."

"Will it hurt?"

"It might. I'll go slowly but it will be uncomfortable. At first. But you want this, right?" His voice deepened, as hypnotic as his slow stroking touch over her backside. "You want to please me? Make me feel good?"

"Yes," she admitted. His thumb came to her asshole and her cheeks tightened.

"No," Marcus turned stern. "Don't tense up. Open for me."

She forced herself to relax. Marcus's thumb pressed rough circles over her sensitive rosebud.

"Good girl." His stubbled cheek rubbed over her ass.

She stilled as his tongue swept between her cheeks, probing her virgin hole, tickling the crease. His free hand cupped her pussy, keeping her from wriggling and escaping his insistent tongue.

Cora didn't want to like it. But she did. Gods, she *did*. Tingles spread over her back and a shot of hot, slick serum leaked from her pussy onto Marcus's hand.

He bit her ass lightly before straightening.

"You...you licked me."

"And you got wet." He sounded so smug. "I think you want this more than you're letting on."

"I want you."

"You'll take me. All of me." Something cool and slippery slopped over her asshole. Lubricant of some kind? Then he probed one finger deep, pushing past the tight ring of muscle.

She gasped. It felt intense. His free hand stroked her pussy and the sensation flipped. It felt good and so fucking dirty.

"Fuck." The swear word slipped out before she could muffle it. She pressed her face into the bed.

"Naughty wife. Shall I spank you? Punish you so the first time I claim your ass it's bright red and sore?"

"Oh gods." Now he was probing her with two fingers. Her tiny asshole was going to be so stretched by the end of the night.

The fingers of his left hand still circled her clit. To her dismay the pleasure rose hotter and higher because of the intrusion in her ass.

"No." She wiggled, trying to escape and earning that spanking he'd mentioned. A few sharp slaps on her rear and she quieted. The subtle sting from his hard hand helped her accept the fingers in her ass.

Marcus got up to three before he stopped and focused on making her cum. Her climax built in every corner of her body, spurred by the light strokes of his thumb around her clit.

When he added a finger in her pussy, her brain shot sparks. Her pussy clenched, begging for more stimulation while her ass did the same, protesting the stretch of three hard fingers.

Cora put her head down and let the climax roll up her spine. Her legs shook, out of her control. Her body was no longer her own.

It belonged to Marcus.

His dick probed the back of her thigh as he pulled his fingers out of her ass. She relaxed even though she knew what was coming. He kept his finger in her pussy as he added more lube to her crease.

A wet squelching sound told her he was lubing his cock as well. Her breath quickened and she rocked forward a little, resisting the urge to scramble away. It wouldn't work. Marcus would catch her and make her pay.

So she waited on all fours for him to claim her ass—

"You ready?"

She almost snorted. Did it matter? "Yes."

She was done waiting. A small part of her was curious how it would feel. An even smaller, secret part of her wanted it... "Do it."

A slap to her thigh. "I give the orders around here."

He did and she loved it. But the wait was killing her so she put her head down and pushed her ass up, presenting the target as best she could.

His half growl told her that was a good choice.

"I'm going to fuck this ass," he told her. "You're going to make me feel good."

Her pussy juiced in response. Something hard probed her asshole. She spread her knees wider. But Marcus wasn't done.

"Beg me for it. Beg me to fuck your ass. To let you make me feel good."

Shit. She couldn't do that.

"I'm waiting, Cora."

"Please..."

"Please, what?"

"Please put your cock in my ass. I'll be good for you. I'll make you feel so good."

"Fuck." The desperation in his voice made the humiliation worth it. Cora smiled to herself...until he started to push his very big thing into her very small hole.

"Fuck." He backed up, added more lube. This time when he pressed, his cock head stretched her. She squeezed but he didn't back out. He pushed forward, millimeter by aching millimeter.

"It's too big."

"Relax, sweetheart." He pulled out. More lube. He swirled the head of his cock around her back hole, stimulating the thin skin. "Breathe, Cora. Remember to breathe."

Right. Her lungs filled on his order. Relief rolled through her and relaxed her enough to let him pop inside. He slid the rest of the way easily.

She waited for him to stop before gasping for air.

"You doin' okay?"

She tossed her head, a half shake, half nod.

"You're doing so good." His free hand stroked her back. She opened to him further and he shoved himself the rest of the way in. A moment to adjust and he gave a shallow thrust.

"Oh gods." He was splitting her open.

"Be good and take it." Fuck if the order didn't make her hotter. His actions belied his words, though; he stroked her back with a gentle hand. His cock moved in tiny increments back and forth, letting her adjust. The discomfort eased, and when he reached down to play with her clit, a flush of pleasure spread over her.

"*Ohhh,*" she moaned into the bed. Her limbs went liquid. Golden honey simmered in her veins.

He started rocking, slow at first, increasing in force as he penetrated her bowels. Her cunt tightened, welcoming the intrusion. She felt full, stimulated and satisfied. "Oh yeah, baby. You're going to cum with me deep in your ass."

"No," she squeaked as her thighs began to shake. She couldn't come with him balls deep inside her ass. It was too embarrassing.

"Yes, you are. I can feel it. Fuck, you're so tight, I can feel you milking me..."

Biting off a string of curses, Marcus braced her hips and sawed in and out of her faster. A few passes later, his dick tripped some switch deep inside her.

Pleasure bloomed, warm and golden, delicious sensation spreading through her limbs. Her body juddered under Marcus's. Her throaty cries filled the room, mingled with her husband's cussing.

"You like that? You love taking me in your ass?"

"Yes," she moaned. Her cheeks burned. Another climax built in her, low and deep, forbidden pleasure rising from secret, shameful parts. Only Marcus could take her to the brink like this. He gripped her throat and held her over the abyss. She might fight him but in the end, she surrendered and embraced the fall—

"My turn, baby." She thought he'd fucked her hard before but no. Now he gripped her sides and rode her, using her body for his pleasure. Climax after climax bubbled through her. She didn't know where one ended and the other began.

Finally, after forever, Marcus seized her tight enough to bruise and brought it home. Hot cum filled her. When he pulled out, it slid out of her, running down her leg, staining the bed. She covered her face as he held her bottom open and inspected her. She knew he loved the sight of her marked with his seed. He was such an animal. She was lucky he didn't pee on her.

When she gave an embarrassed groan, Marcus chuckled and tugged her up. She gave token resistance, more embarrassed than unwilling to have him hold her. Gods, she was a mess. Sweaty, sticky, dripping with cum, face slick from when he fucked her mouth, her makeup smeared—

"You're so beautiful." Marcus looked at her like she was the only woman in the world. He kissed her forehead and tucked her into his chest, holding her tight. Gods, yes, she loved this, it was all she ever wanted...

They lay together in the dark and quiet bedroom. Cora forgot her mussy hair and the cum leaking out of her. Marcus nuzzled her face, brushing his lips over her forehead, cheeks and chin, even eyebrows, before finding her lips. He drew back and breathed her in. Against her leg, his dick stirred.

"Fuck. I can't get enough," he muttered. "I could take you every other minute and it wouldn't be enough."

A smile curved deep inside her. "I know how you feel," she told him softly.

"Do you, baby?" He tucked her close again, draping his heavy thigh over her legs to draw her as near as humanly possible.

"I do." She sighed and lay her head on his chest, ear over

his heart. His heartbeat matched hers. "I know how you feel...because I feel the same way."

"Almost missed this," he whispered, almost too soft for her to hear.

She raised her head. "What?"

His thumb traced her cheek. "This. Love. Us."

Oh. Her heart squeezed. She couldn't take it. "Marcus, I've always loved you."

"I know. You give and give, and I only take." She shook her head but he stilled her with his thumb at her lips. "It's true. But that's gonna end. Now you take as much as you give. And I give as much as I take."

"It's not a competition. You've had a hard life, I understand if—"

"Not an option, Cora. You take what I give you." His gaze heated as she ran her tongue over his thumb. "I've been looking for this all my life, not even knowing what I was looking for. Dropped right into my lap. Beauty, innocent. Pure. You're every good deed I've never done. Every pure thought I never had."

"Marcus, I—"

But he shushed her. "You're the balance, Cora. I'm darkness, but you're light. You fill the room with your presence, and the shadows disappear. Understand?"

She understood. In her own way, Marcus was telling her she had as much power as he did. More. Because didn't darkness always leave before the light?

"I'm here for you, Marcus." Her heart swelled with everything she'd felt for him but never been able to express. "I will always be your light."

TWENTY-THREE

When Cora woke the next morning, paper crackled under her hand. Marcus was gone but his pillow still bore his crisp scent. He'd left a note.

Angel, I have business tonight. Don't wait up. When I return, I'll make it up to you. —Marcus

She pressed her lips to the bold strokes that made the 'M'. He didn't sign it *love,* but she felt it all the same.

Cora flopped dramatically back onto the bed, her hair floofing all around her. Her hands came to her face. She wasn't sure she actually believed last night really happened. He loved her? But when she shifted, the aches in her body confirmed that yes, the night before had indeed not been just her imagination.

She'd never seen so much in his storm grey eyes before as when he told her he loved her. She'd always seen Marcus as the epitome of control before. To the point of stoic and unfeeling.

But she saw the truth now. He felt *so* much. He was a hurricane in a bottle. Leashed chaos. Just like the city he held so tightly in his fist. Only in their lovemaking did she get a glimpse of it. For a moment, the lid came uncapped and she saw what he couldn't hide—at his core, he was a singularly emotional being.

When he hated, he hated so virulently he'd tear whole cities apart to exact his revenge. And when he loved...

She grinned, happiness hanging over her with the hazy morning light. Well, noon light, because when she looked at the clock, she saw it was almost twelve. She was tempted to stay in bed, lounging and reliving the delicious moments of last night, but the joy singing through her pulled her to the closet where she tossed on jeans and a t-shirt, then applied minimal makeup. She'd take it easy today, to be ready when Marcus returned. *I'll make it up to you.*

But then she frowned. She had other things to talk to Marcus about when he got back, though. There was still so much she needed to tell him. About Iris. About Anna. He'd help her find them, she knew he would. AJ was no match for her husband.

She sat up and reached for her phone. Only to find it was dead. A few minutes of scrounging around in her purse and she found the charger, then plugged it in.

She pressed the buttons to wake it up but it took a while to be able to use once it was completely dead. And she wouldn't be able to do anything until Marcus got back later anyway, so she decided to go for a walk.

Not that the Shades guarding the doors downstairs looked happy about it when she tried to leave. When she arched an imperious brow at them and asked, "Shall I tell my husband you're trying to imprison me in my own house?" they were quick enough to move out of the way.

They didn't look happy, but they parted to let her through.

"Stay away from the perimeter," they warned.

"I will," she promised. Easy enough. The grounds were extensive and well-kept, with giant oaks and neatly trimmed green grass. A dark forest surrounding the Estate hid its occupants from the busy world outside.

Cora couldn't imagine Marcus growing up here, a little boy playing with wooden toys or a rubber ball. Well, she couldn't imagine Marcus as a little boy at all. He seemed so solemn and powerful, sprung fully formed from his father's head. Born to run Gino Ubeli's business and grow it to the point where he owned everyone in the city, and through them, everything.

She was too light and happy to dwell on gloomy thoughts for long, though, so she forgot them and browsed around a cluster of rhododendrons. The grounds were quiet, even for the Estate. She found a path and walked leisurely along it as light filtered through the tall oak trees overhead.

About fifteen minutes later, she frowned when she saw a roof peeking out from the huge trunks ahead. The path did twist and turn. Was she already coming back around to the house?

She continued forward curiously. Oh! It wasn't the house at all. The building was large, though, square and fronted with high columns and stone lions. It was like a structure from Roman antiquity had been transported here.

What was this place? With hushed reverence, she tiptoed to the open door. A few dried leaves had blown in but the marble was cool and gleaming, without a trace of mold or dirt. Someone kept this place clean.

As soon as her eyes adjusted to the gloom, she gasped. Three stone coffins stood in a row. Heart thudding softly, she crept close enough to read the names carved into the marble slabs. AMBROGINO UBELI. DOMENICA UBELI. Marcus's father, Gino. And his mother.

She knew the name on the final coffin before she read it. CHIARA UBELI. A weeping angel stood above the tomb, its hands covering its stone face. Forever mourning the atrocities wrought on the girl buried here. By Cora's own family— her uncles and mother.

"I'm sorry," Cora whispered. She wished she had better words, some sort of prayer. Prayers should be the only words spoken here. She retreated, taking in the three sarcophagi.

Her heart ached, but not for them. No, they were at peace. She hurt for her husband, who'd buried them here and grieved them. He'd only been a teen when he lost them but he grieved them still. Some losses you never got over.

For the first time, she realized just how alone Marcus was. He had no one but Sharo and his Shades. And now her. No wonder he was so possessive. She'd hang on desperately to those she cared about, too, if everyone who loved her had died.

As she drifted closer to Chiara's coffin, she frowned at smudges on the edge of the stone lid. The pattern made her glance at the floor, but no, there were no marks there.

Of course not. There was no reason for any marks on the floor, which was well scrubbed and polished until gleaming. The marks on the coffin must have been missed when whoever cleaned this place last came through.

But it nagged at the back of her mind, because the marks almost looked like...like fingerprints—desperate, grabbing fingers along with the spatter on the dark wall. *It couldn't be.* But the faded rust color couldn't be mistaken for anything but what it was.

Blood.

She took a step back.

"You can't be around here, Mrs. Ubeli," a Shade's voice echoed behind her, making her shriek.

"Gods," she gasped, clutching her chest. She backed away, trembling.

The Shade was young, almost as young as she was, and he looked dreadfully uncomfortable. "I'm sorry, Mrs. Ubeli, but you need to come away now. Your husband wouldn't like you here."

Head bowed, she hurried out.

There was plenty of space in the mausoleum for more stone coffins. At least two more. One for Marcus...and one for her.

She shivered and shook her head to dispel the morbid thought. *Not for a long time,* she told herself firmly. *After a good, long lifetime of love.*

But she hurried across the lawn and didn't stop until she reached her room. No wonder Marcus wanted to keep her here, safe.

When she got back to her room, she immediately went for her phone.

There was a missed call from Armand. Several new text messages from a few numbers. Armand's texts popped up first, in shouty caps: OH MY GODS ARE U OK? WHERE ARE U?

Cradling her phone, she texted rapidly. I'M FINE. AT THE UBELI ESTATE.

Her phone blipped immediately with his reply. I WAS SO WORRIED. NEWS REPORTED SHOOTING! WHAT HAPPENED?

WE'RE FINE. WE WERE IN THE BACK. DIDN'T SEE ANYTHING. She paused, deliberating on what to say next. MARCUS IS HANDLING.

After a pause, Cora watched the dots indicating Armand was typing. They just kept flashing and flashing until finally Armand returned: So much going on, but wanna say I'm so fucking sorry for the other day. I woke up remembering everything. I was messed up. Didn't know what I was doing.

Cora shook her head as her thumbs flew over the keyboard. Don't even think about that. It was just an act. To keep AJ from discovering me. And I'm sorry. It was wrong of me to put you in that position.

Maybe. But I'm glad you didn't go alone. And then: Have you talked to Marcus about it? Wanting to help the girl? You can't keep it from him.

Cora's chest tightened. But no, it would be fine. Marcus would understand. He had to. Soon. I'm going to.

Nothing for a second, and then the dots came back and finally Armand's next text. Ok. Really glad you're okay. I'm about to go into a meeting but talk more soon? Come have a spa day with that gorgeous friend of yours?

Cora typed back a laughing face emoji and: For sure.

Then Cora moved on to the next message. She didn't recognize the number but it was a picture message and curious, she clicked on it.

And then screeched and dropped the phone on the bed.

"Anna," she gasped and reached for the phone again. Cora brought it close to her face and looked at the picture of her friend.

Anna had been beaten, that was clear. Her face, her beautiful heart shaped face was beaten black and blue. Her left eye was swollen shut and blood from her temple poured down the side of her face. Her head hung back, slack, and Cora didn't even know if she was conscious. If she was alive.

There was a message underneath the picture. CALL ME. IF YOU TELL YOUR HUSBAND, SHE DIES.

Cora's hands were trembling so hard she could barely manage to keep hold as she dialed the number and lifted the phone to her ear.

The phone rang three times before he picked it up. AJ's smarmy, self-satisfied voice came over the line. "Are you alone?"

"Yes." Cora tried to make her voice cold but she couldn't quite shake her tremors. "Let me talk to Anna."

"Oh, so you *do* know this little cunt. And here she was swearing up and down she had no clue who you were or how that picture of you got on her phone camera. Even after I had my boys work her over."

Cora's eyes sank closed and her body curled in on itself. The picture Anna had taken of her outside the restaurant the first day they met. Of course AJ had taken Anna's phone. Cora put a hand to her forehead.

"What do you want?"

"Five million dollars. Delivered by you personally."

Cora let out a strangled noise. "You're crazy. Where am I supposed to get my hands on—"

"Well you better figure it out. Anna's already endured a beating for you. I'd hate to see what would happen next if I really let my men have their way with her. But if you don't care about her, then I guess—"

"Stop!" Cora jumped to her feet and paced the length of the room, looking out the windows as she went. "Fine. I'll get it but it will take some time. Maybe a few days—"

"Tonight."

"Tonight?" Cora squeaked, her voice going high-pitched. "You can't be serious. That's impossible!"

"Then I guess your friend doesn't mean very much to you after all. She's dead if you don't get me that money personally. It's tonight or never. I'll see you around, Mrs. Ubeli."

"Tonight then. What time? Where?" Gods, what was she doing?

"Eight o'clock on the dot. Underneath the statue of Atlas in the park."

"I need proof that they're alive. Let me talk to Anna."

"I'll be seeing you, Cora."

The line went dead. Son of a—

Cora looked around frantically, needing to do something but not knowing where to start. Marcus. She needed Marcus. He would know what to do.

She reached for her phone but then froze.

She couldn't call Marcus, even if he had his phone on, which she probably didn't. He'd been lining up everything for the shipment for months. She couldn't screw that up.

And if she told Sharo, he wouldn't help her, he'd only tried to get in touch with Marcus. And he definitely wouldn't let her go to the meet.

She huffed out a breath. Because she couldn't do *nothing*.

Anna was only in this mess because of her. She'd screwed everything up and she had to try to fix it.

"Think. Think." She looked back down at her phone. Which was when she noticed the other message she hadn't yet opened. It was from Olivia. Quickly, she tapped her thumb on the message so that it popped up.

It was just two words but Cora knew immediately Olivia was talking about Iris's phone: "Cracked it."

Cora immediately dialed her.

"Good work. Anything useful?"

"Holding your applause to the end, hmmm? Let me see here...the last thing here is a text to the Orphan. Saying she's almost done with moving out. Then a text from a person named Ashley."

"Ashley? Are you sure?" Cora thought of the redhead in the concert hall.

"That's the name. The text reads, NEED TO MEET YOU. ORCHID HOUSE, 1 PM. That's it."

Ashley couldn't have texted her that. She was dead by then. Cora explained this to Olivia.

"Then whoever has Ashley's phone knew her well enough to unlock the password and send it. Or this is the first case of ghost texting ever."

"AJ."

"All roads lead to this guy. It's kinda getting boring." Cora could hear Olivia reach into a bag and eat a handful of chips.

"Olivia, listen. AJ has Anna...my friend."

"The dancer that Armand won't shut up about?"

"Yes. She's probably with Iris. We need to get them out. But first I have to find them."

There was a short silence on the other end. "Well, I might be able to help with that."

"What? What did you find?" Hope rose in Cora. "You know where they are?"

"Not completely. I got a partial address." Olivia gave her the cross streets. "It's somewhere close to that inter-section.

"Thank you, thank you."

Now that Cora knew where AJ was holding the girls, she didn't have to wait for the meet up in the park where he would undoubtedly try to double-cross her. He had no incentive to actually bring the girls and she knew it was a trap.

But if she could surprise him…

"What are you thinking about doing?" Olivia's voice came over the phone. Cora had forgotten she was still on the line. "Because you better not even think about leaving me behind," Olivia continued.

Cora's eyes fell shut. Was she really considering doing this? By herself? Or well, with Olivia, but it wasn't like either of them were master spies. Or trained mobsters. AJ was ruthless and he'd surround himself with the sort of men who'd happily beat up a woman, and worse.

It would be dangerous and Marcus would be furious with her. But he'd be gone all night and Anna and Iris didn't have that kind of time.

So Cora made the decision that needed to be made. "Okay, Olivia, I need you to pick me up. The park by Roman road—as soon as you can. I'll be waiting."

"Ok. Oh my gosh, I can't believe we're doing this! It's so exciting! That was once word for it. But Olivia hung up before Cora could caution her about her enthusiasm.

Then Cora laid back down on the bed. There was one last phone call to make.

She reached underneath the mattress and pulled out the card that she'd thought about throwing away so many times. She still wasn't sure if she was glad she still had it or not.

Dialing the number, even now she didn't know if she was making a mistake. She prayed she wasn't. She prayed her gambles tonight would pay off and that when Marcus eventually learned all she'd done…some part of him would be proud, even if he'd be furious at her for how she went about it.

"Yeah," answered Pete the cop, sounding supremely bored.

Cora bristled. "You're only interested if there's a big bust to be made, right? Well listen up because I've got one that will make headlines. But you need to do exactly what I say."

TWENTY-FOUR

"This is so freaking exciting," Olivia said. They were parked in the street around the corner from AJ's safehouse.

Cora had a hell of a time sneaking off the Estate, but the guards were far more interested about people trying to break in than one small slip of a woman sneaking out through the back kitchen exit. There had been fewer guards on duty, too. Most of them were with Marcus to deal with the mysterious shipment.

Cora had waited for Benito, the guard on outer perimeter duty to turn the corner and then she'd fled toward the woods and past the fence into the public park beyond. She hadn't stopped running until she reached the meet up point with Olivia.

"The cops are ready, too?" Olivia asked. "Is there like some signal?" It had taken hours to set everything up, for Pete to get the SWAT team in place, and the sun was low in the sky now.

Cora's racing heart felt like it was about to leap out of her chest but she managed to keep her voice somewhat calm as she answered.

"I'll give a verbal signal, and yes, they're here, they're just hidden." She didn't know where they were either. Pete said his team would be waiting nearby and for once she trusted him—only because it was in his self-interest to work with her. Him looking out for number one, that she could rely on.

"And the wire, you're sure it's hidden?"

Cora swallowed and nodded.

That had been Pete's stipulation. He still wasn't impressed with her 'so-called detective work'—his words—so the only way he'd agree to help was if she wore a wire and either caught something damning on tape or saw something inside the safehouse she was sure would let them throw the book at the notorious mobster and rumored human trafficker, AJ Wagner.

Luckily the technology had gotten far better than what was usually shown on TV. When Cora and Olivia met with Pete half an hour ago, he'd easily attached a button camera to the button of her jeans and slid a barrette into her hair that doubled as a microphone. No clumsy wires necessary.

And now here they were.

A big part of Cora wanted to turn tail and run away but she wouldn't give into it. Everything was in place. She had back up. And she was far too valuable an asset for AJ to hurt her...at least that was what she was counting on. She'd planned as much as she could.

Now there was nothing left to do but jump.

She got out of the car before Olivia could say anything else. She quickly turned the corner and started towards AJ's safe house. She imagined the house had been cute once, before age and uncaring owners took their toll. Beyond an old iron gate, a concrete walk led to the door. Pieces of the siding hung askew. The windows stared like huge, empty eyes.

She called AJ as she approached, arms up. She kept her distance, though. She was sure she was in range of their guns, but she also knew she was far more valuable to AJ alive than dead. At least she really, *really* hoped so.

AJ picked up right away. "What the fuck do you think you're doing?"

"New rules. You send Anna and Iris out and in exchange, you get me as a hostage."

Silence.

Cora was impatient now that it had come down to it. "Stop with the bullshit because we both know it's what you were planning all along—to snatch me. What's five million compared to having collateral against the infamous Marcus Ubeli? Now send them out or I'm in the wind. There's an SUV parked around the corner, one block down. Once Anna and Iris are both in, I'll come out."

"You think I'm a fool? That I'm just going to give up my bargaining chips?" He gave an ugly laugh.

Cora ground her teeth together. They were *people*, not bargaining chips.

"If you don't send them out, how do I even know you have them? I'm not going to stand out here exposed like this for long. Either you take the deal or I walk." Cora channeled Marcus and made her voice ice.

There was some shuffling on the other end of the phone, then AJ's voice again. "Fine. I'll send out one. As a show of good faith." His voice was mocking. "But I don't release the other one until you come in."

Cora's heart hammered. It wasn't a good deal. Cora wanted both girls safe and out of that house before she stepped in. Who knew what would happen when the

SWAT team stormed the house? Bullets might fly. Cora would be expecting it but whoever was left inside wouldn't.

But Cora knew it was all she'd get out of AJ.

"Send her out," she commanded, "and have the second girl ready to send right when I come in." She hung up the phone before he could reply and stood, back straight, shoulders out, staring down the front door.

Nothing happened.

For long, long minutes, nothing happened.

Shit. Oh shit, what if he called her bluff? What if she'd miscalculated and—

The door opened and Anna stumbled out.

Cora hurried forward. Anna rushed to meet her with big unsteady steps and frantic eyes.

"Cora, what are you doing—"

but Cora just shook her head. Anna looked terrible. Her eye was so swollen and bloodied and her clothes were ripped and—

Cora couldn't think about all that it meant. She just grabbed Anna by the forearms so she'd look her in the eye. "There's a car around the corner. Over there." Cora gestured with her eyes and Anna's gaze followed. "Get in and tell Olivia to drive. Don't look back."

Anna was shaking her head, fat tears falling down her cheeks. "Cora, you can't go in there. You can't—"

Cora dropped Anna's arms and ordered, "Go," in her harshest voice.

Then she turned back to the house and strode straight for the door. Behind her, she heard Anna's footsteps running away. Good girl.

AJ met Cora at the door. His potbelly was barely contained by the sweat-stained wife beater undershirt he had on.

"Where's Iris?" Cora demanded. "The deal was for both of them."

The mobster smirked. "Iris is going to need a little help getting out of bed." He stuck his cigar in his mouth and spoke around it. "She's...not well. Come on in." He moved back from the door to make space for her.

Cora took a deep breath and then wished she hadn't—AJ's cigar plus the inside of the house altogether smelled rancid and turned her stomach. But still, she stepped into the house, turning in a 360 as she did so to give the cops a view of the place after she was in. She didn't immediately see anything incriminating but she was only standing in the foyer.

"Check her," AJ said and two guys came forward.

She gritted her teeth as the two meat-handed thugs frisked her, lingering far longer than was necessary between her thighs and squeezing as they brushed down her chest.

"That's enough." She yanked back when the shorter, squat one went for another pass. "I don't have anything on me." She went to slide her phone into her pocket but AJ shook his head at her.

"Ah ah," he said. "Hand it over."

Cora's jaw locked but she handed the phone to him, eyes tracking it as he slid it into the front pocket of his black slacks.

"Now, where's Iris?"

AJ smiled. "Like I said, she's indisposed at the moment."

Cora stepped forward but the two thugs grabbed her by her arms. She fought against them. "Where is she?"

Because she'd just had a terrible thought. AJ trafficked in women. What if he wasn't using Iris for leverage against The Orphan at all? What if the reason he wasn't producing her was because she wasn't here? He'd considered Iris his girl and she tried to get away, to get out, by marrying Chris. Just how angry had that made him?

"I swear, if you've done something to her or shipped her off somewhere—"

"So dramatic," AJ laughed. "You want to see her, fine."

He motioned the men holding Cora to lead her upstairs. The squat one kept hold of her as the other released her. Squatty dragged her up the stairs but he needn't have bothered. Maybe it was foolish to hurry deeper into this filthy den but she needed to see Iris with her own two eyes. After everything, she needed to see that the girl was okay.

And Pete should still be listening. They'd agreed on a safe word. No matter what, if Cora mentioned the *Fates*, his team was supposed to come in guns with blazing.

It stank even worse upstairs but when they passed one of the bedrooms, Cora looked inside and saw a skinny man with greasy hair hunched over a computer that was connected to several screens. Whatever was on that hard drive could be useful to Pete. Cora made sure to pause with her button camera pointed in the man's direction before Squatty yanked her forward again.

Now she just needed to find Iris and get them both the hell out of here.

"Do you know what the little birdies have been talking about all month?" AJ's voice startled Cora, it came from so close behind her. Cora stepped forward to get away from him, continuing down the hallway and looking in each room she passed.

AJ went on as if she was an active participant in the conversation.

"The shipment. A very special shipment. One of a kind."

Cora forced herself not to react.

"And my guys, we caught a few of them birdies yesterday, locked 'em in a cage and made 'em sing." A short pause. His man had grabbed hold of her and was holding her still while footsteps sounded on the grimy hardwood behind her, no doubt AJ huffing up the stairs. "And you wanna know what they said?"

AJ came around her and spoke, his foul breath right in her face. "They said the delivery was going down *tonight*."

Cora jerked back from his oily face and bad breath. She glared him down icily. "Where's Iris? How long have you had her?"

To her surprise, AJ answered. "Since The Orphan's little hissy fit that nearly cost me the concert deal."

Cora just stared at him. "You wouldn't have been out the money."

"You heard Marcus. I'd lose access. Access to Elysium, access to his home, access to his whole little world."

"Why do you hate him so much?"

"He took everything from me." AJ stopped at a door and pushed it open. Dim light spilled out into the hall.

Cora held her sleeve in front of her face to block the smell as she entered the room. It must have once been a child's room, painted a cheery yellow.

Now the walls were faded and stained, covered in shadows cast by a small lamp by a bed. Trash had collected in the corners of the room. The room seemed cold, and empty, except for a young woman lying on a thin mattress.

"Iris," Cora breathed as she ran over to her. The woman had shadows under her eyes and lank, dirty hair. Her high classic cheekbones now looked skeletal and her beautiful skin had turned grey and sallow. Her eyes fluttered open, then closed again weakly.

"Oh gods." Cora sank beside the bed to feel the

woman's forehead. It was cold to the touch. She checked Iris's pulse next, noting the fresh track marks on the woman's arm.

Cora turned accusing eyes to AJ. "What did you do to her?"

"Gave her a little hit." He shrugged. "Then a little more. After that, she did it to herself."

Cora noted the restraints hanging off the bed. They'd tied her down and forced the poison into her veins. Cora felt sick to her stomach. Had they even fed her? "We need to get her out of here. She could be dying."

"First you deliver."

Cora looked up in confusion but saw him holding out her phone.

"Call him," AJ ordered.

Well past fear, she felt surprisingly calm. "The Fates curse you for what you've done," she spat. This evil bastard would rot for all his sins. He'd admitted on tape to kidnapping Iris and Cora felt sure the computer would give even more evidence against him. Plus Anna's testimony.

Any second the SWAT team would come breaking down the door.

"Oh, on the contrary. I think the Fates are smiling on me. After all, they brought you to my door. And you are going to lead me straight to your husband and the cargo ship full of product that's going to shift the tide of this war."

Cora glared at him, letting all of her hatred shine through. *Just you wait. You'll get everything that's coming to you.*

Any minute now.

Any minute...

Cora glanced around and listened hard.

Silence.

What the hell was taking them so long? Did Pete not hear her? Or was the mic not working? They'd checked and rechecked it. She fought the rising panic clawing up her throat

But only AJ's chuckle filled the silence. "What, nothing to say for once? That's fine."

He reached over and grabbed her hand, wrenching her forefinger to cover the fingerprint lock that unlocked her phone. "All I really need you to do is scream."

AJ pulled the phone back and search through her contacts once it was unlocked. He pushed Marcus's phone number and it dialed.

No! It was never supposed to go this far. No matter what had happened last night, that shipment meant everything to Marcus—

Marcus didn't pick up though and it went to voicemail. Cora felt a jolt of emotion go through her as she heard Marcus's gravelly voice start, "This is Marcus Ubeli—"

AJ hung up and dialed again impatiently. It went to voicemail and he beeped past the voice message.

"Ubeli. Call me now," he intoned, looking at Cora. "I have something you want." He hung up, still looking at her. "You're an idiot, you know? Giving yourself up for this druggie."

Then he slammed the door on his way out and left Cora standing beside the bed.

"The Fates help us," she whispered, and then said it louder, over and over, "Fates, help us. Please, *Fates*, we need you now," as she crouched to check on Iris.

When Cora touched her clammy skin, Iris opened cracked lips and whimpered.

"Iris, shh. Chris sent me. We're going to get you out."

She squeezed the woman's hand gently. "I'm going to get you out."

"C-Chris?" Iris rasped out, crusted and unfocused eyes dragging down to meet Cora's.

Cora nodded even as tears squeezed out of her own eyes. "Yes. Chris loves you. He sent me to help you. We're going to get you out of here."

Behind her, the door knob turned; she jumped but it was only AJ coming back.

He held the phone out. Marcus's voice came from far away.

"Cora. Cora! Are you ok?"

Cora couldn't help but feel a surge of hope at hearing his voice even though she knew it meant she'd screwed up everything so terribly. For whatever reason, the SWAT team wasn't coming. "Marcus, I'm here. I'm ok," Cora barely answered before AJ put the phone back to his ear.

"Proof of life, as requested. We'll meet you at the docks. I know Waters is delivering the shipment tonight. Tell your men to sit tight. My own will take over the heavy lifting. The drugs for your wife, that's the deal."

Cora heard her husband's voice raised in anger just before AJ bellowed, "I'm in charge here." He pulled out a gun. With a shriek, Cora ducked her head as he pointed it towards the bed and fired.

What had he—? Her head snapped up and she looked at Iris.

"No!" Cora sobbed. "*No.*"

Blood soaked slowly through Iris's thin shirt. Cora pressed her hands to Iris's chest, moaning. "Please, no."

"One hour, capisce? No tricks." AJ shut the door hard enough to make the lamp rattle.

Cora almost didn't hear him. She pressed down as the blood ran faster, watching Iris's breathing slow.

The beautiful girl choked once and was still. Her eyes were glassy, staring just like Ashley's. Lifeless.

"I'm so sorry," Cora whispered. "I'm so sorry."

AJ's thugs came for her a few minutes later, pulling her bodily up from the floor. They marched her to the door. One of them stopped to take a picture of the dead woman. He followed Cora and his fellow thug into the hall, cackling. "Sent it to The Orphan. Let's see how well he plays now, the little prick."

Cora let out an animal, guttural cry of fury. How could they be so callous? Her hair had come undone and hung messily over her face. She pushed it back, then realized her hands were sticky with blood from the wrists down, and all she was doing was smearing Iris's blood around her temples.

"Stop dawdling," AJ barked.

He'd put on a shirt and coat like he was a civilized man but Cora knew better now. He was a monster. He glanced once more at her phone, then dropped it into his coat pocket.

"We've got a date with the docks. Time to make a trade."

TWENTY-FIVE

THE DOCKS LOOKED like a black extension of the street until AJ's thugs pulled Cora out of the car. Then she could see the pier drop off into the water, a pit of blackness. She shivered in the chilly night air, wearing nothing but jeans and a soft sweater, now spattered with blood. One of the thugs kept his grip tight on her arm as they walked forward.

Cora felt...blank. The whole drive here she'd tried to think of what she'd say to Marcus, how she'd try to explain it. But then all she could see was Iris's face. Her eyes and that second when the life went out of them. Cora had watched her go. One second she was there and the next she was just...gone.

It didn't make sense. It wasn't fair. Good was supposed to win in the end. Even Marcus, eventually, he loved her. At least he had before he'd known what she'd done.

"See, what'd I tell you," AJ said to his driver, a tall man with a gold earring. "They're using a smaller ship to bring in the goods. Nothing fancy. Waters always was smart."

Cora let them lead her down the sidewalk, into a warehouse where a bunch of crates were piled on a vast stretch of concrete floor.

Three men waited for them in the moonlight, three to match AJ's three. Cora's chest clenched. Marcus, Sharo, and another Shade. AJ approached them confidently.

The thug who held Cora twisted her arm up behind her as he jammed the gun into her back and she couldn't help whimpering.

Even in the moonlight she could see the cold fury in Marcus's face.

Oh, Marcus. Forgive me.

"Let me check this out first," AJ said. He nodded to Gold Earring guy, who took out a crowbar and headed for a crate. After prying it open the man held up a nondescript bottle. "Metamorphoses Spa," the thug read, then looked up at his leader, confused. "It's hair gunk."

"Give it here," AJ ordered. He unscrewed the cap, and shook out a small white pill. He held it up, sniffed it. "Pure," he said with triumphant satisfaction. "The Brothers are going to love this."

"Let's get this over with," Marcus ordered from the shadows.

"Oh, no, Ubeli. You don't get to make demands anymore." AJ waved a hand and Cora was pushed forward, forced to walk to AJ so he could hook her under his arm. His other hand raised the gun to her temple.

"You know why I only shot up the front of that restaurant even though I knew you were in the back? Because I want to see the look on Ivan Titan's face when I tell him Marcus Ubeli's legs are cut from under him, he's got no goods, and his own men are turning on him."

AJ's gold tooth flashed as he grinned. "What are your guys going to do when the shipment's gone and they ain't got nothing to push, no way of getting paid? We'll sell it back to them in Metropolis. And Waters, what's he going to think?"

"Hand over my wife." The vein in Marcus's temple pulsed; Cora could see it from twelve feet away.

"Let me tell you how this goes," AJ continued as if Marcus hadn't spoken. "You get out of here, all of your men, all of you. Then I turn the girl loose and you leave, forever. This is mine."

Cora couldn't stop her trembling anymore. AJ wrapped his arm tighter around her body and rammed the gun into the side of her head. She kept her eyes on Marcus, letting her body go limp. She became a ragdoll. A weak thing. A victim.

But while everyone was watching Sharo and her husband, Cora's fingers slipped between the folds of AJ's coat and found his pocket.

And her phone.

"Stand down," AJ was saying. "I'm not a patient man."

Jerking suddenly in his arms, Cora reached up and stuck the edge of her phone—along with the Wasp that Olivia had attached all those weeks ago—right into AJ's neck.

The voltage hit him a second later, jolting through him with enough force to knock him back. He bellowed in surprise and pain, stumbling backwards and almost falling to the pavement.

Cora staggered too, letting the phone drop. She'd barely regained her feet before someone hit her and brought her down to the concrete, cradling her body against his.

"I got you," Sharo rumbled, and spread his large body over hers. She cringed as she heard bullets flying past them.

Then they were both up and Sharo was running, carrying her out of the warehouse and into the cold night.

Cora couldn't see anything, could barely hear anything, but she clung to Sharo's shoulders. Then they were in an alleyway and the sound of bullets seemed farther away.

A black car pulled in front of them and the door opened. Sharo ducked inside, sliding Cora in before him.

Sharo barely had tucked his feet into the car before he barked to the driver. "Go."

"Wait! Marcus—" Cora shrieked, before she was thrown back into the seat by the car's sudden acceleration. It pulled out of the alley and around to the front of the warehouse, where the Shades were fighting AJ's men.

A dark figure burst out of the warehouse and Sharo threw open the door. *Marcus.* He dove into the car and the driver screeched off from the curb, letting the door slam shut on its own.

"Got 'em," Marcus reported, and checked his gun before turning and taking Cora from Sharo. She threw her arms around Marcus.

A second later, though, he was pulling back from her.

"You ok?" He touched her cheeks and gripped her arms, grabbing her wrists and turning them frantically to inspect her hands.

Oh gods, he must think— "It's not my blood," she said hurriedly.

He pulled her to him, hugging her close.

"Never again," he muttered. "Never again."

Cora sagged into her husband, letting her shaking subside in his strong arms. He was here. He was safe. They were both safe and AJ was gone. It was going to be okay. It was all going to be okay.

That was when she heard the police sirens.

Close.

Too close.

Marcus's muscles tensed. "What the—" he started. Cora looked up to see him glaring at Sharo over her head.

Sharo was already taking a headpiece from the driver and tuning in.

"Police band says an unmarked beige car was followed to the docks. Shots fired."

Marcus cursed. "AJ. Stupid to the last. He must've been tailed here."

Oh. S*hit.*

It hit her all at once. There hadn't been any interference with her mic or the button camera. Pete had seen and heard every single thing that had gone on in AJ's safe house.

And he'd decided he wanted a bigger bust after over-hearing AJ talk about the drug shipment. No matter that Cora had said the safe word and tried to get her and Iris out *before—*

Cora squeezed her eyes shut. The cops had betrayed her. And Iris had *died* because of it.

Blue and red police lights were already washing over the brick walls as the car slunk away down a back alley.

Cora nestled closer to Marcus, feeling sick even as she did it. Because Pete's wasn't the only betrayal of the night.

She'd betrayed Marcus. She lied to him. Conspired with his enemies. Brought the cops to his very doorstep.

"Sir, another report. This one from the club, Elysium," the driver spoke up.

At Marcus's nod, the man continued. "Rioting started right after intermission. The Orphan came on and told everyone he was only going to play one more song. A song for the dead."

The man paused, touching his headpiece as if he wasn't

sure if what he was hearing was true. "Cops tried to settle everybody but they revolted, rushed the stage. The cops were overwhelmed. They got the mayor out first, and helped the people who were getting trampled."

The man grimaced. "But they didn't get to the stage on time. The Orphan was...torn apart. They say there's no other word for it... He's dead."

Cora jerked then, feeling horror jolt through her just when she'd been sure she didn't have any more capacity for grief.

Marcus's arms flexed briefly, as if he was trying to comfort her. *Her.* When she was the one who'd brought this all down on their heads.

TWENTY-SIX

CORA HAD FALLEN asleep in his arms, curled against his chest, his shirt squeezed in her blood covered fists even in sleep. Like she was terrified he'd disappear.

Marcus tried to keep his arms soft and gentle around her but it was hard when every muscle in his body was tense with fury. What the hell had happened tonight? How had AJ gotten his hands on her—

Marcus wanted reports from every single one of his lieutenants but he didn't even reach for his phone. He didn't dare dislodge his wife. Whatever she had been through tonight—

The car slowed and she roused, lifting her head from his chest and slowly blinking, looking around. They were at the Estate. She frowned when she recognized where they were.

"Do we have to stay here?" she said in a small voice. "It's so...dark here."

"The penthouse was bugged," Sharo said. "We had it swept."

It was Marcus she turned her head towards, though. "AJ?"

Marcus didn't answer. He didn't trust himself to speak. When the car stopped, he helped her inside.

She gasped when she caught a glance of herself in a mirror in the foyer. Blood garishly streaked her light hair. And it was all over her hands... Marcus grimaced. He'd hoped to get her in the shower before she saw herself. Her gaze darted away and she started up the stairs.

Marcus wanted to follow her but there were things that had to be attended to.

"I'll be right up, babe."

She nodded, not even looking over her shoulder at him. Marcus's jaw set, but then he turned to Sharo.

"You order clean up?" Marcus asked.

He could feel Cora hovering on the landing, paused just out of sight. For whatever reason, she wanted to hear what he had to say. Fine. He had nothing to hide. He'd tried to protect her from all of this and it had only—it had only—

"What about Waters?" he demanded, glaring at Sharo.

"He's been alerted, but that was before the shipment was confiscated. He'll know now; it's been on the police scanners."

Marcus nodded slowly. "What about our contacts?"

"MIA. Still dealing with the fallout."

"Get them on the phone. I've got to make sure—" Marcus glanced up the stairs, all but feeling Cora shrink back into the shadows.

Sharo said, "Do you have any idea how he snatched her?"

"No," Marcus whispered under his breath. "I'll wait before I ask her."

He heard the softest scuffle on the stairs above. Cora was continuing on to their room. And again the question plagued him: what the hell had happened to put her in AJ's path? The Estate was the most fortified place in the city. Had she gone somewhere? Tried to go see a friend or to visit that damn shelter because of some so-called 'emergency'?

A few minutes later, he finished up with Sharo and took the stairs two at a time. When he got to their bedroom, he found Cora on the bed, head bent over her lap. She hadn't turned any lights on so the room was dark and gloomy apart from the tiniest sliver of moonlight coming in through the blinds.

He went to the bed side table and turned on a lamp, then moved around to view her blood-spattered front.

"Let's get you clean."

She nodded and walked into the bathroom, but froze in front of the sink.

Marcus followed her.

"My hands." She held them out, palms up. "I don't want to get blood on everything."

She retreated as he came to the sink and turned on both taps. He tested the water then stepped away so she could approach. They still weren't touching each other.

He ached to hold her, but her face was blank, still and hollow as a doll's. She might need him or she might need space. He'd wait and see which.

With robotic movements she thrust her hands under the tap, wetting them almost to mid-arm. The water ran red and she jerked her hands out of the flow.

Marcus's throat got thick but he stood behind her then, his arms along hers. He put her hands back in the water, and helped her lather with soap and scrub them gently, until the water ran clean. Her bowed head hung as if she was somewhere else, unattached from her hands.

She was still in the bloodied clothes, though, and that wouldn't do. With gentle hands, Marcus pulled her shirt off over her head.

She let him do it, like a limp rag doll. When he reached for the button of her jeans, she suddenly jerked away and unbuttoned them herself, sliding them down her thighs along with her underwear and stepping towards the shower.

But Marcus wasn't letting go of her that fast. She might have needed to cling to him in the Bentley on the way over here but he— Seeing that gun pointed to her temple—

He yanked his own clothes off and then stepped in behind her right as the spray turned warm.

"Marcus," Cora whispered and in that one word he heard a thousand heartbreaks. She turned toward him, arms folded to her chest, and fell against him. He wrapped a firm arm around her and pulled her to his chest, his other hand pushing her hair back from her eyes.

"Shh, it's all right. It's all right."

She just kept shaking her head. "It's not, though. It's not."

"Yes it is. You were brave. I watched you." He walked her back a little into the spray to wet her hair. Then he lifted her shampoo bottle and squeezed some into his hand.

He talked softly as he began to work the shampoo through her hair, cleaning out the blood. "You couldn't have done more, Cora."

At her name, she shut her eyes and her entire body shook. Like she was reliving whatever AJ had put her through. Marcus had examined her hands in the car and knew the blood wasn't hers, but still. His jaw flexed.

AJ would pay and he would pay dearly. But Marcus couldn't think about that right now. He had to stay in control for her sake. Always in control.

So, with supreme effort, he managed to keep his voice calm as he continued, "He thought you were weak. He underestimated you. Tonight was tough. I don't know what you went through and you don't have to tell me until you're ready. But you're stronger than you know."

He worked his fingers through her hair, washing all the suds out. She leaned her forehead against his chest as he rinsed her hair. Once it was clean, he dropped his lips to the top of her head. "Don't make the same mistake. Know your own strength. You'll get through this."

He waited, but she didn't say anything. That was all right. He would help her through, one day at a time. He would protect her.

Just like you did tonight? He gritted his teeth. She *should* have been safe here. He'd find out what had gone wrong and punish whoever had put his wife in danger. Starting with that motherfucking bastard, AJ. He'd make the man wish he'd never set eyes on Marcus's wife. Marcus would make him wish he'd never been born. He'd —

Cora stirred in his arms and all of his attention came back to her. Large blue eyes blinked up at him, so full of sorrow. And then she shocked him with her next words. "Will you fuck me? I don't want to think any more."

Marcus had been angling his hips away from her for the whole shower. Any time he was around his wife but especially when she was naked, he couldn't help his body's reaction to her. Now wasn't the time though—

But she reached down and grasped him so firmly he couldn't help the groan that slid from his throat. And when she lifted a leg around his waist and positioned him at her entrance, gods, the way her heat tempted and teased the head of his cock—

"Please," she breathed out.

In one swift movement, he turned them around so that her back was to the wall and then he pushed inside her. Usually, he would thrust all the way in, taking and claiming what was his.

But she felt so fragile in this moment. He cupped her cheeks and entered her slowly, so slowly, his eyes tracking her every breath, her every twitch, every flutter of her fingers against his shoulders.

She tried to look away but he guided her face back to his. She might have wanted to fuck but it wasn't what she *needed*.

In this at least, he would not fail her. And as he sank, inch by inch into the sweetest pussy the gods had ever created, he realized he'd needed it, too. When he heard AJ's voice coming from her contact number and then heard her screaming—

He wrapped his arms around her and held her tighter than he'd ever held anything. She squeezed around him like she too was holding on for dear life. Because that's what she was to him. His whole fucking life.

How could he have been so fucking stupid? Lying to himself for all those months and trying to pretend that she meant nothing to him? She meant everything. He didn't deserve her.

Slowly, tortuously, he slid out and then pushed back in again. A shudder went down his spine as pleasure threatened even though he'd just begun. It was easy to hold back, though. He had only to remember the image of AJ holding the gun to her head and her terrified eyes pleading with him for help. But in the end, he'd done nothing. She'd helped herself.

No, he didn't fucking deserve her. He clutched her closer still. But he would.

He'd devote the rest of his life to earning this woman. To earning her trust and love and devotion. He'd give her a world that was beautiful and safe and perfect. He'd give her everything he'd never had. He swore it, now, in this moment. He'd wipe the sorrow from her eyes. He'd make her happy, no matter what it fucking took.

He reached down and grasped her ass, angling her just right so that when he pushed in again, he hit that perfect spot inside her and her mouth dropped open in a silent scream of pleasure.

He pulled out and thrust in again, out and in, grinding against her clit until she was shuddering with her climax and squeezing around him so tight he couldn't hold back anymore. His spine lit up and then he thrust and spilled into his wife and for a moment, everything was as it was meant to be. Her, sated and limp in his arms and him, her conqueror and protector.

But then her legs wobbled and he could tell she was so weak, she almost collapsed right there in the shower where she stood.

Fuck.

He turned off the shower and helped her out, wrapping a towel around her and urging her to sit down on the closed toilet seat while he toweled her off. Her eyes were closed and her face, unreadable. Marcus frowned. Usually after sex her features were soft and she was more pliable than ever. Right now, though...

"Let's get you to bed," he said gently, helping her up off of the seat and taking her to the bedroom. She stumbled along after him. Gods, when was the last time she'd eaten anything? "I'll have one of the men bring something up for dinner," he started but she cut him off with a wave of her hand.

"No," she said, curling up to the pillow drowsily as he pulled the blankets over her. "Just want to sleep."

It must have been true because only moments later, her soft, delicate little snores filled the otherwise silent room. Marcus didn't move from where he sat on the bed beside her, frowning.

Time. It would just take time for her to share all she'd been through so they could work through it together.

And in the meantime... Marcus's eyes shot to the window. He stood abruptly and then looked back down at Cora.

She hadn't moved, not even stirred at his sudden motion. She'd be out for a while. And though he'd managed to block everything out while he was with her, his business couldn't be ignored for much longer. It was a mess now that they'd lost the shipment.

He needed to do major damage control, so, reluctantly, after a lingering stare at his wife from the doorway to make sure she didn't stir, he walked out and closed the door quietly behind himself.

He took a deep breath and held it, letting the mask of Marcus Ubeli settle over himself like a Greek player of old. The part of himself he shared with Cora was sacred. But the world must never see anything other than strength and a leader who crushed his enemies underneath his heel.

He strode down the stairs and straight to the kitchen where he knew Sharo would be waiting. Sharo was indeed there and he handed Marcus a cup of coffee as he came in.

"They have him?" he barked.

Sharo nodded. "It's being arranged. They're estimating three hours, maybe four."

Marcus grabbed the cup and drink it all down without a

word. The liquid burned his throat but it was a good burn and Marcus needed the caffeine.

It was going to be a long night.

TWENTY-SEVEN

CORA WOKE and even without looking at the clock knew it was still hours before dawn. The way the light fell over her hands—they were red-stained. She jerked and stared but they were clean. The blood on them had been washed away, but her guilt went more than skin deep. She'd never get clean.

Marcus's side of the bed lay empty. He was probably downstairs, cleaning up the mess she'd made of his business. At the thought, she whimpered. Iris dead, a shipment seized, and all the Shades brought under police spotlight.

When her husband found out—and he would find out, of that she had no doubt—what happened then? Would he forgive her? She turned her face into the pillow. Gods, she wasn't sure she'd ever be able to forgive herself, so why should he?

She squeezed her eyes shut and thought of how tenderly he'd held her in the shower. How gentle he'd been with her. How he'd caressed her and washed her hair and... made love to her. She'd asked him to fuck her but he hadn't. After all this time she'd gotten the only thing she'd wanted but it was too late. It was too late for them. She'd ruined it all.

She sat up and swiped angrily at the tears falling down her cheeks. Marcus wouldn't look at her that way ever again, not once he knew. Or... She bit down on her lip. Maybe if she could just explain it... How she'd started with good intentions but it had all gotten out of hand so quickly... And then in the end she'd tried— She'd tried—

A sob gulped its way out of her and she threw her hand over her mouth. But there was no stopping it once it started.

And suddenly, she couldn't be here anymore. She couldn't face Marcus when he came back from dealing with the disaster that she'd caused. She couldn't lie to him and she couldn't tell him the truth.

A green light blinking on the dresser caught her eye. Her cellphone.

Marcus or Sharo must have gotten it from one of the Shades, who'd have found it where she dropped it on the warehouse floor. She just needed a little space. She just needed to breathe and figure out her next move. To figure out how to tell Marcus.

She fired off a quick text, then got dressed. Jeans and a tee, under a sweatshirt. By the time she was done, a message was waiting for her.

Maeve: PICK YOU UP NOW?

She texted back. YES.

~

THERE WOULDN'T BE any sneaking out the kitchen exit, not this time. Marcus would have Shades on every door.

So she used a tree to escape the house—one she had

found on her earlier walk. Cora padded through the house until she found the room, unlocked the window and looked out. The tree branch that scraped along the side of the house didn't look so sturdy, but she tested it and then swung her legs out to balance on it. It held.

She froze for a moment. *What are you doing, Cora? Are you really running away? Are you really going to do that to Marcus on top of everything else you put him through today?*

But when she closed her eyes, all she saw was Iris's lifeless face. And the blood. She could still feel it sticky on her hands, no matter that Marcus had washed it away. It would never come off. Never. *Never.*

Her breathing got erratic the more she thought about it and she shook her head, like that could shake the memories away. The only thing that was clear was that she couldn't face Marcus again. Not right now. So she scooted down, grabbed the branch, and then dropped onto the wet grass below.

The darkness grabbed her, and she ran. She didn't stop to hear if she was being followed or if someone in the house had spotted her. She headed towards the path she'd found earlier.

She'd been running for a little while, maybe five or ten minutes when suddenly she heard voices and saw some car lights flashing through the trees behind her. Shit! Did they already figure out she was gone?

Immediately she made for the mausoleum, darting behind a lion statue just before the high beams hit the stone structure above her head.

Flattening herself to the ground, she listened and tried to control her breathing. A car was coming towards the crypt, creeping over the grass.

Cora pressed herself into the little ditch that was just

large enough for her. A couple of bushes helped obscure her. She could just see the marble platform before the steps up to the sepulcher.

As she watched, two Shades dressed all in black got out of the front seats. They left the beams of the car on for light so Cora could see them coming forward to the steps of the mausoleum. One of them was carrying some sort of tool kit. He paused as his partner followed, carrying a chair he must've gotten from the trunk of the car.

"Leave it there," the first one ordered, and the chair was placed in the center on the marble dais, right in Cora's line of site. He opened the tool kit and drew out a coil of rope, placing it on the chair. The other took the tool kit up the steps beyond where she could see.

What on earth was going on?

Cora ducked her head, hoping her hood stayed over her light hair. Her heart pounded against the cold ground as she heard them moving around more. What were Marcus's men doing out here in the middle of the night? Did Marcus know they were here?

She didn't want to know what would happen to her if they found her hiding behind the lion statue.

Slipping her hand into her pocket, she turned off her cellphone, making sure it wouldn't give her away. She hoped whatever the Shades were doing, they'd get it over quickly so she could escape unseen while it was still dark. Maeve was probably already waiting.

More lights flashed and Cora looked up, squinting past the high beams. What now?

"They're coming," one of the Shades called. Cora peered just over her arm as another pair of headlights hit the crypt, high beams casting shadows until someone inside the car cut them off.

That was when Marcus stepped out of the mausoleum.

Cora's breath caught in her chest and she slapped her hand over her mouth to stop her gasp of surprise. What on earth? Sharo was right behind Marcus and just like earlier that night, the two wore long black overcoats. She caught a brief glimpse of her husband's grim expression before Sharo stood in front of her and blocked most of her line of site.

"Took them long enough," Marcus said. He and Sharo stood there facing the lawn, waiting for the oncoming car.

Marcus drew a cigar out of his pocket and lit it. He said something too low for Cora to hear, because Sharo leaned down. She heard Sharo chuckle and shifted her head so she could see Marcus's face better. He looked as he always did when he had a situation under control: confident, an almost-smile on his handsome face.

Suppressing a shiver, Cora wiggled a little bit closer under the bushes. Marcus and Sharo looked for all the world like two buddies hanging out at a tailgate, chatting casually. They barely turned to acknowledge a second car's arrival, even when its doors opened and slammed, signaling a visitor's approach.

A man in a taupe trench coat approached the two men; Cora could see his older face clearly as she looked up now that her eyes had adjusted to the car's low beams.

"Mr. Ubeli," he greeted her husband politely.

In answer, Marcus nodded to him and took a casual drag on his cigar. Sharo's hands were still in his pockets.

The visitor kept a respectful distance. Something in the slope of his head as he nodded to her husband made Cora remember back to the day at the Crown hotel, when the cops were there to guard The Orphan. She recognized the man then; he was the police higher up whom Marcus had acknowledged in the lobby.

What was he doing here?

Meanwhile, Marcus's two men had joined them on the dais. They stood in deceptively casual poses, but the hulk of muscles in their shoulders made Cora think they weren't just there for show. The Shades were weapons, dark and deadly.

The man in the taupe coat cleared his throat. "Mr. Sturm sends his regards. He's grateful for your support."

What did the mayor have to do with this middle of the night meeting?

While the man in the taupe coat spoke, two more men got out of the second car and opened the trunk to get something. Cora couldn't quite see what.

"He asks that you accept this gift as a token of his gratitude. But after this, he requests no more contact."

Marcus removed his cigar and studied it before responding. "Tell him I respect his request, and thank him for his gift."

The messenger nodded curtly from where he stood on the ground before stepping back to allow his two helpers to carry forward their 'gift'.

Cora was about to crane her neck to make out what it was when movement on the steps frightened her and she ducked her head. She trembled for a moment, thinking she was caught.

But then she realized it was only Sharo. He had moved closer to Cora's hiding place, taking a position behind the chair the two Shades had set up earlier.

Then her eyes widened. It was a body. Sturm's men were carrying a body.

It hung limp and heavy between the two of them. A hood covered its head, although the build and size told Cora it was a man.

They sat him in the chair, and Sharo knelt to tie his hands to it with the rope.

When the body was secure, Sharo stepped forward and whipped off the black hood. Oh gods— Cora drew in a breath and pushed a fist to her mouth to keep herself quiet.

It was AJ.

His head lolled a little on his thick neck. His hair was matted down and his coat was gone. His shirt was halfway unbuttoned and he looked the worse for wear. Tied to a chair in the middle of the night, the monster looked smaller, somehow.

"Tell Sturm he has our vote," Marcus said coolly. "And we won't be contacting him, as long as certain...property is returned to us."

The man in the taupe coat nodded. "It's being processed. Give it a week. You'll get your shipment back."

Cora's mind raced. The shipment—returned? And AJ delivered to Marcus's front door as a gift, like a holiday ham.

The man in the taupe coat must be Marcus's man on the inside, a connection to Zeke and the force. Of course, the mayor was higher up than anyone.

Mind whirling, she barely heard Sturm's men get in their second car and creep away, leaving only Marcus, his men, and AJ behind. And her, of course.

For a moment, no one in front of the mausoleum moved or spoke. Above them, the clouds rolled away from the moon and caused shadows to flicker over their faces. It looked like something out of a horror movie, ghouls gathering around the crypt.

And Marcus? He looked like the Grim Reaper himself. She saw nothing of the man who'd held her so tenderly and washed her hair in the shower earlier that night. A shiver skittered down her spine that had nothing to do with the cold.

"Alright," Marcus broke the silence. "They're gone."

One of the Shades stepped forward, handing Sharo a water bottle. The big man unscrewed the cap and splashed it into AJ's face. Marcus's men waited patiently until he woke, sputtering.

"Where am I?" AJ groaned. His hands, bound behind him on the chair, flexed uselessly.

Pulling the cigar out of his mouth, Marcus answered him. "Hello, AJ. Welcome to hell."

"What the—" AJ's voice was cut off as Sharo gagged him. Sharo stepped back, squeezing his fist to crack his knuckles, his eyes on the back of AJ's head.

AJ looked around wildly.

"I want to congratulate you on your good work tonight, AJ," Marcus said softly. "You helped the mayor look strong on crime. He'll get elected. My campaign dollars will be well spent."

Marcus flicked a little ash onto the ground. "Of course, the outcome isn't quite what you wanted. Jail, and now being brought here to the house of your enemy. It's amazing how quickly you can get a man out on bail when you have friends in high places."

AJ made a small noise, barely a whimper.

"Do you recognize the family crypt?" Marcus motioned and Sharo turned the chair to face the intimidating structure.

"My father used to hold meetings here, remember? You were just a young man then."

AJ whimpered again. Cora could see his face clearly, his hair and face dirty and matted with sweat. He looked terrified and Cora blinked, confused. Did she really feel pity for this man?

Then she remembered Iris's dead face. He deserved everything Marcus might do to him. Right?

"I thought I'd bring you here, refresh your memory of old times," Marcus continued. "And also show you where my family lies. You can pay your respects to Old Ubeli. There's even a grave there waiting for me and my wife, when our time comes."

Cora winced automatically at the mention of her. How could this ice cold, unfeeling Marcus even speak of her while he was here, doing what he was about to do? She had no illusions. AJ wouldn't walk out of here alive. And even though she should cheer the fact...watching Marcus... watching him when he was like this...

"Not that it'll come soon." Marcus's voice now held deadly malice. "No thanks to you."

He shook the ash of his cigar over AJ's face and the man squirmed in the chair. Sharo stepped closer to hold it steady.

Marcus took a pull off the cigar and let the smoke curl out of his mouth, savoring it. Then he smiled at AJ. It was a smile that had another shiver rocking through Cora, all the way down to her bones.

"I know you're a man who appreciates cigars." He held the smoking roll up by AJ's face. "You want some?" Marcus's hand dropped carelessly and pressed the burning tip into AJ's chest until the man writhed and bucked, screaming behind the gag.

Cora bit down on her fist again to keep from crying out. But she forced herself not to look away. This was the man she'd married. This was the man she...she loved.

Sharo and the Shades stood watching silently, still as

statues. Meanwhile, Marcus had discarded the cigar and paced a little, waiting for the sobbing man to quiet.

"I wanted you to bring back a message to your masters. The ones who sent you here to see how I rule my city. See, I knew the Titan brothers would need more convincing that their rule here is over. That the bitch who leads them around by their little pencil dicks would need more. And I want them to understand something."

Marcus stopped in front of AJ, right in Cora's line of sight. His face was a cold mask, black eyes boring into the man who'd crossed him. She didn't recognize him as her husband anymore.

"I want you to understand something. I own this city. I own the streets. I own the shops, I own the air. You breathe," Marcus pointed to AJ, "with my permission. And now that your singer is dead—"

AJ jerked and so did Cora. It was business to Marcus. Just business. But Chris was a *person*.

"—it's time for you to leave New Olympus. Permanently."

AJ made muffled sounds behind his gag like he was trying to plead his case, then it quieted. Cora could hear him sobbing. Sharo, who had bent over him, leapt back.

"Pissed himself," the big man muttered.

Marcus's face twisted in disgust. "Face your death like a man."

AJ shook his head wildly, pleading.

And that was when Marcus lost any and all semblance of calm. His features twisted with rage.

"You came to *my* city. Abducted *my* wife. Disrupted *my* business. How did you think this would end? You think you can disrespect me?"

Cora's heart pounded as she watched her husband snarl at his enemy. She pressed her body into the cold ground.

Abruptly Marcus whirled and strode to the car. A third Shade stood there, holding a black case. Marcus threw the case open and then pulled something out. Cora frowned at first and then her eyes widened when he made a fist. He'd put on brass knuckles.

And then before she could even take another breath, he was back on AJ. "You dared," he landed a heavy blow to AJ's face, "to touch," another blow, "my wife."

Blood poured down AJ's face until he was choking on it but Marcus didn't stop.

Over and over again, he pounded AJ's face with a wild madness until the wet, squelching noise of his fist and the brass knuckles on AJ's head and bones and gristle and brain were all that could be heard.

Cora turned away and bent over the grass, throwing up.

Still Marcus didn't stop.

No one said a word until finally, heaving for breath, Marcus stepped back.

"I've decided," Marcus gulped in a breath, standing over the bloody mess that used to be AJ, "how to send a message to the Titans. You'll be that message."

Cora choked her tears down.

"Prep the body," Marcus said, his chest still rising and falling heavily. "Get it to Metropolis."

"Yes, boss." The men answered in unison and scurried forward to carry the chair and dead man into the mausoleum.

"You on clean up?" Marcus asked, and Cora raised her head to see him speaking to Sharo.

The big man shrugged. "Just the tricky stuff. These guys don't know how to get off a fingerprint without taking the hand." His tone was casual, as if he and Marcus were talking about something totally normal, like taking out the garbage. As if they hadn't all just stood around and watched Marcus bludgeon a man's head in.

"If you need help, call the gardener."

Sharo nodded. "Yeah, I learned from him. He was the master."

Sharo handed Marcus a handkerchief and Cora watched her husband calmly wipe off his hands, sliding the brass knuckles off as he did so. He looked beautiful in the moonlight. Even after what she'd just seen him do. Beautiful and so, so cold.

His lips had a satisfied smile, as if he relished the duty of judge, jury, and executioner.

Cora sucked in a breath and saw him, really saw him.

She saw Death.

"He's on standby. He'll sod over everything in the morning, if you can get it done by dawn," Marcus was telling Sharo.

"Will do, boss." Sharo turned and started going up the steps. He paused to ask one more thing. "The message to the Brothers—you want me to write a note?" His back was to Cora but she could hear a joking tone in his voice.

Marcus stared at the ground a moment. His profile was cut clean from the car's headlights. Cora held her breath.

Then he raised his head and his dark hair fell across his face. "Just send the pieces."

Cora waited until the car crept backwards across the lawn. All the men were in the vault; she could hear them joking about their grisly work.

She rose stiffly and hugged the mausoleum walls. Her body felt frozen so she waited at the back of the building, listening to see if she was found out.

No one came to find her though. There were no shouts signaling they'd spotted her. She was about to breathe a sigh of relief when she heard a strange whine start up.

Someone was using a wet saw.

She was going to be sick again. She bolted before she could be seen and didn't slow until she was in the trees, continuing on the path she'd taken earlier that night.

A car waited alongside the road. She approached and rapped on the glass. Maeve woke suddenly. For a moment her friend stared in surprise, but then she motioned for Cora to get in the back.

As Cora opened the door, a large doggy head greeted her. Brutus, the giant puppy.

"He wanted to come," Maeve said apologetically. "Cora, are you ok? I've been waiting..."

"Yes, sorry. My phone died." Cora sat in the backseat and buckled herself in. The large puppy settled down, his head hovering near Cora's.

Maeve was still looking back at her and Cora couldn't imagine what she saw on her face. "You sure about this?"

"Yes," Cora said. *Please don't ask me anything more.* Maeve must have sensed her silent plea, though, because she just pursed her lips and didn't say anything, although it was clear she wanted to. She turned and put the car into drive, then they crept away.

In the backseat, Cora bent over the puppy's head, clutching him tightly. He seemed to know she needed him and held his body still. A few tears spotted the top of his head.

When she'd left tonight, she'd only meant to clear her head. But what she'd seen... She covered her mouth again and struggled to fight back the bile that threatened to rise up.

She could never go back.

"It's just you and me, Brutus," she whispered. "You and me, against the world."

~

THANK YOU FOR READING AWAKENING! There's a darkness in Marcus and now Cora's seen it face to face. He says she's his light. But if their love is going to survive, she needs to be more than just his princess, locked away in a tower. She needs to become a Queen.

ORDER QUEEN **OF THE UNDERWORLD now, so you don't miss a thing!**

THE PANTHEON: WHO'S WHO

A note from Lee: *I've always loved Greek and Roman mythology. 'Innocence' is a retelling of the myth of Persephone and Hades. 'Awakening' goes further, using the story of Orpheus and Euridice as a subplot, and introducing more of the re-imagined Pantheon. I held nothing sacred and pulled from Ovid, Hesiod, Shakespeare, Homer, and even the Bible ('cause why not?). Some of the references are super oblique, but if you're a nerd about this stuff like me, you'll appreciate this cheat sheet (if you don't give a whoop about allegories, ignore this):*

THE UNDERWORLD:

Cora Vestian: Persephone, Proserpina. First name comes from *Kore*. Last name inspired by the *Vestal Virgins*.

Marcus Ubeli: Hades. Last name inspired by the chthonic god *Eubuleus*.

Demi Titan: Demeter. Last name taken from the Titans, the old gods who were the enemies of the Zeus-led pantheon.

Sharo: Charon. Nicknamed *The Undertaker*.

The Shades: Marcus's criminal army.

The Styx: a crime ridden area of New Olympus

Brutus: Cerberus.

The Chariot: Marcus's private club where he conducts most of his business. Contains the office where he and Cora met.

The Orphan: Orpheus.

Iris: Eurydice.

THE REST OF THE PANTHEON:

AJ: Ajax the Lesser.

Anna: Aphrodite. Her stage name is *Venus*.

Armand: Hermes. He has wing tattoos and owns a business called *Metamorphoses*, a reference to Ovid.

Elysium: the popular club and music venue, owned by Marcus. The place to see and be seen in New Olympus.

Hype and Thane: Hypnos and Thanatos. God of Sleep and Death, respectively. They run club Elysium.

Maeve: Hectate, goddess of the Crossroads. She advises Cora.

Max Mars: Mars. God of war = volatile action movie star.

Oliva: Athena. Her company is *Aurum*, the Latin word for gold. Inspired by Steve Jobs. Aurum plus Apple = golden apple.

Philip Waters: Poseidon. Controls the shipping corridors into New Olympus.

Zeke Sturm: Zeus. The esteemed mayor of New Olympus. Last name (Storm) inspired by the lightning bolts Zeus used.

ALSO BY STASIA BLACK

Dark Contemporary Romances

Innocence

Awakening

Queen of the Underworld

Cut So Deep

Break So Soft

Hurt So Good

The Virgin and the Beast: a Beauty and the Beast Tale

Hunter: a Snow White Romance

The Virgin Next Door: a Ménage Romance

Daddy's Sweet Girl (freebie)

Complete Marriage Raffle Series

Theirs to Protect

Theirs to Pleasure

Their Bride

Theirs to Defy

Theirs to Ransom

ALSO BY LEE SAVINO

Contemporary romance:

Beauty and the Lumberjacks: a dark reverse harem romance

Her Marine Daddy

Her Dueling Daddies

Royally Fucked - get free at www.leesavino.com

Paranormal & Sci fi romance:

The Alpha Series

The Draekon Series

The Berserker Series

·

ABOUT STASIA BLACK

STASIA BLACK grew up in Texas, recently spent a freezing five-year stint in Minnesota, and now is happily planted in sunny California, which she will never, ever leave.

She loves writing, reading, listening to podcasts, and has recently taken up biking after a twenty-year sabbatical (and has the bumps and bruises to prove it). She lives with her own personal cheerleader, aka, her handsome husband, and their teenage son. Wow. Typing that makes her feel old. And writing about herself in the third person makes her feel a little like a nutjob, but ahem! Where were we?

Stasia's drawn to romantic stories that don't take the easy way out. She wants to see beneath people's veneer and poke into their dark places, their twisted motives, and their deepest desires. Basically, she wants to create characters that make readers alternately laugh, cry ugly tears, want to toss their kindles across the room, and then declare they have a new FBB (forever book boyfriend).

Join Stasia's Facebook Group for Readers for access to deleted scenes, to chat with me and other fans and also get access to exclusive giveaways:
Stasia's Facebook Reader Group

twitter.com/stasiawritesmut

instagram.com/stasiablackauthor

ABOUT LEE SAVINO

LEE SAVINO has grandiose goals but most days can't find her wallet or her keys so she just stays at home and writes. While she was studying creative writing at Hollins University, her first manuscript won the Hollins Fiction Prize.

She lives in the USA with her awesome family. You can find her on Facebook in the **Goddess Group**(which you totally should join).

instagram.com/intothedarkromance

Made in the USA
Middletown, DE
05 November 2019